To Mac —

DEATH OF THE
ZANJERO

Thank you for all your support!

ANNE LOUISE BANNON

4/8/22

Healcroft House, Publishers

Healcroft House, Publishers, a subsidiary of Robin Goodfellow Enterprises, Altadena, California, United States of America

ISBN 978-1-948616-00-3

Library of Congress Control Number: 2018900817

DEDICATION

For Michael – because this one is all your fault.
Thank you so much!

ACKNOWLEDGEMENTS

One of the challenges of writing a historical mystery is that you have to really get the daily life details right. The problem is that most people don't write those sorts of details down. I was blessed with all manner of excellent help from the librarians at the Los Angeles Public Library. Glen Creason, of the History and Geneology Department, found some wonderful old maps for me that helped me layout the action. Kelly Wallace, the California Subject Specialist, was amazing in helping me ferret out the two most elusive facts about the zanja gates — what were they made of and how did they work? Bob Timmerman, in the Science Department, helped me make sure I had my medical knowledge together. Finally, Kimberley Erickson, of the Cal Poly Pomona Wine and Wine Industry Collection, went the extra mile to find something describing how wine was actually made in the late 19th Century.

Jennifer Younger helped immensely as my beta reader, and Carol Louise Wilde did another awesome job line editing this work. The cover and illstration are the work of Ginko Lee, a truly talented artist.

Finally, thanks go to Los Angeles City Archivist Michael Holland, who is also my beloved husband. The genesis of this story started with his wonderful lecture on the zanja system in Los Angeles. And I had to go and muck it up by adding a dead body. In spite of that, he still pulled city council minutes out for me, dug up tax records and answered endless questions, most of them during his off hours. And that's not even counting all the emotional and occasional financial support.

A NOTE ON THE CAST OF CHARACTERS

This is a work of fiction. However, since it takes place in a real place and time, it only makes sense that Maddie Wilcox would encounter and interact with various people who really did live in Los Angeles in 1870, such as Marshal William Warren and his wife, Mrs. Warren.

As streets and communities are often named after prominent people, I used those names for many of the characters in this book during the writing of my first draft. Then I went back and did some follow-up research and found out more about the some of the various namesakes for some of the people you will meet in this book, particularly, the Ladies of Society.

Mrs. Judson and her husband, **Mr. Judson**, a banker, are purely fictional with fictional names, as is anyone not listed here.

Mrs. Aguilar I presumed existed, since the character is married to Cristobal Aguilar, two-times mayor of the city (and the last Hispanic mayor until Antonio Villaraigosa was elected over 130 years later).

Mrs. Carson, **Mrs. Fletcher**, and **Mrs. Hewitt**, are also presumed to have existed, but the characters, themselves, are purely fictional

Mrs. Glassell is another fictional character with a real name. I know she existed, because her husband, Andrew Glassell, founded both the City of Orange and the Glassell Park neighborhood. Couldn't find anything about her. Yet.

Finally, there was a **Mrs. Downey**, wife of former governor John Downey (he owned the land which became the city named for him). It was reportedly a very affectionate marriage, but I do not know if she had my fictional character's very interesting hobby.

CHAPTER ONE

We knew the value of water in Los Angeles. Back when our great city was still a tiny pueblo, water was scarce and our farms and ranchos were at the mercy of what the heavens produced. Back then we had to pay handsomely to have our fields and vineyards irrigated. Back then the Zanjero, or water overseer, was the most powerful man in the pueblo, which sadly meant he was often the most corrupt, as was Bertram Rivers. I had thought he was my friend.

The dawn was slowly lightening the surrounding hills as we gathered that Monday morning, March 28, in the Year of Our Lord, Eighteen Hundred and Seventy. It had been a fairly dry winter, but not disastrously so. We'd had a good rainy spell the week before, so the Porciuncula River was flowing, and there was sufficient water in the Zanja Madre, the large dirt ditch that led from the river and fed all the smaller zanjas that watered our ranchos and farms.

"Where in tarnation is that son of a b—?" Mr. Worthington snarled, then let loose a stream of tobacco juice.

The expectorant landed near my foot and from the look on my bosom friend Sarah Worthington's face, it appeared that her husband had aimed for me. I suppose a gentle reproof of his language and behavior would have been appropriate. However, it would not have been effective, so I simply stepped aside.

Sarah Worthington had come out with her husband to watch as Caleb Worthington and his men opened the sluice gate to my rancho. She was a tall, sturdy woman, with an elegant bearing and hair the color of freshly tilled earth. Mr. Worthington had been a miner before he and Sarah had come to Los Angeles and bought their lumber business. She was so dear to me, the first woman to befriend me when I'd been brought to this desolate place.

We were both anxious for the gate to be opened. I had been up all night and had yet to see my bed. Indeed, I was wearing my work dress, instead of a decent walking suit. Sarah had some matter troubling her deeply, probably Mr. Worthington. I suspected she wished to unburden herself to me, although I did hope that I could convince her to wait until later that day so I could spend at least a few hours in slumber first.

There were five of us gathered at the edge of the Zanja Madre. Besides myself and Mr. and Mrs. Worthington, there were Sebastiano and Enrique Ortiz, the men who ran my winery and vineyard. The only person who was missing was the Zanjero, Mr. Rivers. He was needed to verify that the receipt I had gotten the previous Saturday did, indeed, reflect the amount of time I had paid for that Friday and to approve the opening of the gate.

As Deputy Zanjero, Mr. Worthington already knew that I had paid for my allotment, but Mr. Rivers refused to let anyone else open a sluice gate without his presence. Mr. Rivers said it was to protect the good citizens of the pueblo. I thought it a fine sentiment, but at that moment, one that was quite inconvenient.

"Perhaps, Mr. Worthington, you shouldn't wait," Sarah said, after hiding a small yawn behind her hand. "Else Mrs. Wilcox might not get her full allotment."

Mr. Worthington glared at her. He was as big and burly as one might expect of a former miner, with dark blonde hair and small, dark eyes. He was wearing his usual dusty black suit and black tie. He spat out another disgusting stream, this time landing close to Sarah's foot.

"Hombres," he said, with an accent that was truly

dismal. "Um, viy-eenay casa Rivers and officina. Diga Señor Rivers, uh, we're waiting."

As it happened, both Sebastiano and Enrique spoke English better than most Americans. Nonetheless, the two brothers looked at each other, then Enrique nodded and turned to do Mr. Worthington's bidding. However, they were saved by the appearance of Will Rivers, Mr. Rivers' youngest son.

He was a lad of thirteen, a tow-head with bright blue eyes. The boy usually wore what his three older brothers cast off, never mind that his father could afford to buy him new clothes. Will was very slight and his pants were generally tied on and his shirts constantly billowing about him as a sail on a merchant ship. One wondered how soon it would be before the wind would catch the garments and blow the lad away with them.

Will was barefoot, as he generally was, and approached at a dead run from the road leading into the city proper.

"Where's your pa?" Mr. Worthington demanded.

"I don't know," Will gasped. "He, uh, never came home last night."

That statement would have elicited a great deal more concern, but the pueblo was a rough place, filled with many temptations for those men who were weak-minded enough not to resist. That a husband and father should stay out the night was, sadly, not that unusual. I wouldn't have thought it of Mr. Rivers, but it didn't surprise me, either.

Mr. Worthington cursed loudly.

"Ma said to tell you to go ahead and open the gates today," Will said, trying to look braver than he was. "Pa will be madder than a wet hen if you miss your scheduled times."

Mr. Worthington glanced over at me, then at Will. Mr. Rivers did prefer that things be done properly. However, there were other rancheros waiting for their water and Mr. Worthington had other duties to tend to, as well. The tolling of the bell from the Clocktower

Courthouse softly floated over the Zanja Madre from the center of town. It was six in the morning and time to give me my water.

"Hombres," Mr. Worthington finally yelled and gestured that they should open the gate.

It was a large panel of wood, painted over and pitched many times to keep the wood sound in the wet. Enrique scrambled down the dry part of the dirt zanja on my side of the gate and back up to the other side of the bank. Together, he and Sebastiano tried lifting the panel, but it was stuck solidly. Mr. Worthington took a long pole and began jabbing it around the bottom of the gate. The gate remained stuck. Enrique and Sebastiano jiggled the panel and Mr. Worthington jabbed and suddenly the gate pulled free, upsetting the men. Water poured quickly into my zanja, rushing and whispering as it went past.

Then through the froth and foam, a dark shape rose up. It was the body of a man, clad in a dark suit of clothes. Sarah screamed but stayed standing. With Mr. Worthington pushing it with his stick, Sebastiano and Enrique reached out and as the water rose, were finally able to pull the body out of the zanja.

The man had been tall and broad-shouldered with dark blonde hair. There was a good solid cut and bruise on the back of his head, just above where his hairline had receded. His suit was torn in spots, presumably from the time in the water, as it otherwise looked to be of good quality. I looked over at Mr. Worthington, whose face had taken on a queer look. My stomach felt just as queer.

"Maddie, stay back," Sarah whispered, holding my arm. "It's too terrible."

I shook her off as Mr. Worthington turned the body over and confirmed that we had found Bertram Rivers.

Sarah wailed in anguish.

I knelt down and opened the corpse's mouth. There were no plants or other debris lodged in his throat that I could see. I was not able to discover more because

Sarah had fainted dead away.

I waved my foreman over.

"Sebastiano," I said softly, giving him my handkerchief. "Please get this good and wet so that I can revive Mrs. Worthington."

"Yes, Ma'am." Sebastiano was an average-sized man with broad shoulders, a drooping black mustache, and usually laughing eyes. He was a good friend, though reluctant to show it in front of others in town for fear of hurting my reputation. "Do you want me to get the rig for the lady?"

"Yes, please. Thank you, Sebastiano."

He returned in seconds with the wet handkerchief. Laying Sarah's head in my lap, I dribbled some water onto her wrists, then bathed her forehead. I would have to wait to loosen her corset strings.

Meanwhile, cursing and bellowing, Mr. Worthington had Enrique help him gather up Mr. Rivers' body and load it onto his horse to take to the undertaker's. I looked around for Will. It was a terrible way to find out one's father was dead.

The boy had fled, I guessed, to his home. Sarah moaned softly.

"Gently now, dearest," I crooned, almost under my breath. "You've fainted and it won't do to get up too quickly only to faint again."

I reached into my leather satchel. It was as big as a saddle bag with a single strap that I wore over one shoulder and across my torso. It wore my dresses dreadfully, but the tiny bags they made for ladies were far too small to carry all the things I needed. I was after my flask of angelica wine. It was our local version of sherry. I knew Sarah didn't usually approve of spirits, but some are good for shock, and my angelica was quite delicate.

I fed her some and she coughed lightly, then struggled to sit upright in the dust. It wasn't long after that when Sebastiano brought my rig around, hitched to my roan mare, Daisy. The both of us helped Sarah onto the seat since Mr. Worthington had already left to take Mr. Rivers' body to the undertaker's.

The Worthingtons had a house near the town center, between the city hall and market and the town square. It was a large, two-storied house with wood siding painted bright white, including the trim on the shutters and the cutouts decorating the eaves. We arrived in good time and after hitching the mare, Sebastiano helped me get Sarah, who was improving but still weak, inside and onto the sofa in her front parlor. I asked him to wait for me, he nodded and went outside.

Hannah, Sarah's colored maid, came in and I sent her for some tea. I waited only long enough for Hannah, a short, stout woman with a round face and skin as dark as a night out on the desert, to return with the reviving beverage, accompanied by some freshly-baked biscuits and cactus pear jam. As soon as Hannah was gone, I poured the tea and heavily sugared it even though Sarah generally drank hers without any, then insisted she drink it. She, in turn, insisted that I pour myself a cup and eat some biscuits, as well.

"I'm more concerned for you," I said, as I helped myself to a cup, added my usual teaspoon of sugar, and added jam to a biscuit.

Sarah shrugged. "I am almost recovered. Such a shock, though, to see a body in the zanja."

"It is hardly the first time a body has been found there," I pointed out. "Nor is it like you to faint dead away at anything. Have you tied your stays too tightly again?"

Fortunately, Sarah and I were on the sort of terms that allowed for such intimacy. Yet still, she blushed.

"I don't believe so. Actually, they could use a bit of tightening," she sighed. "My waist positively bulges."

Sarah yawned widely and excused herself.

"Were you out chasing after Mr. Worthington last night?" I asked more severely than I intended, possibly because I was trying to stifle a yawn of my own.

It was Sarah's habit to chase after her husband in the late hours of the night in the hopes of bringing him home before he came to grief. Given the violence of the rough men in our saloons and houses of ill-repute, and there were many of them, I often feared for Sarah's well-being.

"It is my wifely duty to see to it that my husband returns home safely," Sarah said a little defensively.

"Where did you find him?"

"I didn't," Sarah said with a sniff. "He came home of his own accord, though he was smelling of cheap perfume again." She blinked her eyes. "Is it such a terrible thing to hope for a husband who does not waste himself away at saloons and... and..."

"Houses of ill-repute," I finished for her.

"Oh, Maddie, he is such a trial to me. I could almost wish I were a merry widow like you," she said, starting to sob.

"I would not say that I'm all that merry," I replied, although I was, in fact, quite content with my bereft state. "And I do understand your anguish. My Albert spent easily as much time drinking and whoring as your Caleb."

Sarah gasped at my coarse language, then sniffed softly. "I remember it well. I even thought how lucky I was that Caleb did not do such things. I should have known he was simply better at hiding it. How could I, who grew up in a mining camp, have remained innocent of such knowledge?"

I shook my head. I had little regard for Caleb Worthington and had known of his frequent drunkenness well before Sarah did. If I had refrained from telling her, it was out of tender concern for the grief it would cause her since she had little recourse.

Sarah suddenly sighed deeply. "What a terrible thing, to be shot and dumped in the zanja."

"But he wasn't shot," I said. "At least, I don't think he was. There was a nasty cut and bump on the back of his head."

"Oh," said Sarah, sounding surprised. She thought this over. "I guess I must have simply assumed…"

I chuckled grimly. "It wasn't a bad assumption."

And, indeed, it wasn't. As I noted, the pueblo was a rough place at that time and shootings were all too common.

"Still," I continued, "It seems more likely that he met with some misadventure. He quite probably fell, hit his head, and rolled into the zanja and drowned."

I must admit that the thought did not sit well with me, although I couldn't, for the life of me, figure out why.

Sarah let out her breath and nodded. "What a terribly sad thing to have happen. I must plan a visit to Mrs. Rivers today." She yawned again. "But first, I think I should sleep a little. I didn't last night, even after Caleb came home."

I squeezed my eyes shut, reminded again that I had yet to see any rest, myself. Still, I also had my duty to Mrs. Rivers to perform. It was a sign of just how tired I was that I did not consider changing my work dress to something more suitable first. I got up.

"Then I shall see myself out and leave you to your rest," I told her.

Outside, I had Sebastiano drive me to the Rivers' home, even though it was only over on the next street, Calle Primavera. It was another clapboard house, two-stories, and obviously owned by someone of considerable status and wealth in the community. Mr. Rivers certainly had been such. He had built and owned the largest wool mill in the town and owned several houses that he rented out. The newly-widowed Mrs. Rivers would have ample means for her support, assuming she could get the local magistrate to grant her the half of her husband's property to which she was entitled by state law.

One of the oddities of California's property laws, actually a holdover from Mexican and Spanish rule, is that all property acquired during a marriage is held jointly by both the man and his wife. However, that didn't mean that judges always granted a widow her rights. Fortunately, I had insisted that my Albert write down his extravagant promise that I should have all his property should he die before me, saving half for any of our children. I had kept the letter because I had not believed him, and when he died without a will, that letter saved my life.

A black wreath already decorated the door of the house of mourning. It had been done with surprising dispatch, considering that we'd found Mr. Rivers less than two hours before. The wreath was why I fully expected to be told that Mrs. Rivers was not receiving by the Rivers maid, Susanna, a short, stout Negress with the same dark, dark skin and round face as Sarah's maid. But I was admitted to the front parlor, where Mrs. May Rivers was sitting, dressed in a black poplin day dress. There was a black veil laid across the back of an overstuffed chair on the other side of the fireplace. Like her four sons and her husband, she was quite fair, although her golden hair was obviously longer. Her eyes also differed in that they were a more faded blue than her sons'. She was an average sized woman, with the sort of pleasingly curved figure that other women in the pueblo envied.

"So good of you to come, Mrs. Wilcox," she said pleasantly, gesturing to the sofa. "Please sit."

"I am so sorry for your loss," I sat down wondering where her sons were.

"You're very kind," she said. "It is terribly sad, but we must manage."

Her eyes were red, as one might expect, and the skin below them was darkened as if she hadn't slept the night before, which I could well imagine, if Mr. Rivers had not made it home. Still, her eyes were dry and did not appear to be ready to overflow.

"Is there anything I can do?" I asked. "Anyone I can write to? Perhaps send a telegram?"

She smiled softly. "No. The boys have taken all that

on, thank heavens. Mr. Sutton has already assured me that he will make all the arrangements for the funeral. And Mrs. Miller has already sent over a stew for my luncheon today. Do you know Mrs. Miller?"

"I believe so, but not well."

"She's our minister's wife. A very dear woman. She sent a most gracious note as soon as she'd heard."

"News does appear to move swiftly," I said. "Well, I shan't trouble you further. But I am at your beck and call should need arise."

She smiled as I got up and Susannah showed me out.

It was a very good thing I'd asked Sebastiano to drive me into town. I had not seen my bed since the morning before and it was all I could do to sit up straight in the rig for the short drive to my rancho and adobe house. Nonetheless, my mind was awhirl. I rather resented Sarah having fainted when she did. It had kept me from getting a better look at Bert Rivers' body, although why it should worry me so, I could not understand. Perhaps it was due to my exhausted state.

Juanita Alvarez, my maid, helped me undress, scolding me for neglecting my rest as she did so. I slid between the sheets of my fat goose-down bed and instantly fell asleep. And by the time I awoke, I knew why I was so worried about Bert Rivers' death. I couldn't be absolutely certain. But I was fairly sure Rivers had been dead before he landed in the Zanja Madre. Which meant it was more than likely someone had helped him into the irrigation ditch. Which in turn meant that he'd mostly likely been murdered. And I had no idea what to do about it.

CHAPTER TWO

There were those who said we saw a murder a day in our fair pueblo. I will grant that such dastardly deeds were far more common than one would like, but perhaps not a daily occurrence. And when murder did happen, it was most often the result of a fight gone bad or some other public dispute. In short, one knew who the miscreants were and justice was quickly served.

However, in the case of Bertram Rivers, I had little more than a solid inkling that he had met his end by the means of foul play. Just because I hadn't found any of the plants or gravel or other debris that drowning people generally swallow didn't mean he hadn't drowned. But something felt dreadfully wrong about it.

It could have been my regard for Mr. Rivers. I had yet to learn the full measure of his perfidy, and that morning of his death, I still regarded him as a capital fellow. He had always treated me fairly and politely, which was more than I could say for others in town. We were not close friends, nor were his wife and I. We did not go to the same church (I believe they were Methodists). But we knew each other well enough for pleasant conversation at gatherings and other parties. And Mr. Rivers and I spoke to each other almost every month when I paid for my water subscription.

I was most uneasy in my thinking as I went over the day's activities with Sebastiano, the main one being to assign two of our workers to watch the sluice gate in case Mr. Worthington came back earlier than six of the evening to shut it down. He had attempted such before, even though there was little he stood to gain by it. It was simple meanness. He did not approve of my friendship with Sarah and especially did not approve of me as a woman of property.

I owned Rancho De Las Flores, which consisted of fifty acres of vines, the winery that went with it, and the two houses where I and my servants lived. Back in 1860, when Albert Wilcox dragged me out to the benighted wilderness that was then our city, he bought the rancho, planted the vines, and then did me the enormous favor of getting himself struck by lightning one Sunday morning while I was in church. I had told him there was a storm brewing. But Albert never listened to me. Fortunately, there were several witnesses to what had happened and to the fact that I was piously listening to Reverend Elmwood when the bolt came out of the sky. I still had to endure a great many unkind jokes that I had called the lightning down on Albert, even though I had maintained the appearance that we were fond of each other and that I was unaware of his drinking and, well, whoring.

As I pondered my past, it occurred to me that Mrs. Rivers was behaving much as I had those first hours and days after Albert had been killed. It had been desperately hard to appear as grief-stricken as I should have been, which may have accounted for some of the joking. I'd met several widows who had been genuinely fond of their husbands, and it seemed as though their eyes brimmed with tears at the least mention, even months and years after the man's passing. But if Mrs. Rivers was as relieved by her husband's death as I had been by mine, I could not help but wonder why.

Even more curious was my visitor who arrived just before tea-time. Regina Medina was possibly the most notorious woman in the pueblo. How do I say it? Well, there is no polite way to speak of her profession. She owned a house of ill-repute and engaged in that most evil and pernicious trade of selling women's flesh for the illicit pleasure of men. She was also my friend.

I am as shocked by that as any right-thinking woman would be. I had avoided her for over five years, but there came a time when a man patronizing her house shot one of her girls. The girl had survived the wound initially, but then infection took hold. Regina's maid had told her that I had the healing way about me. Regina begged me to come help, and while I could not condone her way of life, I believed that the girl was still a child of God and it was my duty to go to her aid. Fortunately, I was able to stop the infection and the girl lived and married a teamster, as I recall.

Regina knew my secret and I later learned hers. Even as our friendship grew, we made a point of avoiding each other in public. There were few in the pueblo who would understand our friendship. I barely understood it, myself, and wagging tongues are often vicious. Those rare times when Regina came to visit me, she generally did so after dark, when the local town folk were not about to see her. For Regina to come during daylight hours meant something was terribly wrong.

Maria, my housemaid, had seated Regina in the front parlor before fetching me from the winery where Sebastiano and I were debating whether we should rack, or move, that fall's cabernet sauvignon into the barrels where it would finish its fermentation and aging.

"Will I need my bag?" I asked Maria as I crossed the compound.

"I don't know."

I hurried to the front parlor, asking Maria to bring us tea and sweet breads. Regina sat, in her full glory and ramrod straight, on my red velvet sofa. She was a very tall woman, with luxurious dark hair that she kept pinned up on top of her head. Adding the tall, straight hats she favored, she looked even taller. She wore a blue bombazine walking suit, with an upper skirt swept up and gathered in back and black lace decorating the ruffles on her underskirt. There was, as usual, plenty of lace in the jabot under her chin. It was her other trademark. It frequently took months, if not years, to get the latest fashion books from the East, but somehow, Regina always got them first. Her clothes were the most stylish in the pueblo and many an upright wife often found herself blushing when it came out that her very latest dress had already been modeled by Regina.

"My darling Maddie," Regina cooed in her deep, breathy voice. She had the light lilt of the Irish, and I believe she had probably been born there, though she would never say.

"My darling Regina," I sat down on the nearest chair. "It's lovely to see you, but it's considerably earlier than your usual visits. Is something wrong?"

Regina sighed. "I don't know. I hear tell Mr. Rivers was fished out of your zanja?"

"Not quite," I said, and paused as Maria brought in the tea and sweet bread. "Your usual?"

"Yes, please."

I busied myself pouring and adding the two lumps of sugar that Regina preferred. Maria left quickly.

"I was there when Mr. Rivers was found," I continued. "However, his body was in the Zanja Madre and only surfaced after they opened the sluice gate."

Regina frowned as she stirred and sipped her tea. "Were you able to look at the body?"

"Some. Why do you ask?"

"Rumors are starting float about that Mr. Rivers met his end by foul play." Regina rested her hands and tea cup daintily in her lap.

"I must say that I've been thinking the same," I said.

Regina's perfectly shaped eyebrow quirked up. "That, I'm afraid, is bad news, indeed."

"I'm not certain, mind you."

"I would hope for your sake that he did meet with an accident." Regina looked at her tea. "It will, of course, be very hard for you to account for your whereabouts last night and there are those who might think the worst of you."

She was right about that. Suddenly nervous, I put my cup down.

"You know I didn't kill him." I got up and started pacing. "I had no reason to, anyway. He was my friend. We were always on cordial terms."

"That may be, but we both know that won't settle the wagging tongues in town."

"And why would I have to account for last night? There's no telling how long he was in the zanja."

"According to Mr. Mahoney, Mr. Rivers was last seen leaving Mr. Mahoney's saloon shortly before nine o'clock. Apparently, Mr. Rivers was in quite a state, but still able to walk."

"How terrible! The poor man."

Regina smiled and shook her head. "It was quite the usual for him."

"Mr. Rivers? He's always been sober when I've seen him. And fair and upright."

At this, Regina laughed out loud. "Oh, dear, dear Maddie. You're not the only one to have had the wool pulled over her eyes by Bert Rivers. He does, indeed, know when to be charming. Or did. But he was a most despicable man. I had to ban him from my house. He was too hard on my girls." She stirred her tea and took a sip. "Discretion being an absolute must in my trade, I probably shouldn't tell you this. But you've patched up more than one of his victims."

I sat, aghast and trying to understand this new portrait of a man I had thought reasonably kind and fair-minded.

"And I'm not the only person in town with a grievance against him," Regina continued. "Bert's position as zanjero allowed him to take ill-advantage of quite a few people, most of them weaker than he. And that made him quite a few enemies." She reached over and patted my hand. "Please, Maddie, you had no reason to believe he was other than the upstanding civic benefactor he presented himself as."

"This is most distressing," I mumbled, then sat up straight. "I appreciate your concern, Regina. And your honesty." I smiled weakly. "You are one of the few people I know that I can count on for that."

Regina smiled and rose. "I'm very happy to do it. After all, Maddie, all these fine, upstanding Christian women in town, and there isn't one who won't cross to the other side of the street when she sees me coming. Except you. You may not agree with my profession, but at least you had the decency to hear me out. And you're always there when my girls need you. I find it amusing that of all the women written about in the gospels, Jesus was friends with the prostitutes."

I stood also. "Thanks to you, I have noted the same. However, I suspect we are to assume that they all reformed their lives."

"Well, you know why I can't." She smiled and kissed me quickly on the cheek. "I must be on my way. It's going to be a difficult night. One of my girls is having her courses and another is croupy."

I blushed. "Do you need some tonic?"

"No. I've plenty. I'll send for you if it gets worse, though."

"I should be here. And how are..?"

"Both doing wonderfully well, thanks to you." She smiled, then slid through the front door of the adobe.

That was the difficulty of the adobe. There was no front hallway. The front door opened directly into the front parlor. The house was square and built around a patio. From the front parlor, there was a corridor that led to the other rooms, specifically, the dining room and a library. Around the corner was my bed chamber. Juanita's chamber was on the far wing. The other two chambers housed my cook, Olivia Ortiz and her husband Sebastiano, and their children, and my housekeeper, Magdalena Ortiz and her husband Enrique, and their children. The rest of the ranch hands and their families lived in the barracks house.

I heard horses and a carriage rumbling away from the yard. Regina had left me with a great deal to ponder. However, I had little time to do so. Shortly after she'd left, a messenger came round with a note from Mrs. Sutton, the undertaker's wife. Mr. Rivers would be laid out for viewing in his parlor the next night and the funeral would be the day after that, Wednesday. In addition, Mrs. Sutton asked me to stop by the funeral parlor sometime that evening after supper. That was even more puzzling.

"I have a matter that I wish to discuss with you privately and which requires the utmost in discretion," the note read.

I wrote a quick reply that I would be there by seven o'clock and sent the note back with the young Chinese boy who'd delivered it.

To say that I was in considerable turmoil by the time I presented myself at the funeral parlor's front door would not be an understatement. The young Chinese messenger admitted me and led me through the front viewing parlor to the back chamber where Mrs. Sutton prepared the bodies for viewing before placing them in their caskets.

Angelina Sutton was small in stature, which utterly belied her steely strength. Like me, she was just barely considered acceptable in town society. She and her husband, Mr. Miles Sutton, did provide an all-too-frequently needed service, and she was known for her tender concern for the bereaved families. She would probably have been embraced wholeheartedly by the ladies of our town's society if it were not that she was Mexican, from one of the wealthier founding families, it was true, but Mexican nonetheless. The ladies of town barely tolerated me because of my widowhood, widows supposedly being notorious for turning the heads of married men. However, I was a good church-going woman, I held considerable property, and I made some of the best wine in town, so they had to be kind to me, and I did count a few friends among the group.

Mrs. Sutton had lit the preparation chamber with several lamps. Mr. Rivers' body lay on the table in the middle. The body was undressed and she had discreetly covered the torso and nether regions with a sheet. Shelves and glass-fronted cabinets lined the walls of the room, cluttered with glass bottles and jars of varying shapes and sizes.

Mrs. Sutton, herself, was wearing a light blue work dress. The bib of her white apron was pinned to her bodice. Her full, glossy black hair was pinned up and her dark eyes glowed with intelligence.

"Ah, Mrs. Wilcox. I'm so glad you're here," she said, looking up from a chair near the corpse where she'd been sewing something, I couldn't see what.

Though not close friends, we were on friendly terms, mostly because we shared the same social status. Mrs. Sutton and I mostly knew each other from my sick visits about town, usually crossing paths when the patient I was tending had died. I'd had no reason to believe she'd held me in any particular regard, which was why I was so perplexed and curious about her summons that night.

She set her sewing down and stood.

"I hope you don't mind," she said. "I have found something that has caused me to be unhappy in mind and I thought you might have an idea of what to do about it."

"And why me?" I asked.

"You, I can trust," she said. "You know anatomy and you are clear-headed. They will listen to you, perhaps. My husband will not even listen to me, so he is useless."

"What did you find?"

Mrs. Sutton pulled the sheet away just enough to expose the right side of Mr. Rivers' torso. In the center of the left side of his chest was a small hole.

"He'd been shot," I said with a small gasp. I looked up at her. "Do you think that's what killed him?"

"Maybe," she said. "The doctors can't do an autopsy.

Mrs. Rivers did not want one and Marshal Warren obliged. He's already ruled the death an accident."

"Even with that bump on the head?" I asked.

Mrs. Sutton shrugged. "It could have been. Here, look."

She put the sheet back across the torso, then lifted and turned the head. The wound was a straight line across the back of Mr. Rivers' balding pate, just above the ring of dark blond hair. Mrs. Sutton brought a lamp closer and I could see that not only was there a fair amount of bruising along the line, the hair below it had been singed.

"Are we supposed to believe he had fallen against something?" I asked.

"Could he have?" Mrs. Sutton asked back.

"It's possible." I mentally reviewed all the sorts of sharp edges a man could fall against. "What about drowning? Did you find anything that could say he had?"

"I did look at his mouth and inside his nose. I found nothing. Usually, you find plants and other things. And the nose will often bleed." Mrs. Sutton sighed. "He hadn't been in the water that long, only overnight."

"And he was last seen at nine o'clock last night." I shook my head.

"Nine o'clock?" Mrs. Sutton frowned. "And you found him at six in the morning? I've seen plenty of bodies that have come out of the zanjas, and I would say he'd been there at least twelve hours."

"And there is that gunshot wound," I added. "This was no accident. He was most definitely murdered."

"I am not surprised," Mrs. Sutton said, gazing at the corpse. "The only surprise was that it did not happen sooner."

I looked at her. "You are the second person to say so. I had no idea Mr. Rivers was held in such ill-regard."

"You are not Mexican. It's a good thing Mr. Sutton does not require much water beyond what we need to drink and wash in. I should have had to give myself to

Mr. Rivers to get it."

"What?" I stepped back in utter shock.

"Most of the society ladies do not know. But if a farmer's wife is pretty enough, Mr. Rivers would impose himself on her. You do not believe it? That's why he was able to. No one would believe he'd done that, except the farmer or his wife."

I took a deep breath and let it out slowly. "He was still murdered. We can clearly show it. We must talk to the marshal."

"I'm not talking to him," Mrs. Sutton said with a sniff. "He's only interested in chasing down escaped prostitutes for the bounties. I do know one deputy who is honest. Mr. Walter Lomax."

"Mr. Navarro is also honest."

Mrs. Sutton smiled. "My cousin. He is too young and too much interested in chasing sweet young girls. Chin Tai!"

The young Chinese boy came running in. "Yes, ma'am."

"You go find Mr. Lomax and ask him to come visit me here at once. Before Mr. Sutton gets home, please."

"Yes, ma'am."

The youth, a lad of twelve, ran off.

I looked back at the body. "Shall we see if there's anything else we can learn from the corpus?"

"I have not found anything else except the bullet hole and the head wound."

I went ahead and examined the body anyway, even feeling the skull under the head wound. It was intact, possibly cracked, but I doubted the wound had killed Mr. Rivers. The bullet wound was also very deep. I found a glass rod on one of the shelves and gently inserted it into the wound. It may not have been the approved method, but it told me what I wanted to know.

"It was probably the bullet that killed him," I told Mrs. Sutton, pointing at the rod. "I can't say for certain, but there appears to be a straight path to the heart."

Mrs. Sutton nodded in agreement. "And the hole

is so small. I would say it was a derringer that was used, and that it was shot at close range, directly into the chest."

"You would?" I asked.

"I've seen a lot of gunshot wounds, Mrs. Wilcox."

"Indeed, you have."

Chin Tai opened the back door and led in Policeman Walter Lomax, his dark brown hat in his hands. He was an average-sized man with brown hair, broad shoulders, and a square jaw. He had the calm reserve of a much older man, though he couldn't have been older than thirty-five or so. Most folks thought him aloof and unfriendly, including myself. When I greeted him on the street, he seemed wary and as if he was wondering what I intended with my greeting.

I let Mrs. Sutton explain what we had found. When she had finished, Mr. Lomax fixed his deep brown eyes on me.

"And why are you here?" he asked, his voice deep and slightly raspy.

"She is my witness," Mrs. Sutton said. "Mrs. Wilcox knows anatomy and she is an honest, upstanding member of our community."

"They say he came out of your zanja," Mr. Lomax said to me, as he turned his hat around in his hands.

"Not quite," I said. "He was in the Zanja Madre and only floated to the top after they opened the sluice gate. They'd had trouble getting it open. I suspect the body had caught on the gate somehow. You can ask Mr. Worthington. Or better, his three helpers."

Mr. Lomax quirked an odd smile. "You don't trust Mr. Worthington?"

"He has never given me reason to," I replied, feeling annoyed. "On the other hand, Mr. Rivers never gave me reason to doubt him or his regard for me. But the question here is not who can or cannot be trusted but what do we do about this murder?"

Mr. Lomax shrugged. "Nothing much we can do. There's no telling who shot him."

"And let the killer go free?" I asked, my pique rising. "What about justice for Mr. Rivers?"

Mr. Lomax and Mrs. Sutton looked at each other, then at the body.

"I'd say Mr. Rivers got his justice," Mr. Lomax said.

I sank back. "Was he truly that evil?"

Again Mr. Lomax and Mrs. Sutton looked at each other.

She reached over and patted my hand. "Mrs. Wilcox, I know you considered him a friend. But he was no friend to many in this pueblo."

"Then why was there no outcry? Why didn't somebody speak up?"

"Because he was the zanjero," Mrs. Sutton said. "And people like you and the mayor and the city council and the men who own businesses in town, they all thought he was a good man."

"And those who knew otherwise didn't care," Mr. Lomax added with a shake of his head. "As long as he did his job and kept the peace, it didn't matter how he went about it. It's a harsh truth, and I beg your pardon. I do respect your delicate sensibilities."

I snorted. "My sensibilities aren't that delicate. Still. No one deserves to be murdered in cold blood. Not even the worst heathen."

Mr. Lomax gave his hat one final turn. "I'll talk to the marshal and ask around. Maybe somebody saw something. But, Mrs. Wilcox, it doesn't seem likely we'll find anything out."

"I thank you nonetheless, Mr. Lomax," I said. "Now, if you'll excuse me, I'll say good night. I am extraordinarily tired and this has been a most disturbing day."

Mr. Lomax followed me out of the funeral parlor and insisted on seeing me home. He remained taciturn, but I appreciated his kindness. Once home, I went straight to bed. It had, indeed, been a most disturbing day

CHAPTER THREE

My mind was in no way quieted the next day, but with wine to be racked and other chores on my rancho, I had little time to brood over it. I went to the viewing Tuesday night and couldn't help looking for who seemed genuinely grieved and who seemed to be merely giving the appearance of grief. I like to think myself an excellent judge of character, but it is also my nature to assume the best in those I meet.

The next morning, I returned to the Rivers' house for the funeral. Sarah Worthington, who had seemed genuinely grieved the night before, sat next to me. Her grief was still raw, but she seemed in better control of her faculties that morning.

Reverend Miller, whom I did not know well, gave the eulogy, heaping all manner of praise on Mr. Rivers. I do not know why, but it seems as though men of the cloth tend to fall into one of two categories. There are the large and imposing sorts, often handsome, with full heads of hair, and the small and bookish sorts, who usually wear glasses, are balding, and bear their authority like a shield. Reverend Miller conformed to the latter category, although he seemed more confident than others of his ilk.

"Bertram was a most caring and tender husband," the reverend intoned.

It was so soft, I thought I was imagining it, but I thought I heard a snort. Mrs. Rivers was sitting directly in front of me, her widow's weeds draped over her. The snort seemed to have come from that direction.

"He was a devoted friend and a kind employer,"

the reverend went on. "Indeed, he and his deputy, Mr. Worthington, were more than cousins, but as brothers to each other."

I definitely heard Sarah snort and hoped no one else had. There was little I could do about it at that moment, but after we'd all gone to the cemetery and were walking back, I made a point of walking with Sarah, slowly nudging her apart from the others in the group. She was wearing her light blue poplin and I was wearing my brown bombazine visiting dress. The light breeze lifted the ribbons on the black cockades we wore pinned to our sleeves.

"Did I hear you snort during Reverend Miller's eulogy?" I asked, trying to sound more amused than appalled.

"No," said Sarah. She looked at me. "Yes, I'm afraid I did. When the reverend said that Mr. Rivers and my Mr. Worthington were as brothers." She snorted again. "I suppose they were if the brothers were named Cain and Abel."

"I didn't know Mr. Worthington didn't care for Mr. Rivers," I said.

"They hated each other. They were cousins and grew up together, though I do not know what dispute started their enmity. I know Mr. Worthington was most distressed when Mr. Rivers was appointed zanjero. Mr. Worthington wanted the appointment, you know."

I hadn't known, but that was of little consequence. We were interrupted at just that moment by Mrs. Warren, the city marshal's wife, and Mrs. Judson, whose husband was the owner of the primary bank in the pueblo and also sat on the city council.

"Good afternoon, ladies," Mrs. Judson said. She was an average-sized woman with gray hair and was wearing a full skirted yellow dress with an overskirt draped to the back. "Have you heard the news? It's going around that Mr. Rivers met his end at the hands of another."

"What?" Sarah gasped, going pale.

Mrs. Warren, a dainty petite Mexican woman in dark blue, smiled like a satisfied cat. "Mr. Warren said that he'd received some intelligence that Mr. Rivers was actually murdered. Can you believe it? A murder? Here?"

I was about to remind Mrs. Warren that murder was actually all too common in our little pueblo, but held my tongue. After all, when a murder occurred, it was almost always the result of a fight, with the participants well-known. A killing by an unknown assailant was relatively rare, or at least rare enough to be remarked upon.

We paused as the widow, escorted by her sons, walked past. They say a widow wears her veil to spare her the embarrassment of others seeing her tears. I was glad of mine so that others couldn't see that I wasn't shedding any. Oddly enough, I got the impression that Mrs. Rivers' veil was also hiding a lack of grief.

"Poor thing," said Mrs. Judson softly.

"Indeed," said Mrs. Warren. "She's suffered so much."

"Mrs. Wilcox, Mrs. Worthington," Mrs. Judson said. "I am having a small tea party this afternoon and would be honored if you ladies would join us at two o'clock?"

"Why, yes, thank you," I said.

Sarah suddenly came to attention. "Yes. Thank you. It's very kind of you to ask us."

"You seem distracted," I said to Sarah as the other two ladies moved on.

"Hm? Oh. I'm afraid I am." Sarah sighed and tears threatened to spill onto her cheeks. "Poor Mr. Rivers. I thought the marshal had ruled the death an accident."

"Mrs. Worthington!" Caleb Worthington's approach prevented me from answering.

"Yes, Mr. Worthington?" Sarah answered, her disdain for her husband showing badly.

"Enough shilly-shallying," Mr. Worthington snarled. "There's work to be done. Get yourself home now."

Sarah glared at his retreating back then looked at me. "He is in a state. I fear I shall have to miss the tea party. I've tried explaining to him that my being social helps to advance his position in town, but he simply refuses to listen. Please offer my regrets to Mrs. Judson."

She left with a sigh and my heart yearned to ease her sorrow.

I went on my way and was shortly joined by Deputy Lomax.

"Mrs. Wilcox," he said quietly with a tip of his hat.

"Good afternoon, deputy. A sad day, isn't it?"

He nodded. "I talked to the marshal yesterday."

"I gathered. Mrs. Warren was saying just now that Mr. Rivers had been murdered, although she did not say how."

"Marshal Warren and I decided to keep that between us. Find out who knows more than he should." The deputy stopped walking and the toe of his boot poked at the dirt in the street as if he didn't want to say more. "You know how the marshal doesn't take notice much of women?"

"Unless one has a bounty on her head," I said.

Mr. Lomax quirked a wry grin in spite of himself. "I let him believe that it was Mr. Sutton who brought the bullet hole to my attention and didn't say you were there at all. Just to keep your reputation, ma'am."

"Thank you kindly for that. Deputy," I said.

"I'd be careful around the marshal, Mrs. Wilcox," Mr. Lomax's boot began poking at the dirt in the street again. "The man is still alive because he always shoots first." Mr. Lomax paused and gazed at his boot. "He asked me about the body being found in your zanja. So I talked to Mr. Worthington about it. He said it happened as you said."

"Indeed." That surprised me. "I had thought there was no love lost there."

"There isn't," said Deputy Lomax. "Which is all to

the good, since that's why Marshal Warren believed him. And Mr. Worthington is an honorable man, even if his temper sometimes gets the better of him."

The deputy looked like he wanted to say more but apparently decided against it.

"Indeed," I said again.

"In any case, ma'am, take care around the marshal," Deputy Lomax said. "He wants the matter cleared up as quickly as possible and will blame the first convenient person, guilty or not."

I nodded. Mr. Lomax had the right of it, and with the body having shown up so close to my rancho, one could make a case that I had left it there.

We said our goodbyes, and I made my way home to change clothes for the tea party. Juanita was in a foul temper and I suppose, as her mistress, I should have admonished her to keep her temper to herself. But even as Juanita served me, she was also my confidante and one who was wise beyond her twenty-one years. She'd only been with me for three years but had proved herself more than valuable as a maid and dare I say a friend. I was dreading the inevitable day when some young swain would court and marry her. It was only a matter of time. Juanita was very pretty, with a round, cheerful face, full black hair and a petite, rounded figure.

"No, no!" she protested, when I proposed to wear my green tea dress. "Wear the blue-flowered lawn. You wore the green one last time. They will remember and talk about it."

I sighed. Juanita was right.

"I do not see why you have to waste your time with those gallinas," Juanita continued in Spanish as she helped me out of the brown bombazine. "You are always in such a bad mood when you do."

"As the best hostesses in town, they buy a great deal of wine," I pointed out, as I usually did.

"Not as much as Governor Pico did for his fancy new restaurant and hotel. Or the saloons. Or the other

hotels. And you did not have to be friends with any of
their wives. And what about the agents buying wine to
sell in San Francisco?"

"And it was thanks to the introduction from las
gallinas that I was able to meet those agents, saloon
owners, and Governor Pico." My voice was slightly
muffled as Juanita threw the blue lawn dress over my
head. I pulled it around me and stood patiently while
she buttoned it up. "In addition, isn't it better to know
what those gossips are talking about? Forewarned is
forearmed."

Juanita hissed her annoyance. She continued to
scold, and I perhaps should have shushed her. But I
couldn't admonish her for what were largely my own
thoughts, as well. And it was an excellent reminder
that I needed to guard my tongue very carefully upon
arriving at Mrs. Judson's home.

"A small tea party," in Mrs. Judson's
understanding, was actually a fairly large party,
involving as many as twenty women, all wearing their
best hoops. There could be as many as ten of them in
the front parlor, all seated, as it was almost impossible
to move around so many whalebone hoops otherwise.
The later arrivals spilled out onto the veranda in front
of her magnificent white clapboard house. It hadn't
escaped anyone's notice that Mrs. Judson's own close
circle of friends always seemed to have arrived first.
The rest of the women tried to get there as early as
possible, as it was quite an honor to join the ladies in
the front parlor.

Mrs. Judson, herself, was a convivial old thing,
and with her surviving children grown and married,
she had little to do besides throw parties whenever
occasion warranted. With the mysterious death of Mr.
Rivers, occasion more than warranted.

I arrived in good time and still looking fresh, even
though the spring weather was beginning to warm up
already. I did not bring my leather satchel with me.
I couldn't around these ladies. They wouldn't have

understood. I was lucky enough to arrive sufficiently early to be seated in the front parlor in one of the better chairs near the fireplace, a bit of fortune I'd never previously achieved. But then it occurred to me that it was well-known that it was the opening of my sluice gate that had revealed the body.

Even more suspicious was that Mrs. Aguilar, the wife of our former mayor, was there as well. Mrs. Aguilar was one of the few women of position in our community who did not normally accept Mrs. Judson's invitations. Shortly after Mr. Aguilar had been elected the first time, Mrs. Aguilar was invited to a tea and did not arrive early enough to be seated in the parlor. For some reason, she took it rather personally. That she had come that day, and early enough to be admitted to the front parlor, was most curious, indeed.

Mrs. Judson, wearing another yellow lawn dress, had already greeted her guests on the veranda and settled herself near the parlor entry. Mrs. Carson, wearing a green-sprigged poplin gown over her plump figure, had been dominating the conversation, as she often did at gatherings. It was one of her usual themes, namely who would next set her cap for Mr. Prudent Beaudry, a wealthy landowner in town who also happened to be unmarried. That he seemed to have little inclination to marry failed to deter Mrs. Carson and her friends from either chasing him for their daughters or, if widowed, chasing him, themselves. Now that Mrs. Rivers was widowed, Mrs. Carson seemed to think that the late zanjero's wife should take up the chase.

"Of course, poor Mr. Rivers' death is such a tragedy," Mrs. Carson said, after noting that Mrs. Judson was in her seat and sipping tea.

All eyes in the room fastened themselves on me.

"It is, at that," I replied and, after a sip from my cup, decided to give them what they wanted. "And so shocking. There we were, my zanja perfectly dry and waiting. But the sluice gate was stuck and once it opened, he floated up out of the Zanja Madre. Poor Mrs.

Worthington fainted dead away."

Several of the women gasped in delicious shock.

"So terribly upsetting for you," Mrs. Judson said soothingly. "How will you ever get over it?"

I smiled at her. "It is difficult, but I am managing. Thank you ever so much for your concern."

"But how did the poor man end up in the zanja, I'd like to know," piped in Mrs. Downey. She was tall and dark, with a gaunt face and was wearing a lavender gown, which meant she was ending her year of mourning for her brother's death.

"We all thought that he'd fallen," Mrs. Warren said. She, too, was rarely seated in the front parlor and seemed quite pleased to be there. "There was that knock on the back of his head. Mr. Warren said that Mr. Rivers had probably fallen, struck his head and rolled into the zanja."

Mrs. Glassell, almost the twin of Mrs. Carson, simpered over her tea cup. "But he didn't fall, did he? Mrs. Warren, do you know who gave testimony that Mr. Rivers had been murdered?"

"I did," said Mrs. Aguilar. She was a relatively tall woman with dark black hair, and very imposing in her dark blue bombazine gown. "I was sitting up late that night. One of the children had the ague and I was looking out my window to pass the time. As you know, our house is across the street from Mahoney's Saloon."

"It's so terrible that they build those horrid places so close to where we decent people are living," complained Mrs. Fletcher, a stout woman with a high-pitched voice and a chronic cough that she mostly hid. "I do wish there was something the city council could do to stop it from happening."

The other women agreed noisily while I held my tongue. The city council had no interest in keeping the saloons at a distance from their homes because the men of the council enjoyed patronizing the saloons.

"It is a terrible thing," said Mrs. Judson over the babble. "But Mrs. Aguilar was telling us what she saw that night."

"Thank you, Mrs. Judson," Mrs. Aguilar said, with a brief smile. "Even though it was Sunday, there were plenty of men going in and out of the saloon. Sometimes I think the city council meets there more often than they meet at the city hall."

Here, the women tittered, as did I, because Mrs. Aguilar was absolutely correct about that. Even the Temperance men visited the saloon.

Mrs. Aguilar smiled again and continued. "Mr. Aguilar was there that night, although he came home around eight-thirty. Alicia was restless and wanted a cup of water sometime after the clock struck ten. While she was drinking it, I looked out the window, and there was someone lying on his back in front of the saloon. Not very unusual, I must say, sadly."

Again, there was a general murmur, this time of sad agreement.

"So," Mrs. Aguilar said. "I did not think much of it. I kept looking, just to look, and he was still there even after eleven. I also saw two women, at different times, both walking away from the saloon toward our houses."

This sent the hens fluttering as nothing else had. After all, what decent, God-fearing woman went abroad alone that late at night? Well, I knew of many reasons why one would, in my own case, going to the aid of a sick or injured loved one after sending whatever messenger on ahead. Or Sarah Worthington, trying to bring her husband back home before he became too far in his cups to walk.

"But, Mrs. Aguilar," I asked loudly over the general outcry. "Why do you believe it was Mr. Rivers who was out there?"

"Because just as Alicia began to settle down and sleep, I saw that the man was gone. It was almost midnight. I heard something dragging from outside and looked down from the other window. I could not see who it was, just the body being dragged under the window toward the zanja."

"It had to have been Mr. Rivers!" coughed Mrs. Fletcher over yet another round of flustered cackling.

"I fear so," said Mrs. Aguilar. "Although I did not think so, at first. I assumed someone was dragging the fallen person home. It could have been Mr. Worthington lying there, or someone else."

"But if it were Mr. Worthington, he'd have been dragged in the other direction," Mrs. Carson pointed out.

"I didn't know for certain if it was Mr. Worthington." Mrs. Aguilar said, smiling pleasantly even as her eyes shot daggers at Mr. Carson. "Actually, I had no idea who the fallen person was. I only said Mr. Worthington by way of example. It could have been anyone. It was a dark night and well past time that we are required to keep our lanterns lit."

"That's right," said Mrs. Downey. "The moon is on the wane."

"Assuming it was Mr. Rivers that Mrs. Aguilar saw," I said, nodding my head in courtesy toward her. "Which given the circumstances, one would have to think it probably was, how did he end up in front of the saloon on his back and then in the zanja?"

"I think the better question to ask is who killed him?" sniffed Mrs. Carson.

"But who would want to?" asked Mrs. Judson. "I mean, he had his failings, like any other man."

Here there was a round of knowing looks.

"Poor Mrs. Rivers," sighed Mrs. Hewitt, who was decidedly mousy in appearance and even demeanor. But she was known for the ferocity of her temper when crossed. "She suffered so much."

"Still," said Mrs. Glassell. "I have heard that there are others in town who might not have found Mr. Rivers quite so congenial. Mrs. Elmwood, for example, is known to be less than charitable toward him."

"The minister's wife?" asked Mrs. Fletcher.

"Yes," said Mrs. Glassell.

"I've always found her to be the most Christian of

women," Mrs. Warren said.

There were more knowing looks and I began to realize that they were all among Mrs. Judson's personal circle of friends. I wondered what they knew that I didn't. That's when I began to understand that the privilege of sitting in Mrs. Judson's parlor had less to do with a timely arrival on my part and more to do with what she and her friends wanted to know. I tried to quash the unworthy feelings that arose at that moment. Mrs. Judson had a right to choose how she entertained, and I couldn't imagine how she arranged everyone's arrivals.

Still, there was a reason I always returned from her parties feeling as though I had been vaguely insulted. I had thought it was merely the chatter of the other ladies. But in reality, it was because I somehow knew I was being snubbed. And being offered the front parlor seat only because I was of interest to this flock of gallinas, well, I must say, that made my pique rise considerably.

I took advantage of the clock chiming to put down my cup and rise.

"Look at the time," I said with a brief smile. "Ladies, do forgive me, but I must be headed home."

"I will join you," said Mrs. Aguilar, also rising.

Mrs. Judson followed us to the front hallway. "Dear Mrs. Wilcox, thank you so much for coming. And, Mrs. Aguilar, it's always a pleasure to see you."

"Thank you, Mrs. Judson." Mrs. Aguilar's smile was properly pleasant, but her eyes did not mirror any warmth.

"It was a lovely tea," I said, also pleasantly. "Thank you for having me."

Mrs. Judson glanced up as Mrs. Aguilar was let out by the maid, then took my hand.

"I hope you were not too put off by the discussion," Mrs. Judson said with sincere kindness. "I suppose it was a bit unseemly for women to be discussing a murder. But they do get so excited and, like me, haven't much else to absorb their interest."

"Thank you for your concern," I said. "And I really must be on my way."

The maid let me out and I noticed Mrs. Sutton sitting on the veranda watching me as I left. I waved and gestured that I could not stay, then hurried down the street after Mrs. Aguilar.

She chuckled as she saw me come alongside her.

"You had enough of las gallinas, too?" she said amiably.

"More than enough." I sighed and looked back toward Mrs. Judson's house. "I have no idea how she managed it, but I got the distinct impression that she arranged it so that I'd be on time to be seated in the parlor."

"She tells people she wants there to come at an earlier time," Mrs. Aguilar said. "I came early that first time and was told that Mrs. Judson wasn't ready. I saw Mrs. Carson come by and be admitted immediately. Then Mrs. Sutton came by and was told that Mrs. Judson wasn't ready. When we showed up at the time we'd been asked, we were told the front parlor was full and were seated on the veranda."

"Oh, dear," I sighed. "How unkind."

"It is the way of the world," said Mrs. Aguilar. "And I think it is Mrs. Judson's way of trying to be kind while still keeping everyone in their place."

I shook my head, trying to rid myself of all the sordid feelings coming up. "How is Alicia doing?"

"Quite well." Mrs. Aguilar smiled with genuine warmth. "Thank you so much for bringing the quinine and sitting with her during the worst of her fever last week."

"I'm glad she made it through," I said.

It was a little early in the year for the ague, but not unheard of. Nor was what we now call malaria a rare disease in the pueblo, especially since back then we did not know that mosquitos were the cause. Many young children did not survive it. Alicia, at 10 years old, was, fortunately, a strong child.

"Mrs. Aguilar," I said, as something suddenly occurred to me. "Mrs. Hewitt said something, and I heard Mrs. Warren say the same earlier, that Mrs. Rivers had suffered so much. Do you know what that suffering was?"

"We women suffer from a lot of things, not least, our husbands." Mrs. Aguilar chuckled. "I know Mr. Rivers was often drunk, and I have heard he was less than kind to many here. But I do not know how much of that Mrs. Rivers knew about."

"Well, thank you kindly for the talk." I handed her my visiting card. "Please feel free to call on me at your leisure."

"Thank you. It is very kind of you." Mrs. Aguilar handed me one of her cards. "And please call on me at any time. I know Alicia will want to say hello."

With a pleasant nod from each of us, we parted ways and I walked quickly back to Rancho De Las Flores.

Chapter Four

There, los hermanos Ortiz had everybody working at full tilt. Supper would be late again. Sebastiano and I had concluded that we should rack the cabernet sauvignon and he wanted to get as much of the laborious process done as possible while there was still daylight to see by.

Racking is the process of moving wine from the fermenting vats or barrels into the barrels where the wine will finish aging and then be sold. It is a long process that takes a certain amount of attention because, as wine ferments, it leaves behind all manner of lees and detritus, none of which makes the wine taste any better. So, it's best to rack at least once after the first fermentation is done, and then a second or third time. I believe we were doing a third racking that year. Or was it the year we did the fourth racking? I do not recall now and Sebastiano kept all the notes from the winery.

Sebastiano's brother, Enrique, had Rodolfo Sanchez and Wang Fu in the cornfield, getting the ground ready for planting. I noted that the beans looked as though they'd already been planted.

Sebastiano and Enrique were the rancho foremen. Sebastiano was in charge of the winery and everything that went on there. Enrique cared for the vineyard. I had tried calling each brother Mr. Ortiz but every time I did, the one I did not require was the one who answered. So I used their Christian names and they often used mine.

It is, perhaps, a dreadful habit to be so familiar with

one's servants. But my late and much-lamented mother was equally familiar with hers, which drove my father to fits of apoplexy. Mother was a transcendentalist and firmly believed that all humans were equal in the sight of God, and as such, deserved respect. I do not know if Mr. Thoreau or Mr. Emerson or Mr. Alcott extended that philosophy to Negroes and Chinamen and Indians but my mother did. Which also drove my father to fits of apoplexy. Nonetheless, our servants were fiercely loyal to my mother, and when I became a woman of property, I followed her example and have been largely blessed that I did.

Olivia, Sebastiano's wife and the cook, was busy in the outdoor kitchen on the adobe's patio. Since it was still a fine day, she already had the tables set up in the yard between the adobe and barracks house, where the rest of the servants and hands lived. Normally, I would have dressed for dinner, but we only had supper unless there were guests. I hurried into the adobe and my bedroom and exchanged my tea dress and hoops for a work dress. Then I returned to the winery, where our Chinese hands, Wei Li and Wei Chin were solemnly watching the wine pouring from the great fermenting barrel into the smaller aging ones. Sebastiano almost had the last of the cabernet sauvignon racked, so I took over checking barrel seals for Hernan Mendoza. Hernan's cousins, Emilio and Pascual Mendoza, were slowly moving the newly filled barrels the to the cart that would take them to the cold room, which had been built into the side of a small hill not far from the eastern edge of my property.

It was getting on for seven o'clock when the last of the barrels had been filled. Sebastiano had Emilio and Pascual push the carretta back into the winery, as it was still cool enough at night that the wine would not be harmed.

In the meantime, Wang Fu and the Wei brothers took their leaves to go back to town, since they did not live on the property as did the others. It was their choice, and I thought at the time that it was because there were quite a few children on the rancho, and with them, a fair amount of noise. Not only did Sebastiano and Enrique have their wives working for me (Magdalena, Enrique's wife, was my housekeeper), their children lived with us until they got married and had their own homes. That spring of 1870, the Ortiz children were mostly youths, with three of the eldest living in the adobe but working elsewhere. In addition, Hernan's wife, Maria, helped Magdalena with keeping the household, and Anita, Rodolfo's wife, was the nanny to all of the children, especially Maria's, since they were quite small at the time. Juanita, my personal maid, was still single.

The other reason my Chinese laborers went to their homes at night, I thought, was that conversation at suppertime was as likely to be in Spanish as it was in English, and it generally overflowed from all ages and stations. I was never one to hold with the idea of children being seen and not heard, at least, not all of the time.

As I have already stated, the weather was quite fine, so we ate at the tables in the yard, under the lanterns strung from several poles. As we finished, the children, or anyone still going to school, were dismissed to the library to practice their lessons. Then we adults enjoyed a less restricted conversation, which that evening could only have been the murder of the Zanjero, Bertram Rivers.

"It's all anyone is talking about," Enrique said. Unlike his older brother, Enrique was tall and did not wear a mustache. His face was bronzed even darker, thanks to all the time he spent under the sun in the vineyards.

I don't recall if we were speaking in English or Spanish or both that night, but I'll relate the conversation in English.

"I'm not surprised," I said.

Olivia, a stout woman with a sour face that belied

her sweet nature, snorted as she gathered empty dishes from the table.

"The poor man," she said.

"Pah!" spat Magdalena. As thin as Olivia was stout, she had a round face that was usually smiling. "He got what he deserved. He was an evil man."

"Ay, he was," Maria jumped in. "Did you hear about the Vasquez family?"

"Baldo and Constanza?" Magdalena asked.

"Poor Constanza," Anita said. "She has no children, either." A truly beautiful young woman, with exceptionally glossy dark hair, she wore her suffering like a shawl about her shoulders. She was barren and it troubled her a great deal, never mind that she raised almost all of the children of the household.

"There, there, Anita," Juanita reached over and patted Anita's back. The two were cousins and very close.

"So tell us!" begged Magdalena. Being the housekeeper, she didn't get away from the rancho that often. "What about Baldo and Constanza?"

Maria was the most likely to be sent on errands, and as such, was the most likely to hear the best gossip in town.

"Señor Rivers cheated him," Maria said. "Never got a full day's pay for any of his work on the zanjas. He wanted to quit, but Señor Rivers wouldn't let him. He doesn't have any help on his rancho and Señor Rivers wouldn't let him pay someone to do the work for him."

All the farms around the city that got water from the Zanja Madre were required to supply a certain amount of manual labor to keep the zanjas in good working order. It seemed fair enough until you realized that not every farmer, including Mr. Vasquez, had the men to spare.

Olivia waved at Maria, who picked up the stack of dirty dishes and hurried them to the kitchen while Olivia flopped down into her seat.

"It's a sad thing that someone who had so much

responsibility abused it so badly," she observed.

"Eh, Basto," said Enrique. "Tell them what Señor Mahoney told us this afternoon."

Sebastiano shifted slowly. "We were at his saloon, making our usual delivery. Oh, Maddie, he wants a barrel of angelica delivered tomorrow. There's going to be a party."

"We'll select one in the morning," I said. "Thank you."

"So, after we put the delivery in the strong room, Señor Mahoney offered us each a beer," Sebastiano continued. "We were at the bar drinking it, and everyone was talking about Señor Rivers. Then Señor Mahoney told us all that Señor Rivers and Señor Worthington had a terrible fight at the saloon the night Señor Rivers was killed."

"Did he say what about?" I asked.

"No. Just that the two began hitting each other and Señor Worthington said he wanted to kill Señor Rivers,"

I frowned. "I had heard that they were not the best of friends."

"Sad for two men who looked so much alike," said Rodolfo. "You'd have thought they were brothers."

"They were cousins but they hated each other," Hernan said. "When I was working with them last year, we kept waiting for them to start beating each other up. They never did, but you could tell they wanted to."

"Maybe that's why the city council hasn't made Señor Worthington zanjero yet," said Maria, returning to the table.

"They've certainly had a meeting or two since then," I said, pausing to reflect on that.

It did seem a little odd that the council hadn't made the appointment but it was not unheard of. I couldn't help but wonder if Mr. Mahoney's upcoming party would have some bearing on the decision, as most of the councilmen would likely be there and talking about it.

The conversation moved to other topics, including the laying down of the cabernet sauvignon wine and whether to rack the latest vintage of the angelica. The fortified wines were rarely racked until they were added to the sherry barrels in which they would be sold. But there was the occasional vintage where the lees, or other detritus, were heavier than normal and could queer the wine. But while the lees were rather heavy that year, they weren't so heavy that we had cause to worry and we ultimately decided not to rack.

After the meal, I went to the library with Anita to hear the children's lessons. We did have two school houses in the pueblo but they were run by the Americans, so Mexican children often got short shrift. Anita was an excellent teacher and I helped out as much as possible. Already I could see that Sebastiano's daughter Elena, who was 15 at the time, would have made a wonderful doctor. I was trying to figure out how to send Ramon, Sebastiano's eldest and a strapping lad of 19, to college. He had gotten a job at the new Pico House, serving as a maitre d'hotel in the restaurant, however, and was proving to be quite the astute businessman. It was probably just as well, as I was unable to find a man to champion Ramon's cause. Or that of any of the Ortiz children. It was hard enough to get those of them who were amenable into the Normal School, attitudes being what they were and, alas, still are. But I digress. The Normal School wasn't even started until well after the event I'm relating here.

Work started early on the rancho. I rose before dawn the following day, as is my usual practice. As soon as I was dressed, I met Sebastiano in the adobe patio so that we could break our fast, then select a barrel for Mr. Mahoney and decide whether to rack the angelica and which barrels would require it. I had learned the hard way that it is better to have eaten before performing this most pleasant of duties, as one must taste from the barrels to make a good selection. I also made no plans to be out and about, since the smell

of sherry would be rather strong on my breath, even if
I spit out a goodly bit of it.

Therefore, it was with no little irritation that I
learned heard in the midst of the sherry-sampling
that Mrs. Elmwood was waiting in the front parlor of
the adobe for me. Mrs. Elmwood was the wife of my
church's pastor. If I am truly honest, I must concede
that I never found her company all that pleasant. If
anything, I regarded her as pleasant but vapid. She
was a rather rotund woman and had a rather fluttery
aspect about her. Her hair was a deep brown, shot
through with gray, and her eyes were green and
constantly looking everywhere but at the person to
whom she was speaking.

I almost told Maria to tell Mrs. Elmwood that I
was not in. However, given that Mrs. Elmwood did not
particularly care for calling on her husband's flock, her
doing so unannounced during the week meant that
there was a matter of some consequence afoot.

"Please tell her that I am not dressed to receive," I
told Maria. "If she does not mind, then I will be happy
to speak with her. Or I can have her to tea tomorrow,
or speak with her after services on Sunday."

Maria appeared a minute later to say that Mrs.
Elmwood's business was most urgent and she was not
concerned that I was wearing my work clothes. As I
left the winery, I grabbed a fistful of mint leaves from
the patch next to the winery and rinsed them in the
small fountain in the patio that we use as a well. I
took a moment before entering the front parlor to chew
furiously on the leaves. I doubted it would cover the
smell of sherry, but it could not be helped and I knew I
was blameless.

If Mrs. Elmwood noted the smell on my breath,
she had the good grace to say nothing. Perhaps it was
because she was too preoccupied with her own concerns
at that moment.

"It's good of you to see me, Mrs. Wilcox," she
said in her soft, fluttery voice. "I know I am intruding

abominably, but I truly had nowhere else to turn." She paused and leaned forward from her perch on the sofa. "I need to speak to someone who is discreet."

Which, at last, began to make sense. I will engage in the usual tittle-tattle when there is no harm to come of it. However, I refuse, then and now, to engage in gossip. I try not to listen to it, but no one can expect to have friends in society and not hear the full breadth of local rumor. That I would not spread it is was known in the pueblo, and thus Mrs. Elmwood's visit.

"How can I help you, Mrs. Elmwood?" I asked, sitting on the chair across from her.

She sat up straight, laid her hands in her lap and gazed out the front window. "I am concerned. You will have heard by now that two women were seen walking abroad the night Mr. Rivers met his untimely death."

"I have," I said.

"And, as such, those two women must be looked upon with suspicion of at least having seen something amiss." She paused, her eyes flicking up to meet mine briefly, then she gazed straight ahead. "I am not one of those two."

"I had no reason to believe that you were," I said. "So why do you come to tell me this?"

"I have two reasons. One is my concern for you, my dear. You are known to go abroad alone at night." She held up her hand before I could protest. "True, it also well known that you do so for the most charitable of reasons, although you might wish to be a bit more discerning in your charity. But you do go abroad at night and alone. That means you could have been one of the two women who were seen."

"I suppose," I said. Fortunately, since she was looking everywhere but at me, she did not see me bite my lip as I considered. "But while I was not at home, I was off the streets all that night. I did not leave until almost six o'clock the next morning when I oversaw the opening of the zanja that revealed Mr. Rivers body."

"Oh." She fell into herself, utterly deflated. "That

brings me to my second reason for speaking with you. I was hoping you had seen something. You see..." Her gaze fell onto her lap. "I was not one of those two women who were seen. I was nowhere near Mr. Mahoney's saloon. But I was abroad that night, and alone, myself. I was hoping you had seen me and could testify to my good character should need arise. It was for charity's sake that I was out."

"I don't doubt that," I said.

"Poor Mrs. Hemphill," Mrs. Elmwood sighed. "She went wandering again that night, searching for her husband and sons. Her daughter, Mrs. Ontiveras— You know her, don't you?

"I do."

Mrs. Elmwood fixed her gaze on her hands again. "Mrs. Ontiveras has her hands full with her children, six of them, you know. But she has graciously taken in her poor widowed and ailing mother. We found Mrs. Hemphill quickly enough, not far from the hill near Mr. Beaudry's property. But it was no small struggle to get her home. And once there, she was so very agitated, she could not be left alone. We gave her some chamomile tea, and finally had to tie her to her bed." Mrs. Elmwood shook her head in dismay.

I pressed my lips together and held silent. It was my opinion that Mrs. Hemphill could have used a dose of laudanum. There was no question that the drug was often overused, being given to women for even the least of the vapors, a practice I deplored even then. Mrs. Elmwood, herself, had good reason to disdain the drug, as her sister had become addicted and died of it. In Mrs. Hemphill's case, however, it would have been a Godsend. But it was not my place to say so, so I forbore to make any comment.

"In any case," Mrs. Elmwood continued, straightening up and gazing at the wall. "It was well after ten o'clock before Mrs. Hemphill fell asleep and I could leave her. I suppose I could have sent the house boy for Mr. Elmwood, but I didn't care to disturb the reverend's rest. I was only going home, two streets away and nowhere near any of those despicable saloons or other such places. Why should I disturb Mr. Elmwood's rest, especially when I could go to my own that much more quickly?"

"Perfectly understandable," I said.

"But if someone saw me and drew the wrong conclusion," Mrs. Elmwood shuddered and put her hand to her mouth. "I should be horrified."

And thus you can see why I do not and will not spread gossip. Here was a woman doing an act of Christian charity who merely wanted to get to bed quickly without disturbing her husband, and yet she feared for her reputation simply because of the malicious nature of idle women who had little better to do than assign the worst motives to the even most innocent of acts. Thoughts of Mrs. Judson's tea party the day before sprang, unbidden, into my mind. I decided then and there that I would not attend another unless there was a good, solid, needful reason to go.

"There, there, Mrs. Elmwood," I said calmly. "Should the need arise, I will be happy to testify to your good character. But I don't see the need arising. I think most people in this town are well aware of your goodness."

Mrs. Elmwood sighed. "I do hope so." She stood. "I have intruded abominably. Pray forgive me. And thank you so much for the kind words and for your discretion."

"You're very welcome."

I saw her out, then returned to the winery. By the time Sebastiano and I had picked out a cask for Mr. Mahoney, Hernan and the Wei brothers had returned with the now-empty carretta after loading the cabernet sauvignon into the cold room, which was actually an underground cave built into a small hill not far from the eastern edge of the property. We did not mention to anyone that it was there as there were those of malicious intent who thought it amusing to destroy and taint barrels.

The carretta still being hitched to one of the two mules, Sebastiano had Hernan load the cask we'd selected for Mr. Mahoney, and Sebastiano left to deliver it. Meanwhile, I started organizing the next barrels that we were going to rack of the merlot, I believe, while Hernan and the Wei brothers set about washing the barrels that would receive the wine.

I do not know how many other wineries followed that practice. The concept of sanitation in the care of the sick and injured was still relatively new then. However, I saw no reason not to apply it to my winemaking. So while Sebastiano had questioned it many years ago, I insisted and we had fewer bad barrels, I believe.

We had just finished and I was about to commence racking when there was a great rattling clatter from the road. I stepped into the yard just in time to see Sebastiano trotting the mule and the empty carretta through the open gate. He pulled the mule up and tossed the reins to Wei Chin, then jumped from the seat.

"Maddie!" he called, running up. "Your friend, Mrs. Medina. She has just been arrested for the murder of Mr. Rivers."

CHAPTER FIVE

Idid not know if the members of my household approved of my friendship with Regina Medina, but they did respect it. I was horrified by Sebastiano's news, not the least because I knew that she was, in fact, completely innocent of the murder. Leaving the racking in Sebastiano's capable hands, I immediately went to my room and summoned Juanita.

She helped me into my best green bombazine walking suit, a treat I'd had made for myself for Christmas the prior winter. As I fastened the jet brooch I wore with it onto the rather neat lapel, I choked. Regina had given me the color plate from her own collection of fashion books, and I'd had my dressmaker work from that. It was quite a cunning and smart suit, featuring a swept-back skirt and ruffles of matching silk ribbon, with still more ribbon ruching over the bodice. Fortunately, I only needed my smaller hoops underneath, as where I was going was not sympathetic to hoop skirts at all.

I decided to walk. It would take too much time to hitch the rig to Daisy, not to mention taking Sebastiano away from the critical work of racking the merlot. I could have driven myself, but ladies driving generally gave rise to far too much comment. So I made my way to the Clocktower Courthouse, which was essentially the city hall.

It was a brick building with two floors and a white cupola clock tower on top, a very impressive addition to our little pueblo. The bottom floor held the marketplace, where on any given day, one could buy produce, leather goods, all manner of necessities and oddities. Upstairs were the county courtrooms and city offices. The police office and jail were behind the building. That is where I went.

The office was open, but City Marshal William Warren was absent. The front of the office was a long room divided lengthwise by a tall counter with a gate at one end. There was a desk behind the counter with a door next to it that led, I guessed, to the jail.

I called out and Mr. Lomax appeared from the back.

"How do, Mrs. Wilcox," he said, looking as though he wanted to ask why I was there, but wouldn't.

"I need to speak to Marshal Warren immediately," I told him. "He's got the wrong person in jail."

"You mean Mrs. Medina?"

"Yes. She did not kill Mr. Rivers," I said. "Have you talked to her, Mr. Lomax?"

"Some," he conceded.

I looked him in the eye. "Does she know how Mr. Rivers was killed?"

He glanced back at the cells. "Don't rightly know."

"Let me talk to her," I asked. "I'll see if I can find anything out. You can listen at the doorway, so there's a witness. Just please don't let her see you listening. She may not reveal anything."

Mr. Lomax mulled this over for a full count of ten, then nodded. He let me through the gate, then through the door in the back wall. It led, as I had surmised, to the three jail cells. Two were fortunately empty. Regina was in the far cell, alone. She wore a sprigged lawn at-home dress, but her long, luxurious tresses were down.

"Good day, Mrs. Medina," I said in full voice.

"Ma- Mrs. Wilcox!" Regina gasped, then straightened up. She glanced over at Mr. Lomax. "To what do I owe the honor?"

"Mr. Lomax, would you excuse us, please?" I asked.

He nodded and left the doorway but did not close the door.

"Maddie," Regina whispered angrily. "What are you doing here? Have you no thought for what the town biddies will say when they find out?"

"I'm trying to get you out," I whispered back, then lifted my voice to normal speaking tones. "I have good cause to believe you to be innocent of the murder, Mrs. Medina. Therefore, I would like to secure your release from this odious place as soon as possible."

"Don't give yourself up for me, Maddie," Regina whispered, tears forming in her eyes. She looked over at the doorway. I nodded. She raised her voice. "That's very kind of you, Mrs. Wilcox. But I fear that my convenience as a woman of ill-repute in this town will bear more weight with the marshal and the judge. That's the only reason I am accused. No one saw me abroad that night, as I was not. And why, in Heaven's name, would I waste my time bashing in Bert Rivers' head?"

I broke into a smile. "Indeed, Mrs. Medina. I agree. That is why I am here. I realize it is not a popular opinion. But it is the Christian thing to do. If you will excuse me, I will make my case to the marshal."

I nodded and left Regina hanging on the bars looking after me, utterly distraught.

On the other side of the door, Mr. Lomax stood, that odd quirked smile of his on his lips.

"You never said how you knew she was innocent," he said.

"Well, I think we've just proved it," I replied. "She, like everyone else, thinks that it was the head injury that killed Mr. Rivers."

He glanced back at the cells. "I'll talk to the marshal."

The which, as fortune would have it, walked into the office at just that moment.

"Talk to me about what?" Marshal William Warren demanded.

He was a medium-sized man, with dark hair and eyes, an unruly, overgrown mustache and beard, and a perpetual sneer on his face. He wore the usual dark suit, which was, as usual, covered in dust. He was well-known for his tendency to shoot quickly and his overwhelming interest in hunting down runaway prostitutes for the bounties offered by the men who owned their contracts.

The latter was, perhaps, not entirely his fault. His pay, and that of his police deputies, partly came from commissions on the fines and bounties that they collected.

"Well?' Marshal Warren demanded. "And what is she doing there?"

"Mrs. Wilcox came to offer Christian comfort to Mrs. Medina," Mr. Lomax said. "And during their conversation, it became apparent that Mrs. Medina does not know how Mr. Rivers actually died."

"That's very interesting," the marshal growled. "But I don't see as how that means much."

"She's innocent," I sputtered in spite of myself. "At least of the murder. How can you keep her locked up when she didn't kill anyone?"

"I can do what I want." Marshal Warren hitched up his pants. He sidled past me to one of the desks and got out a can of tobacco. "Besides, there's plenty of folks who think Mrs. Medina is guilty of something worth hanging for, so I expect they're not terribly worried what the actual charge is."

I gaped in horror as the Marshal not only rolled a cigarette in front of me, a lady, but lit it. I looked over at Mr. Lomax for some explanation for this incredible display of rude behavior. But even as I did, as the sun breaks over the hills on a clear morning, I came to understand the marshal's interest in keeping Regina in jail. A goodly portion of his pay came from collecting bounties on runaway prostitutes. Regina, however, was uncommonly good to the women in her, ahem, employ, and so they seldom ran away on their contracts. As for the few that did, Regina simply let them go. Hence, she was not a source of income to the marshal, and it appeared that he was aggrieved because he thought she should have been.

As distasteful as that realization was, it did provide me with an appeal which might interest the marshal more.

"I suspect our esteemed city council might be concerned if Mrs. Medina is detained unnecessarily," I said.

I had little expectation that the members of the city council would stand up for Regina of their own accord. However, I also knew that they preferred her house over any in the pueblo. It was, by far, the cleanest and the most pleasant. While Regina had never said anything, I'd heard them many times from the front room whilst I was helping a sick or injured girl in another.

"They do seem to like Mrs. Medina's place," Mr. Lomax added, which surprised me.

"Mr. Lomax!" I gasped, in supposed shock that our city council would frequent such a place. I was trying to preserve the illusion that I was too ladylike to even know about such things.

It was a fine point that entirely escaped the notice of the city marshal. He glared at me then glanced at Mr. Lomax.

"All right," he grumbled, glaring at me again. "So tell me who I should put in jail for the murder."

"Why the guilty party, of course," I said.

"And who would that be?" Marshal Warren demanded. He let out a loud, satisfied snort when I could not answer. He tossed his cigarette butt to the floor and smashed it with his boot toe. "What you fail to appreciate, Mrs. Wilcox, is that it's my job to keep the peace in this town. But since you're so all fired up for the cause of justice, I'll make you a deal. You bring me someone I can hang for Bert Rivers' murder and I'll let Mrs. Medina off. I'll give you 'til... When does Judge Sepulveda get back from riding circuit?"

"Wednesday," Mr. Lomax said.

"Wednesday, it is." Marshal Warren slapped his tummy in satisfaction. "And just to show you good faith, I'll let Mrs. Medina go now. Of course, if she bolts, I'll take that as evidence that she's guilty and I will find her. And that won't do your reputation in this town any good at all."

"As long as my reputation is that of a compassionate Christian woman, that's all that matters to me," I said with far more conviction than I actually felt.

I see now that I cared far more for the good opinion of the ladies of the pueblo's society than, perhaps, I should have. It was also true that I did have my winery business to maintain. So it is perhaps understandable, though not to my credit, that I wavered in my resolve for a moment. It was only a moment, however.

Marshal Warren did not seem to notice, nor would he have cared if he had. He tossed the keys to the cells at Mr. Lomax, who went to the back and retrieved Regina. Marshal Warren settled himself into the chair behind his desk and rolled another cigarette. He had good reason to be satisfied. He'd saved himself from angering the city council by closing down their favorite house and put all the blame for whatever outcome squarely on my shoulders.

I shuddered inwardly, wondering why, in Heaven's Name, I'd done what I'd done. My mother often said that my biggest fault was to rush in without consideration of all the consequences, and it appeared I had done so yet again. Still, if one was going to follow the dictates of Our Loving Lord and Savior, one stood up for the cause of justice. Which meant I had to find the guilty party in only five days, and I had no idea how I was to go about it.

Mr. Lomax, God bless him, took care of seeing both myself and Regina outside. The streets were empty, but I had no doubt the pueblo would soon be abuzz with the news of Marshal Warren's "deal." I tried not to worry about my reputation. It was already whispered that I offered my charity to any who asked or needed, and there were those who disapproved of this practice. But I did have friends within Mrs. Judson's inner circle, and the outer circle, as well. Or so I thought. Fortunately, I now realize I wouldn't have done anything differently had I known just how duplicitous my so-called friends would turn out to be.

Regina held her head high as we left the police office. But I caught her looking at me and it was clear she was quite angry at what I had done. I suspected I knew why she was and tried to forgive her. Still, I was somewhat nettled at her lack of gratitude.

As we landed on the Calle Principal, I called out to Mr. Lomax.

"I'm going to make a call first before I return to my rancho," I told him.

He nodded and gestured at Regina to lead on.

I made my way to Sarah Worthington's house. She was quite happy to receive me and we shortly found ourselves comfortably situated in her front parlor, with tea and biscuits and cactus pear jam.

"So have you heard about Mrs. Medina being arrested for the murder?" Sarah asked me as soon as her maid Hannah had left us alone.

"Not only have I heard, I have seen to her release from jail," I announced. "She is not guilty of that particular crime."

"You what?" Sarah almost shrieked, then recovered herself. "Maddie, my dearest friend, have you taken leave of your good senses? Everyone in town will be talking about you and it will not be kind."

I sighed. "I know. But it cannot be helped. She is, as I noted, innocent of the murder. What kind of Christian would I be if I let an injustice like that come to pass? The worst of it is, Marshal Warren has given me only a few days to find the true killer."

"And how do you propose to do that?" Sarah asked with a skeptical sniff.

"I haven't the faintest idea." I set my teacup on the sofa's end table and stared at the plate of biscuits.

"I suppose my first step should be to find those two women that Mrs. Aguilar saw that night. They must have seen something."

"Or you could look at who had reason to kill Mr. Rivers," Sarah said, thoughtfully picking up a biscuit. "Though who that might be, I have no idea. Perhaps Mrs. Rivers would know."

"I can't disturb a newly widowed woman in her grief," I said, more for the sake of propriety than reality as I had reason to believe that Mrs. Rivers was not grieving overmuch. "Still, her house is not far from the saloon where Mr. Rivers was supposed to have fallen. Maybe she saw something that night." I looked over at Sarah. "It comes to my mind that you were abroad that night, searching for Mr. Worthington."

"Are you accusing me?" she snapped.

I was taken aback by her vehemence.

"No," I said, slowly. "I just wondered what, if anything, you saw that night."

Sarah sniffed and took out her handkerchief. "I'm so sorry I snapped, Maddie. Mr. Worthington simply gets more and more tiresome every day. He has no regard for my feelings or for my position in the town's society. I was so pleased to hear of Mrs. Medina's arrest if only because he would not be able to visit her house anymore."

I decided not to tell Sarah that I'd never heard or seen her husband over at Regina's. I didn't care to reveal even to her that I had more than a passing familiarity with the house, never mind that it was purely in the interests of Christian charity. Nor was I there that often, so it was entirely likely I had missed seeing Mr. Worthington there. I also decided not to opine that closing Regina's house would not do much good in terms of deterring Mr. Worthington. Or any of the men in the pueblo. They had simply too many other options and there was little likelihood that the pueblo would ever be rid of such places of ill-repute. But then, something else occurred to me.

"Sarah, aren't you afraid to be out so late at night, around men who might be shooting at each other?" I asked.

Sarah allowed herself a smug grin. "I have my trusty derringers." Then her aspect changed and she sighed. "Oh, Maddie, what's a woman to do?"

I shrugged. "I suppose you could divorce Mr. Worthington. Given his frequent drunkenness, I suppose you might even get a good settlement. At the very least, you'd have a chance to find a more tender husband."

"But I would never be acceptable to society. I would be humiliated." Sarah took out her handkerchief again, her distress growing. "And that would be if I could get a settlement and then a new husband. What if I couldn't get a settlement? What if I was thrown out to fend for myself on the streets?"

"You'd probably fend very well, if I know you," I said with a small smile. "You're a strong woman, Sarah. Still, I suppose it might not be worth the risk of attempting a divorce unless you can prove that Mr. Worthington is unfaithful and not seeing to your care."

"Alas, there's little likelihood of that. Mrs. Temple had bruises all over her body and witnesses to Mr. Temple's liaisons and the judge refused to grant the writ, let alone give her a settlement. I don't wonder that she ran away."

"It was quite the scandal," I agreed.

"There are those who say that Mr. Rivers used to beat Mrs. Rivers," Sarah said with a confidential nod. "So if you're looking for someone who had reason to kill Mr. Rivers, you might want to consider her."

"There is that." I winced and frowned. "I've heard there are many others who had cause to hate Mr. Rivers."

Sarah sighed. "He was always very kind to me."

"I dare say, most of us in polite society found him to be quite congenial," I said. "I've been told that he was quite charming when he wanted or needed to be. I certainly found him so."

"Then why would anyone want to kill him?" Sarah asked, clearly among those who believed Mr. Rivers to be an honest and fine man. "It makes no sense. You could say Mrs. Judson or Mrs. Aguilar killed Mr. Rivers."

I paused. "What about Mr. Worthington? As you told me, their enmity was quite pronounced."

I fully expected Sarah to take great offense at my suggestion. After all, one can disparage one's own and still become quite angry when another says the same, and Sarah had been known to do just that. Still, she surprised me.

"What a horrible thought," she gasped, then considered. "It would be too terrible. And yet..." She shook her head. "I have no idea. I don't think he'd been in a fight when he came home that night. I can usually tell." She began weeping again. "I tell you, Maddie, he is such a trial to me."

It is not to my credit, but I began to lose patience with this, my dearest of friends. I looked up at the clock on her mantle.

"Oh, dear. Is that the time?" I asked, setting aside my tea cup and standing. "It has been pleasant, Sarah, but I simply must get back to the rancho."

Sarah rose also. "Oh, of course. Thank you so much for calling."

Hannah showed me out and I hurried back to my rancho, feeling rather guilty about abandoning my friend in her hour of need.

It was true, Sarah had few alternatives. It is appalling how few rights we women still have, even with the vote. In this enlightened day, if our husbands are not kind to us, or worse, abandon us by leaving or dying, we are blamed, even the most virtuous of us. Nor are we given many opportunities to support ourselves should we be widowed.

Back then it was still worse, for we didn't have many offices where we could find jobs. And if we chose not to marry, well, there was nothing more horrifying and unnatural than a maiden aunt. I remember reading a story in our then new newspaper a couple of years after Mr. Rivers' death about just such a horror and feeling quite piqued by it. Which was why I usually bore Sarah's complaints with a great deal of patience. However, that day, I began to think that she could have borne her plight with more fortitude.

It was probably my agitation and concern for Regina, who was certainly in a far more perilous situation. You might wonder at my regard for such a woman, indeed, I wonder at it, myself. But I believe at that point, I had come to understand that Regina was essentially a very good person at heart and was in her most distasteful of professions because she had no other alternative.

My beloved mother often noted that I was kindest to the outcasts of our society, and I realize now that it was because I had so often felt outcast, myself. As a young girl, I was far more interested in books and plants and the natural world around me than the rest of my playfellows and I was often spurned for it. My Grandmother Franklin (my father's mother) despaired of me ever becoming a proper lady and begged me to be more accommodating to the others of our set. But I found it hard to pretend to like people who had so little regard for me.

As I approached the gate to my rancho, I shook off such depressing thoughts, changed into a work dress and helped finish the racking and a dozen other chores one had to manage on the rancho.

It was well past dark when Regina came to call. The children's lessons had been heard and I was in my library, working on my accounts. Regina had recovered some of her usual aplomb and wore her blue walking suit and tall hat. But she was still very distressed.

"Maddie, what in Heaven's name possessed you today?" she demanded the second we were alone.

She had taken the sofa across from my desk, a

usually very pleasant nook surrounded by book shelves. Maria had left us with a decanter of angelica and the small glasses.

"You did not kill Bert Rivers," I told her calmly as I poured a glass for each of us. "We both know it. What kind of person would I be if I did not step in and give evidence? I will not allow an innocent person to be hanged."

"I'm not an innocent person." Regina pressed her lips together as if to avoid saying more, then took a sip of her drink.

"Well, you are of the murder," I said firmly. "Honestly, Regina. Are you so eager to meet your doom?"

"No." She sank into herself. "I know I'm headed for the flames of perdition. And if I'm completely honest, I don't doubt it will come at the end of a rope." She slid her hand along the top of her throat then along the jawbone. Her eyes filled with tears. "And since I fully expect it, it doesn't really matter if it happens sooner rather than later." She looked at me. "But if you lose your reputation, Maddie, you will be forced to move elsewhere and I will have lost my only friend in this wretched place."

"You have friends," I said, embarrassed by her sentiment.

"Not like you." She sniffed and sat up. "And you certainly proved it today. As terrified as I am that you will come to rue it, I am grateful."

I shifted, even more embarrassed. "Even if we weren't friends, I still would have done it. Injustice is injustice and no Christian worthy of the name should stand for it, no matter the character of the victim."

"As long as the rest of the town thinks that's why you stood up for me, your reputation may yet be saved."

"That would be nice." I sipped my angelica and gazed at the light golden liquid in my glass. "However, my reputation is only secondary."

Regina laughed softly. "And that, Maddie Wilcox,

is why you are my friend." She quickly finished off her angelica then looked at me. "So, given the good marshal's bargain, we only have a scant few days to search out the real killer. What can I do to help?"

I leaned back in my chair. "Well, you seem to have a more accurate appraisal of his character and you know a lot more of the men in the pueblo. Who would have a reason to kill him?"

"That's a very long list, Mrs. Wilcox." Regina held out her glass and I poured her a second helping. She settled back on the couch to think. "There's the Samples family. They have a farm a little to the north and east of here. They're a colored family, came here after the war. My housemaid Sybil is Mrs. Samples' sister. Sybil was exceedingly happy when I banished Mr. Rivers from my house. I don't remember the totality of her complaint, only that Mr. Rivers had not been very gentlemanly toward Mrs. Samples."

I pulled a fresh sheet of paper from my desk drawer and dipped my pen.

"Samples family," I muttered as I wrote. "And there's the Vasquez family, as well."

"You might as well check the entire enrollment of the Zanjero's office."

I glared briefly at Regina. "That will be far too cumbersome a task."

"And now that I think about it, possibly not that fruitful in terms of uncovering a reason to kill Mr. Rivers," Regina said, then sipped thoughtfully.

"How do you mean?" I asked.

"Well, even if he was cheating everyone, which we know he wasn't, from what I've heard, that kind of cheating is so common that one expects it to happen."

I set my pen down and picked up my glass. "I do believe you have a point, Regina. Remember that awful pound master who went around letting everyone's animals loose, then impounding them and charging us for the impound fees?"

"Oh, do I!" Regina laughed loudly. "I paid him

several times, thinking I really hadn't tied up my horse securely."

"I had locked my stable and he opened it. I was going to petition the city council about it when he agreed there had to have been a mistake." I finished off my angelica, then poured my second glass. "But no one was all that surprised. We were all angry but hardly enraged enough to take his life. So the people we need to focus on are those whose complaint with Mr. Rivers was far more serious than simple cheating."

Regina smirked. "That will still be a long list, and might still include the Samples family. I will ask Sybil about it later this evening." She paused and set down her glass. "I don't know how you will take this. I know Mrs. Worthington is your friend. But Caleb Worthington particularly hated Mr. Rivers."

"I know." I frowned. "I mentioned it to her, fully expecting her to chastise me quite soundly."

"She does have a temper, I've been told."

"Yes, she does. But she didn't get angry at me," I said, musing. "She was properly horrified by the idea, but didn't dismiss it, She was also abroad that night, looking for Mr. Worthington."

"Oh, such a pointless and heartrending endeavor." Regina shook her head. "We've plenty of ladies in town who do that. They would never admit it, I'm sure. And I don't know why they continue to waste their time coming to my door. I can't tell them if their husbands are inside."

"They consider it their wifely duty to make sure their husbands get home safely."

"Yes, that is the lie they tell themselves, poor things."

"And there are other reasons to be abroad," I pointed out.

"Oh?" Regina looked at the decanter and lifted an eyebrow. "I perhaps shouldn't. Your angelica is rather deceptive in its mild flavor."

I pushed the decanter toward her. "It has been a

most trying day."

"Indeed, it has." Regina all but pounced on the decanter and quickly filled her glass.

I couldn't help but laugh. Regina could hold her spirits better than most of the men in the pueblo. She had polished off quite a few more than three of my small glasses many times before without ill effect.

"You know who else was abroad that night was Mrs. Elmwood," I said. "In fact, she made a point of calling on me this morning to make sure I knew that she was nowhere near Mr. Mahoney's saloon."

"You mean the minister's wife? How very suspicious. And yet, I've never seen Mr. Elmwood."

"I should hope not!" I sat up in righteous indignation.

Regina laughed, full and throaty. "I suppose one would hope not. But, darling Maddie, more than one man of the cloth has darkened my door. I assure you."

"Nonetheless." I shifted and pulled the decanter toward myself. Regina knew I did not approve of her trade, but I tried not to remind her of it. "Mrs. Elmwood was on an errand of mercy that night, helping Mrs. Ontiveras with her mother. At least, that's what she told me. She was also wondering if I was one of the two women Mrs. Aguilar had seen."

"Well, we both know you weren't." Regina suddenly groaned, emptied her glass and reached for the decanter. "And that reminds me. The worst of tragedies. Our girl died last night."

I gasped. "What happened? Why didn't you send for me?"

"It was too late. She'd had a bit of fever over the past few days, and she complained of some belly pain but it wasn't much and none of us thought much of it. I went to check on her around midnight and her fever had increased incredibly. I was just about to call you when she died."

"And the little one?"

"He'd already been taken by the sisters at St.

Vincent's."

"Childbed fever," I said. "You should have called me sooner."

"With all the rumors already being bandied about? I didn't dare. Not for a small fever and a bit of pain. And there's nothing you could have done, anyway. I was writing you a note about it when that dreadful Marshal Warren came by to arrest me."

I sighed deeply. There is nothing to be done when childbed fever strikes and thank Heaven, it's not as common as it used to be. But I still take it personally whenever I lose a mother to it.

Regina took a long, slow sip of her drink, then set the glass down and stood.

"I'm afraid I must make my way back home while I can still walk," she said.

I followed her through the house to the front parlor. Before I opened the door, Regina turned and grasped both my hands in hers.

"My darling Maddie, I can't thank you enough for today. But, please, let's not have any more of this nonsense about risking your reputation to save my miserable skin. I know I do not deserve it."

"Everyone deserves justice, Regina," I said.

I kissed her cheek and opened the door. She slipped into the night.

CHAPTER SIX

I was just about to make my way to the Samples' farm the next morning when I received a note from Mrs. Judson asking me to call upon her at my earliest convenience. I returned the message that I was taking a ride that morning and should be there shortly.

I must concede that I found the summons quite puzzling for a number of reasons. However, I resolved not to speculate needlessly as I would soon arrive at the Judson home. Fortunately, I already had on my best brown riding habit. It was quite a charming little piece, with a plain skirt, but cunning ruffles on the bodice. I had a lovely full bonnet to wear with it to keep the sun off my face and fairly new black boots. My gloves were getting a trifle worn, I'd noticed, but not noticeably so.

Mrs. Judson was ready to receive me and I was shown into the front parlor where she offered me tea and biscuits with strawberry jam. I settled myself onto the sofa, shifting my big leather bag as I did so.

"That is quite the bag you carry," Mrs. Judson remarked.

"It carries things I need sometimes," I replied. "And since I cannot know when I'll need which thing, I frequently carry several of them at once."

"What forethought," Mrs. Judson said, sipping her tea.

"Thank you. Now, how might I help you?"

"Oh." Mrs. Judson set down her tea cup and I suddenly realized she seemed somewhat distressed. "I suppose you've guessed that the entire town is talking about how you rescued that poor Mrs. Medina from jail yesterday."

"I don't doubt there's been some talk of it."

"That was awfully brave of you, my dear. But why risk your reputation in such a way?"

I smiled. "I learned, through perfectly honorable means, that she was innocent of the murder. As a woman striving to be worthy of the name of Christian, I could not shirk my duty."

"To be sure."

Apparently, my answer satisfied her. She picked up her cup and sipped, then said,

"It is most curious what Mrs. Aguilar saw that night, isn't it?"

"Yes." I set my cup down and smiled. "In fact, if you know anything about who those two women might have been, I'd be very obliged if you'd tell me."

Mrs. Judson gasped. "You're not actually going to look for the real killer, are you?"

"I must. The marshal only gave me until Wednesday to do so."

"How utterly dreadful!" Mrs. Judson was clearly properly appalled. "What a despicable man!" She stopped and put her hand on her chest. "Oh, dear. Pray forgive me for saying so. I would not for the world hurt dear Mrs. Warren."

"Nor would I," I replied. I also failed to add that I was of the same opinion regarding Mrs. Warren's husband.

Mrs. Judson seemed pleased at my intimation that I would not go spreading her lapse about town. She leaned forward.

"It is possible Mrs. Hewitt saw something," she said. "You may have heard that she does go abroad of an evening to bring her husband home from Mr. Mahoney's saloon."

"I hadn't heard about Mrs. Hewitt, but I have heard of the practice," I said. "So terribly sad that women find themselves having to do that."

"Indeed," said Mrs. Judson. "I cannot tell you how

grateful I am that Mr. Judson has never put me in that position."

I smiled. Mr. Judson was one of the principals in the largest bank in town, had extensive property throughout the county, and was on the city council. According to Mr. Mahoney, Mr. Judson was not well-liked by his fellow councilmen. He was perfectly circumspect and correct in everything he did, and in addition insisted that his fellows behave likewise. This latter aspect of his personality did not sit at all well with his colleagues on the council.

I would not have said so to Mrs. Judson, of course, for that would have been a dreadful thing to say. However, as I smiled and sipped my tea, it occurred to me that there was considerably more beneath her fluttery conviviality than I'd ever suspected and that Mrs. Judson was well aware of what was said about her husband. Moreover, she seemed to have a knack for managing people to her preference and benefit without them noticing that they were being managed. For example, her management of the tea party arrivals. I could not tell, however, whether this was to the ill or to the better. I did know that I was going to be far more wary around her than not.

"Your husband is a most upstanding man," I said. "Do you know if anyone else was about that night?"

Mrs. Judson paused. "I can't say. For one thing, I don't know for sure and I shouldn't like to cast the dark shadow of suspicion on someone who is quite probably completely innocent."

"And yet you cast it upon Mrs. Hewitt," I said.

Mrs. Judson tittered. "Oh, dear. I only mentioned her because her habit of going abroad searching for her husband is rather well-known. I assumed you already knew about it, and if you hadn't someone would tell you soon enough. Besides, I have good reason to believe that she was doing nothing more than trying to get her husband home from the saloon while he could still walk."

"I've heard she has a temper."

"She does, indeed." Mrs. Judson sighed. "I'm afraid I may have spoken in error. Mrs. Wilcox, I do hope you will believe me when I tell you that I did not want to cast suspicion on Mrs. Hewitt when I mentioned she was abroad that night. I thought you already knew and I do truly hope that she saw something that might help you find the villain who killed Mr. Rivers. Besides, it's perfectly obvious that she couldn't have killed him. She's far too short to have hit him over the head."

"She is at that," I replied. I almost added that Mrs. Hewitt's height was not relevant to who killed Mr. Rivers, but then realized that even though Mr. Rivers had been shot, the angle at which the bullet had entered the body (from what I remembered of it) was almost 90 degrees. Tiny Mrs. Hewitt would have had to hold the gun almost above her head to have hit a tall man such as Mr. Rivers at that angle.

Besides, Mrs. Judson wasn't supposed to know how Mr. Rivers actually died and obviously didn't.

"Mrs. Wilcox?" Mrs. Judson asked, interrupting my musings.

"Pray forgive me," I said. I looked down at my tea cup and saw that I had finished my tea. "Your observation about Mrs. Hewitt is quite apt. In fact, I hadn't considered that aspect of the affair at all. Thank you most kindly for suggesting it."

Mrs. Judson looked exceptionally pleased. "I'm glad I was able to help."

"However," I said, putting as severe a look on my face as I could manage. "I must ask you not to repeat this conversation to anyone, especially Mrs. Hewitt. As you pointed out regarding the dark cloud of suspicion, even the kindest remark could well be taken the wrong way. I would rather give the killer the chance to reveal himself by knowing more than he should about the circumstances of Mr. Rivers' death. And if he knew what we discussed regarding Mrs. Hewitt, he could well take advantage of it to lead us in the wrong direction."

"My goodness, you're right," Mrs. Judson said. "And to think I was going to beg for your discretion. I should have known I could count on it."

"And I can count on yours?"

Mrs. Judson tittered again. "Of course, Mrs. Wilcox. I am much better at keeping secrets than you might think given the ladies of my salon."

"I beg your pardon?"

"The ladies who populate my front room during tea parties. I find it not only instructive, but safer to have them there than on my front porch." She tittered again then became sober. "But be that as it may, I do understand the meaning of discretion and our conversation will remain between us, I assure you.'

"And I shall not say anything unless I must to prevent another injustice." I stood. "I thank you again, Mrs. Judson."

Her maid showed me out. Mrs. Judson had proven to be quite the puzzle. Without question, her mind was far sharper than her demeanor would suggest. And she was certainly no stranger to duplicity. Yet, I got no sense of malevolent intent from her. As I mounted Daisy, my roan mare, I shook my head. I had another visit to make and needed to focus my energy on the upcoming interview.

The Samples' small farm was on a little plain on the northeast edge of the city. They mostly grew beans, corn, and other vegetables, but a goodly portion of the land was given over to a large herd of sheep. I approached slowly from the road and waved as soon as I saw Mr. Samples in the bean field. He, alas, had good cause to be suspicious of strangers, but he knew me. He was of average height, with dark skin and his hair was cut close to his head. The scars of his former life in durance vile formed lighter ridges along his arms and one ran the length of his face.

As I came down the road toward the small unpainted clapboard house, Mr. Samples also headed for the house, carrying his hoe on his shoulder and a small rifle in his other hand. I saw three of the five Samples children running toward the house and hurrying inside.

Mrs. Samples emerged from the house, wiping her hands on her apron. Her skin was lighter, and what scars she bore were probably hidden by her clothes and the faded red kerchief she wore wrapped around her head.

"Ted!" she called. "Put that gun of yours away. It only be Mrs. Wilcox acomin'."

I rode into the yard and dismounted while Mr. Samples set the rifle next to the small porch.

"How do you do, Mr. and Mrs. Samples," I said pleasantly.

Mr. Samples remained wary, but Mrs. Samples dusted off a wooden rocking chair on the porch and offered it to me. She sat down on another rocker and waved at Mr. Samples to sit, as well. He glanced at her, then glared at me and stayed standing next to the porch stairs.

"This is most awkward," I began. "You must have heard about Mr. Rivers' murder. And your sister, Mrs. Samples, has said that Mr. Rivers used you ill."

Mrs. Samples shrugged. "He weren't no worse than any other white man. Treated us like slaves. Forced me to be with him."

"Good Heavens!" I gasped.

"I'm used to it," Mrs. Samples said with a sad shake of her head.

"And you, Mr. Samples?" I asked.

"What are you after?" he demanded.

"The truth about Mr. Rivers' murder," I said, suddenly realizing that I was not approaching this interview with the utmost of tact. "I apologize. I only have until Wednesday and I've been told there were a great many people in the pueblo with grievances against him. And I was told you were among that number."

"Don't know about that," growled Mr. Samples.

"He was hard on us, but he could've been worse."

"But he took liberties with your wife," I gasped.

"It weren't nuthin' worth getting Ted's neck stretched over," Mrs. Samples said.

"See them sheep?" Mr. Samples pointed. "Mr. Rivers done said I had to raise 'em. I got to pay for their keeping, too. And shear 'em. But he got the wool. I needed the water so he got the wool. But can't do nothing about it. Nobody going to believe us. Or do nothing. It's the way of the world."

"But you're a free man," I said. "You have rights."

Mr. Samples laughed bitterly. "That's right. I is free. That be true. And my childrens is free. We wanna leave here, we can go. Ain't no massa with no whip standing over us. I even own this here property. But rights? Ain't no one giving me any rights. But I'm still better off than I was. I got my wife. I got my children. Ain't nobody taking them away to sell to somebody else. I was powerful mad about the way Massa Rivers done treated me and Miz Samples. But what good would it do to get him killed? They'd just string me up and ask no questions."

"Ted done said it," said Mrs. Samples. "It's the way of the world. Ain't nothing we can do except keep working on and raising our children to be good, God-fearing people. And that's what we're going to do."

"And what about the sheep?" I asked. "Have any of the Rivers family contacted you about them?"

Mr. Samples shook his head.

"Then there is something I can do about this atrocity," I said, standing up. "I will speak to the Rivers family on your behalf and there will be reparations if I have to pay for them, myself!"

Mrs. Samples got up and grasped my hand. "Miz Wilcox, you are a powerful good woman. Thank you." She nudged her husband.

"Thank you, Miz Wilcox," he said. He was smiling, but with a very skeptical glint in his eye.

I got back on my horse, feeling quite out of sorts.

As appalling as the Samples' story was, I had to concede it was not all that surprising. The war years had been quite awkward for me here in the pueblo. Even though California had been admitted as a free state, here in Los Angeles, the Americans were largely Confederate sympathizers. I'd had to tread most carefully because of my abolitionist beliefs. It seemed as though some folks still sympathized with the fallen South, which actually made sense since it would be unlikely that someone's beliefs would change overnight simply because a treaty had been signed.

I was so absorbed in my thoughts that I almost missed the cries coming from the next farm over. Perhaps it was because the cries had started as the exuberance of children at play. But they shortly turned to terrified screams and I immediately turned my horse toward the children.

There were five American children, three girls and two boys, gathered around their playfellow, although as I got closer, it became apparent that these were not merely playfellows, but siblings. Their clothes were ragged, but had been mended many times over and looked mostly clean. They were thin, though not emaciated, suggesting that they had food, but only barely enough. The fallen child was a boy, about six years old. He was crying loudly and his right foot was listing at an odd angle.

"Good Heavens!" I exclaimed, getting off my horse. "What a loud fuss you're making, little man. It can't be all that terrible."

I know that sounds somewhat unsympathetic, but I find startling young children with such admonitions often quiets them faster than anything else.

"My— My leg," he sniffed.

I knelt beside him. "I see that. We'll have to get you home very carefully, won't we?"

I looked up. Of the older children, one looked to be a girl about 12 and a boy about 10.

"You two, how far away is your house?" I asked.

The girl pointed toward a smallish house some distance away, on the other side of a bean field.

"Very good," I said. "The two of you run fetch a large blanket and your mother and father, if he's here."

The children nodded and ran for the house. I dug in my bag for a bit of angelica. One of the remaining girls, who was probably around nine, pointed at the bottle.

"Is that spirits?" she asked.

"Hush, Hannah." Her other brother, a lad who looked to be about the same age, nudged her hard.

"We're not supposed to take spirits," the girl insisted, her eyes growing wide with fear. "They're from the devil."

I sighed. Scaring the children would not help the injured boy, whose face was going pale and sweaty.

"This is medicine," I told her. "It will help your brother."

I poured some of the angelica into a small cup, then got out my bottle of laudanum. I poured just a tiny trickle into the cup and swirled it and the angelica together.

"He's hurting a great deal right now and this will help ease his pain a little so that we can move him without him going into a faint," I explained.

Hannah was not entirely convinced, but I remained firm and got her young injured brother to take some of the medicine. The two oldest children returned carrying the blanket between them, with two women about my age following quickly behind. Actually, one looked a bit younger, but both were work-worn, with neatly mended dresses.

"Oh, no!" cried the younger one, a fair-haired beauty. "Oh, no! Jacob!"

She slid down next to me in the dust, which I had to admit was doing nothing for my brown riding suit.

"Hush, Sabrina," said the older of the two, who was much rounder and dark-haired. She put her hand on Sabrina's back.

"But, Ruth, he'll be a cripple," Sabrina wept.

"Not if I can help it," I said firmly. "We'll get him gently on the blanket and take him back to your house. Then I'll set the bone. I've some skill, I'm told."

"But, but we can't," Ruth said, looking frightened.

"Do you want to leave the boy a cripple?" I demanded.

"Ruth, please." Sabrina held the little boy's hand and looked imploringly at the other woman.

Ruth finally nodded. "Quickly then. And children, you will hold your tongues."

"She gave Jacob spirits," Hannah said.

Ruth pulled Hannah aside and spoke quietly. "She doesn't know about us and you must keep still so she doesn't learn."

We got young Jacob onto the blanket without disturbing his leg any more than absolutely necessary. The children helped to lift their young brother and we got him back to the small house quite quickly. I was puzzled by the way Sabrina and Ruth had reacted but tried to stay focused on caring for Jacob. I certainly understood Sabrina's fear for the child. Jacob had clearly broken his leg, and there was a very good chance that he could take sick from it. That was assuming I didn't have to amputate it, which was even riskier. We knew so little then, and even these days, there are still many things that can go wrong.

The house was decent-sized, with five rooms. Ruth had us lay Jacob on the sofa in the front parlor, which was next to the kitchen. Fortunately, the laudanum had taken effect and Jacob had fallen asleep. I had to convince Ruth to light a lamp by offering to pay for the coal oil.

As it turned out, the break was a clean one and I was able to set it relatively easily. I had a harder time finding a splint and sufficient bandages to keep the leg immobile.

"I'll have to come back later this afternoon," I said, as I tied the last knot on the bandage. "I have some plaster of Paris at home and can make a cast so his bones will heal better."

"But you can't," said Ruth. "You shouldn't be here at all."

Both women looked at me, their eyes wide with fear. There was the sound of a step on the porch and the room brightened as Mr. Lomax came in the door.

"Pa! Pa!" The children ran screaming toward him, babbling about Jacob's injury and the fact that I was helping him. And Hannah was complaining yet again that I had given Jacob spirits.

I would never have considered Mr. Lomax a warm man. He had always been aloof prior to that afternoon. But as the children rushed up to him, he smiled warmly and laughed, swinging young Hannah to his shoulder. At least, he laughed until she pointed at me.

He slowly let the little girl down to the ground, his bearing even more aloof and wary than I'd ever seen it before. I looked over at Ruth and Sabrina. It was hard to imagine two women who looked less alike. The children all seemed to have their father's chin and nose, but each child's coloring matched either one woman's or the other's. All of a sudden, the wariness and aloofness and Hannah's worry about spirits began to make sense.

They were Mormons. While Mormons weren't as virulently persecuted in the pueblo as they had been elsewhere, they were not popular, largely because of their practice of polygamy. And their theology was not, to my mind, particularly sound. Nonetheless, I had to remind myself that given my friendship with Regina, I had little room to point a finger.

"It would seem young Jacob has broken his leg," I said, choosing my words carefully. "As I was explaining to the ladies here, I can make a cast to hold the bones in place until they heal, but I need to go home and fetch some more bandages and my plaster of Paris."

"And you plan on returning?" Mr. Lomax's eyebrows rose slightly.

"Of course," I replied with a self-righteous sniff. "I wouldn't have said so if that wasn't my intention."

"Folks don't always do what they say they will," Mr. Lomax said.

"I do. I should think you would have heard that much about me,"

"I hear a lot of things." Mr. Lomax slid his coat back from his six-gun, holstered at his hip. "But this time, I have to be sure."

I was fairly certain he wasn't going to shoot me, but not entirely. Even as I stiffened my resolve, it suddenly occurred to me what he was really saying.

"I am well known for my discretion, Mr. Lomax," I said. "And for being less than discriminating about where I provide charity. So if I am going to stand up for a wanton like Mrs. Medina, why would I scruple to avoid caring for a young innocent child just because his religion is not popular? Or place his family in danger, for that matter?"

Sabrina gasped and began weeping.

Mr. Lomax offered me his small side-of-the-mouth grin. "Didn't think so. Good to know I was right." He let his coat fall over his gun. "I've got plaster of Paris in the shed."

"And bandages?" I asked. "I could go home."

Jacob let out a little moan as he began to wake up.

"Best not make him suffer any longer than we have to." Mr. Lomax looked at his wives.

"We have our last good sheet, sir," Ruth told him.

He sighed heavily and nodded. "We'll make do."

I made a mental note to see to it that the sheet was replaced and set to work cleaning and wetting the strips as the women tore them. Mr. Lomax got the plaster of Paris mixed at my direction. Many hands made light work and we had the cast molded and drying around Jacob's leg in good order. Jacob's brothers and sisters looked on in awe at the marvel. Well, it wasn't all that common then. The Europeans had been using casts for some years, but the American medical men had remained wary, although I couldn't understand why.

Mr. Lomax walked me outside to where my horse was tied. Daisy stood patiently but flicked an ear to let me know she was ready to go again.

"I owe you a great deal," Mr. Lomax said, smiling softly. "Thank you."

"I'd have done it for anybody," I said, looking down at my riding habit and inwardly sighing over the scolding I was sure to get from Juanita when she saw it. "In fact, I did. I had no idea this was your family."

"We don't mix much." He shrugged, then looked at me curiously. "Where'd you learn that trick with the plaster of Paris?"

"Oh, here and there," I said, reluctant to say more. I untied Daisy's reins. "Now, I've left some willow bark with his mother so that she can make some tea for him. It will taste very nasty, but it should help ease the pain some. And he will be hurting for a few days."

"He'd be hurting more if we'd had to take care of him." Mr. Lomax held his hand out, then grunted as he helped me into my saddle. "Thank you again."

"Thank you for standing by me with the city marshal yesterday. I didn't get a chance to say so then, but I did appreciate it."

Mr. Lomax nodded. I offered him a small wave, then headed Daisy back into the town center.

CHAPTER SEVEN

I tied up Daisy, extra securely, outside of the market at the Clocktower Courthouse. I wasn't sure exactly with whom I wanted to speak next, but Mrs. Hewitt was a possibility, and I was also considering speaking with Mr. Mahoney, the saloon owner.

Fate, however, intervened, in the form of Mrs. Carson and Mrs. Glassell. They saw me tying up Daisy and scurried over to me from the front of the marketplace.

"Mrs. Wilcox, as I live and breathe," gasped Mrs. Carson, her plump face beginning to glow in the mild warmth of the afternoon.

She wore a blue walking suit with black lace and ribbon trim and carried a black parasol over her blue straw bonnet. Mrs. Glassell wore a similar suit, but in dark yellow with matching trim, a natural straw colored-bonnet, and carried a matching parasol.

"So brave of you to stand up for that dreadful Mrs. Medina," Mrs. Glassell simpered.

Mrs. Carson raised her hand to stop my response. "We know, your Christian duty. Still terribly, terribly brave."

"And now you're going to find the real killer." Mrs. Glassell glowed with excitement.

"Well," said Mrs. Carson. "We know our duty. The least we can do is give you our own poor observations."

"For example, there's Mrs. Downey," said Mrs. Glassell with considerable satisfaction.

"You know how she always knows what phase the moon is in?" Mrs. Carson added.

Mrs. Glassell jumped in without waiting for my response. "She's a spiritualist. Or pagan. Or some such nonsense."

"It's mostly harmless," said Mrs. Carson. "But she is up watching most nights. From the widow's walk on her house."

"It's near the hill, next to Mr. Beaudry's parcel, you know," Mrs. Glassell added. "She must have seen something."

"Oh, and don't forget to speak to Mrs. Worthington," said Mrs. Carson.

"And Mrs. Hewitt," added Mrs. Glassell.

"Poor things," said Mrs. Carson. "Always chasing after their husbands."

"Not that we believe they did anything," said Mrs. Glassell.

"Of course not," said Mrs. Carson. "But they must have seen something."

"And don't forget Mrs. Elmwood," said Mrs. Glassell solemnly. "You know how her daughter up and got married and moved to Santa Barbara so suddenly?"

"It was shortly after that, I mentioned Mr. Rivers to her and she turned quite red in the face and refused to say another word to me," Mrs. Carson said. "Now, why would that be?"

"And she hasn't had a kind word to say about him since," said Mrs. Glassell. "And then there's Mrs. Rivers, herself."

"Perhaps we shouldn't," said Mrs. Carson. "On the other hand, it would not be just to ignore her."

Mrs. Glassell sighed. "Poor, poor dear. He beat her, you know. I've seen the bruises. Not only on her but on her boys, too."

"Of course, you expect a boy to get a beating or two as he goes along," said Mrs. Carson. "But you don't expect a husband to beat his wife quite so severely."

"Or so often," said Mrs. Glassell. She turned to Mrs. Carson. "Is that everyone, dear? Mrs. Fletcher?"

"Too simple to know anything," said Mrs. Carson.

"Ah, but Mrs. Judson. She knows a great deal more than she lets on."

"Well, we've done our duty, haven't we, Mrs. Carson?" Mrs. Glassell simpered with great satisfaction.

"Yes, we have. Good day, Mrs. Wilcox."

The two scurried off toward their houses while I stood, staring after them. I was so shocked that even if I'd had the chance to ask anything, I couldn't have. I'd been under the impression that the women they'd told me about were their friends. But to say such things. I recalled Mrs. Judson's remarks about finding it instructive and safer to have them in her parlor and realized what she'd meant by that.

I shook my head and decided to go to the dry goods store. A wagon train from the port was supposed to have arrived that day, and I was hoping a certain shipment had been delivered. I would not have been able to take the wooden crate on my horse. But better to be sure it had arrived before I sent Sebastian or Enrique on a fool's errand after it.

And, indeed, my shipment had arrived. I paid Mr. Del Rosario for the goods and asked him to hold the case until one of the Ortiz brothers could pick it up, to which he agreed.

I had barely turned to leave when Mrs. Hewitt came bearing down on me from the street.

"Mrs. Wilcox, please hear me out!" she hissed at me as she skidded to my side.

"Here?" I asked, aghast that she'd accost me in such a public place.

She glanced around. "No. We can talk on the street."

Once outside, the tiny woman turned on me.

"Are you accusing me of murdering Mr. Rivers?" she demanded.

"Good Heavens, no," I stammered. "I have heard you are about at night and was only hoping you'd seen something."

Mrs. Hewitt snorted. "Oh, I saw him, all right.

Passed out in front of the saloon. It's a disgrace. A disgrace, I tell you. There must be something we can do to get rid of those dreadful places. But what can we do? We're only women. And I did not kill Mr. Rivers. I had no reason to. I suppose the time might come when my passions consume me and I take a frying pan to poor Mr. Hewitt's head. Which reminds me, you should be talking to Mrs. Rivers. I don't think you'll be disturbing her bereavement all that much if you know what I mean."

"I believe I do."

"And while you are asking around, you may want to speak to Mrs. Carson. She's not so blameless as she'd have you believe. In fact, speak with Mrs. Glassell. She'll tell you more than you'd want to hear. In fact, I don't doubt it was those two biddies who told you about me."

"It is a sad state of affairs that you are faced with," I said as soothingly as I could.

Mrs. Hewitt sniffed and moved on.

I thought about it for a moment, then decided it would be worth speaking with Mrs. Downey if only to get it over with, and since the house was nearby. So I untied Daisy and rode up the street to the Downey home.

It was another mansion, as befitted the family status. Mr. Downey was a former governor of the state, and in addition to his many business interests in the pueblo, he traveled a great deal. He was off on another trip, so Mrs. Downey was quite happy to have me come in to tea.

"I've been told that you often watch from your widow's walk," I told her once we were settled. "I'm hoping you saw something the night that Mr. Rivers was killed."

Mrs. Downey chuckled. "I don't watch the streets, I'm afraid. And I probably couldn't have seen anything from this distance, anyway. The moon was on the wane that night and everything supposedly happened well past the time for lamps to be lit."

"Oh, dear. I was so hoping." I stirred my tea just to be doing something. "This house has quite the view from on top."

"That's what I love about it." Mrs. Downey smiled and looked up at the ceiling. "But I much prefer the view of the sky to that of the streets. You seem quite a sensible woman, Mrs. Wilcox. Can I tell you a secret?"

"Of course."

She paused, held herself up straight and smiled. "I study astronomy. In fact, Mr. Downey will be bringing me a telescope, once he is finished with his business. I've been doing rather well, charting the constellations with my naked eye, but a telescope will help a great deal. Of course, I don't say much about it amongst the ladies of Mrs. Judson's salon."

"To be sure. I suspect they would not understand."

"Well, there you have it. I have almost no interest in what happens on the ground. If I tell the ladies anything it's only to make them happy."

"Ah. Well, your astronomy sounds fascinating, but I'm afraid the sheriff only gave me a few days to find the killer. Perhaps after all this is over, you can call on me and we can talk about it further?"

"I'd like that very much. And please feel free to call on me."

I left quickly, then realized I was not far from the Ontiveras home. It was well past tea time by that hour but I felt the urgency of my time limit. Nobody had seen anything and it seemed as though I would never find out who had killed Mr. Rivers.

The Ontiveras family was one of the oldest in the pueblo, and had been one of the most distinguished, with extensive land holdings throughout the county, some fifteen years before when Eliza Hemphill had married Arturo Ontiveras. As more Americans had moved here, and the Californios had lost more and more of their lands to lawsuits and tax sales, the family had become less distinguished. Mr. Ontiveras did, however, still do an excellent trade in tallow and cow hides, among other things, and controlled a very productive tar pit, which produced most of the pitch and the kerosene for the community.

Mrs. Ontiveras was an average-sized woman with light brown hair. She was wearing a plain striped work dress and a worried frown as she waited in the parlor for the maid to admit me.

"Poor Mother," she sighed. "She's been quite agitated all day."

As if to prove her daughter's point, the elderly Mrs. Hemphill came rushing into the parlor, the ribbons on her nightgown flying. She saw me and pounced.

"You must help me escape," the old woman cried piteously. "They're trying to poison me. They've hidden me away from my husband and sons." She turned, frantically. "I've got to find them. I've got to find them."

"Mother, please!" Mrs. Ontiveras tried to gently grab her mother by the waist, but the old woman would not let go of my riding basque.

"I'll help you, Mrs. Hemphill," I said, gently but firmly taking her wrists. "Now, would you be so good as to pour me some tea, so that I can find out all about what's happening here?"

The old woman blinked and settled down.

"Oh. Tea. Yes, that would be lovely. Will you join me?" she asked, as if she had been planning tea all along. "Where are the tea things?"

"They're coming, Mother," Mrs. Ontiveras said, hurrying to the door of the room and signaling the maid.

Mrs. Hemphill gazed at her daughter with a confused look on her face.

"She doesn't recognize me," Mrs. Ontiveras whispered to me, almost in tears. "She hasn't for months now."

I nodded and led the older woman to the sofa.

"I cannot thank you enough for inviting me to tea, Mrs. Hemphill," I told her. "You have such a lovely parlor."

"Yes, it's so nice, isn't it?" Mrs. Hemphill said, seating herself. "My husband, Mr. Hemphill, is so kind to me."

She nattered on about her late husband and her life, albeit, as it had been many years ago. I reached into my bag for my little bottle of laudanum. When the maid arrived with the tea things, Mrs. Hemphill busied herself pouring tea, still chatting away amiably.

I gave Mrs. Ontiveras the little bottle.

"Is this..?" Mrs. Ontiveras looked at me, her eyes opened in fear. I nodded. "But Mrs. Elmwood says we shouldn't. That she'll become dependent on it."

I sighed. "That's possible and Mrs. Elmwood has good cause to be wary. Her sister, you know. But there's a big difference. Mrs. Elmwood's sister was a young, vibrant woman. Your mother is quite old and nearing her end and mad already. A little laudanum when she's agitated will not make things worse and may even calm her down. Just a few drops, mind you, in some angelica or other strong drink. That way, she won't taste it as easily."

Mrs. Ontiveras nodded.

"Oh, is that the time?" I asked loudly and turned to Mrs. Hemphill. "This has been a wonderful afternoon, Mrs. Hemphill. I'm so glad you invited me. Oh, do be sure to try the lovely angelica I brought for you. It's one of my best, if I do say so, myself. I hope you like it."

"I'm sure I will. I'll have Carrie bring some immediately," Mrs. Hemphill replied, then went back to nattering over the tea service.

Mrs. Ontiveras walked me out to the front veranda. "How did you do that?"

"I have no idea," I replied, quite honestly. "It merely seemed like the best thing to do. I do wish you well, Mrs. Ontiveras. Such a terrible burden."

"It is, but possibly even worse for her. Thank you for your kindness, Mrs. Wilcox."

I hurried back to my horse and untied her. As I

swung into the saddle and arranged my leg over the pommel, it occurred to me that I had not been able to verify Mrs. Elmwood's account of the night of the murder. I decided to leave that for another day, as it was getting perilously close to dusk and I had one more visit to make.

I knocked at the back door of Mr. Thomas Mahoney's saloon because I was not allowed in the front, where the patrons were. I know nowadays that it's getting more common to see young women drinking spirits in public, but I'm afraid I'm still shocked by it. Mr. Mahoney's daughter Alice opened the door for me. She was a tall, gangling lass of sixteen years and she worked with her twin sister, Annie, in the kitchen behind the saloon, cooking the stews and baking the bread that Mr. Mahoney served his customers. The girls had three young Mexican girls to help them, and the kitchen was filled with chatter in both English and Spanish as the young women scurried to prepare for the onslaught of a busy Saturday night out front.

Alice showed me to her father's office, which was just behind the bar. The door to the front of the saloon was open, as usual, but I didn't bother to look through it. I could hear well enough what was going on out front, and I didn't want to be seen there, never mind that I had perfectly legitimate business to conduct.

Mr. Mahoney was a tall man with broad shoulders, graying dark hair, and bright blue eyes. His chin was frequently covered with the stubble of a gray beard. But that evening, he'd apparently found time to visit the local tonsorial parlor, because not only was he beautifully and freshly clean-shaven, his hair was neatly slicked down and the scent of pomade hung heavily about him.

The office was crowded, with a large but rather beaten up kneehole desk taking up most of the rear wall. Crates of liquor, barrels of wine and beer, and other items Mr. Mahoney would need were stacked about carelessly. Another door at the far end of the office led into a storage place, and Mr. Mahoney's Indian servant, a tall, proud fellow with black eyes and blacker hair named Jim, came through the office just after me and went to the storeroom.

"How do, Mrs. Wilcox," Mr. Mahoney said. There was just a hint of a lilt in his voice that betrayed his Irish birthplace, although he'd been in the United States since he was a young lad. "What brings you here this late of a Saturday afternoon?"

"Nothing good, I'm afraid," I said, taking the chair he'd pulled out for me.

He eased himself into his desk chair. "Let me guess, that business with finding Bert Rivers' killer?"

"Yes," I sighed. "I'd like to know as much about that night as you can remember."

Jim came through the room, carrying a wooden crate on his shoulder, and turned toward the kitchen. I assumed that Henry, the other Indian servant, was watching the front of the saloon. Henry usually did. He was several inches shorter than Jim and Mr. Mahoney, but built much like a bull, with thick, solid shoulders and a wide face. He had quite the knack for settling down drunken and angry customers, or so I'd been told. I could well imagine it.

Mr. Mahoney held to the common, but deplorable, belief that serving an Indian liquor was simply asking for trouble. It was a ridiculous prejudice since the Indians were no better nor worse than any other man when it came to liquor. Any man suffering the oppression we offered our Indian brothers would be prone to drowning his sorrows in the grape or grain, as it were. And certainly, there were plenty of American men who did the same without feeling nearly so oppressed. In any case, Henry and Jim were not allowed to even touch the liquor unless it was in a corked bottle, and by all accounts, did not. Mr. Mahoney felt it was a sure way to keep his liquor stock from disappearing down his employees' throats.

"It was an ordinary night," Mr. Mahoney said.

"Most of my usual patrons had come by. The Mayor left sometime around eight, eight-thirty. Mr. Rivers left right after the clock struck nine. He said he had to make an early day of it to be sure the ranchos got their water."

"I understand there was a fight between Mr. Rivers and Mr. Worthington."

"There was always a fight between those two." Mr. Mahoney wiped the corners of his mouth with his thumb and forefinger. "It went way back to when they were growing up in... Now, where were those boys from? Ah. I remember. Pennsylvania someplace. Not sure how they both happened to land here. They were cousins, but there was no love lost between them. Mr. Rivers told me he'd been teasing Mr. Worthington since they were boys. In fact, he even bragged that he'd stolen Mrs. Rivers away from Mr. Worthington. I think that's when Mr. Worthington went to the gold mines and eventually met Mrs. Worthington. Can't remember what brought Mr. Rivers out here."

"How odd," I said. "From what I heard, it was a particularly violent fight, that the two almost came to blows."

Mr. Mahoney shifted. "I'm afraid, ma'am, that there was no 'almost' about it. They did. I pulled Mr. Worthington off of Mr. Rivers, myself."

"Do you know what the fight was about?"

"Nope." Mr. Mahoney's face suddenly closed off.

His reaction startled me. There was naught I could do about it, however.

"Mr. Mahoney!" called Henry from the front.

Mr. Mahoney sighed, and I gestured that he should go and tend to his business. He eased himself out of his chair and smiled at me.

He wandered through the door into the saloon, from whence came a stream of language so virulently foul, I imagine a teamster would have been offended, let alone a lady. It was Mr. Worthington. I'd heard similar from other men in the saloon. Still, it wasn't merely the depravity of the actual words that unsettled me. It was the pure anger.

"Dad blame it, Mahoney!" Mr. Worthington complained very loudly between other, far worse, swear words. "It's the second time this week, and I secured that stack, myself!"

"I don't understand," Mr. Mahoney said. "What stack?"

"Stack of logs that came out of the Tejon Pass the other day," Mr. Worthington paused, presumably to take a drink of something intoxicating. "Near fell on me again. Bad enough, I almost lost them Friday, when the mules came in. Almost got run over 'cause the dagnabbed mules spooked. Then not half an hour ago, the whole stack came rolling down as I was walking past. I could have been killed, I tell you!"

I suppose Mr. Worthington's adventures made his foul language understandable. Indeed, I would have been hard pressed not to use strong language in such a situation, myself. However, his complaint did little beyond confirming my already low opinion of the man. It was, perhaps, not fair. Still, it was this very coarseness that so grieved my darling Sarah.

"Let me get you something to eat," Mr. Mahoney said.

"I already ate," Mr. Worthington snapped. "Just give me the bottle, will you? I aim to make a night of it after this miserable week."

"Here you go, then. Well, how do, Mr. Carson. Good to see you here tonight."

In fact, several men of the pueblo had just wandered in and it became apparent that Mr. Mahoney would not be able to see me out. So I left on my own, greeting his daughters as I did.

The night was almost full on, but everyone's lamp was lit, per city regulations, so I did not have a difficult time making my way home. And, as it turned out, Sebastiano was waiting for me with a lantern at the turning of the road to my rancho.

"There you are, Maddie," he said, with a grin. "We were almost ready to start searching for you. So, who got sick now?"

"Only one broken leg and a mad old woman," I said, sighing. "And I haven't had a thing to eat since breakfast except tea and biscuits. I was mostly talking to people about Mr. Rivers. What a loathsome business this seeking out a killer is!"

"Well, tomorrow is Sunday. You can't go asking after killers on Sunday, can you?"

"I suppose not," I said. "But I do have a young boy to check on and I might pay a call to Mrs. Rivers, to see if she's up to company. It would be the kind thing to do."

"Of course, Maddie," Sebastiano smiled and gently kicked the mule into a walk.

It had been a long day and it didn't appear there would be any relief the next day, either, never mind that it was Sunday and supposedly a day of rest. Nor did I look forward to my proposed visit with Mrs. Rivers. She was in full mourning, and one generally made the assumption that she would not want to be bothered by visitors. I never quite understood the practice of grieving in private, as if our sorrow were somehow shameful, although I could understand that one might not be up to entertaining visitors if one were actually buried in one's grief.

I remembered the very long days of my own year of bereavement after my husband's death, not being able to go anywhere, no company to speak of. Since I hadn't been all that grieved, it was all very dull, and I had longed for the day when I could put my widow's weeds aside and re-join the world of the living. It had been a very long year, indeed.

The memory of all that led me to wonder about Mrs. Rivers and the rumors that she was less than devastated by the death of her husband. There were many who thought that a woman could never kill her own husband, and it was true enough that we were kept so utterly dependent on our husbands for our livelihood that a woman had to be very desperate to dispose of the man who had her keeping. But it did happen.

I tried to imagine Mrs. Rivers in such straits and found it impossible to do so. If she had been beaten by her husband, he had never beaten her so severely she couldn't go out in society. There was considerable parsimony in the way she and her children were kept, but we all assumed it was simple frugality, and if the younger boys weren't as well turned out as one might expect from a family of their position, then it was because of a virtuous desire to save and to encourage humility. Still, I had to concede I did not live in that household and there were many ugly secrets behind many a closed door.

CHAPTER EIGHT

Sunday morning dawned with clear blue skies, devoid of clouds or even interest, I thought. Fortunately, the morning air carried the coolness of the night, but while it would not be terribly hot, I didn't doubt that I had a warm day ahead of me.

I suppose after a lifetime of harsh, frozen winters, one could most certainly be entranced by the evenness of our weather here in Los Angeles. I know I found my first winter here quite pleasurable. However, I soon began to long for the changing of the seasons. The heat of summer cooling into glorious crisp and colorful autumn, then the sudden change from a barren landscape into a white wonderland with the first snow. True, the cold became quite tiresome after a couple weeks or so. But then it melted into glorious springs filled with a riot of bright colors from flowers of all kinds. Here, the hills merely became green, and as I looked them over that morning before leaving for church services, I saw that the ever-present golden brown was even then setting in.

I walked to the Congregational church, of which I was a member. It wasn't far and the street around it was often crowded by the carriages and wagons of the other members. I noticed several of my fellow church-goers watching me as I made my way to my regular pew. I also noticed Reverend Elmwood eyeing me, as well. He was of the bookish sort of preacher and generally mild in his exhortations. However, he could be quite the fiery man of God when he got worked up about something, usually the sinful goings-on in the pueblo.

After the first hymn and invocation, the Scripture lesson was read, from the prophet Hosea, which I thought an exceedingly odd choice, and the cleansing of the Temple story. How odd that I should remember those two readings, even after all these years, and yet, they had quite the impact on my next few days, and the good reverend read them with great relish.

I should have known he had some ulterior motive. Indeed, he based his sermon on the text from Hosea, decrying the infidelity of the prophet's wife and the way she prostituted herself to any and all.

"We have in our fair little city far too many places of sin and carnality where more and more of our poor men are dragged into temptation by the wiles of wanton women," the reverend intoned. "Last night alone, two of our brothers lost their lives in a brothel, fighting over a wanton, a woman of ill-repute. And still another such woman, one of even greater unrighteousness in that she is the owner of the house of ill-repute, leading more young women into her snares and setting even more traps for our good men, this woman, this sinner and wanton, wanders among us free in spite of committing that most foul and heinous sin of murder in cold blood, killing our beloved zanjero just last week. And yet, she has not been called to justice."

Here, the reverend looked straight at me.

Oh, how I wished I'd had then the wisdom and the grit gained by years of living a mostly blameless life. I was, perhaps, more confident in my mission and my place in life than most other women I knew. But at that moment, I quailed. My face grew hot as I felt the stares of my fellow church-goers. I wanted to bolt from the church right then and there. Fortunately, I had enough backbone to hold my head high and my back straight as Reverend Elmwood continued on, detailing the horrors of damnation for those who murdered and those who assisted them in their escape from justice.

I had to remind myself several times that Regina

was quite innocent of the murder of Bertram Rivers and that I was fully invested in finding the real killer. That did not mean the rest of the community believed the same, however. If anything, I felt an undercurrent of anger ripple through the congregation and caught several women looking quickly away from me once my eye fell upon them. I debated withholding my offering that morning but thought better of it. However, I left the church the second it was decent to do so. The small organ had barely gasped the last notes of the hymn and I was already out the door and would have been well on my way when Sarah Worthington hailed me.

I paused, debating whether I should pretend that I hadn't heard her and hurry on. It was that pause that saved me. For I had no sooner turned when a horse hitched to a nearby buggy suddenly reared, whinnying frantically. The hooves swung perilously close to my head and I barely had time to scramble backward before the beast fled, the empty buggy bouncing behind him.

I stepped back again and fell on my backside.

The women of the church came flowing out and gathered around me, chattering as they did. I felt a strong hand on my arm.

"Here now, Mrs. Wilcox," said Mr. Glassell. He was much thinner than his wife and much more jovial in spirit. "Are you hurt?"

I collected myself. "No. It seems I'm quite all right."

"That horse could have killed you!" gasped Mrs. Glassell.

"May I help you up, Mrs. Wilcox?" Mr. Glassell asked.

"Why, yes, thank you."

I was wearing my best kid gloves, along with my green bombazine walking suit. Fortunately, the hoop had only briefly lifted when I fell, thus saving me from exposing my nether limbs. I re-arranged my skirt so that I could get up without standing on it, then took Mr. Glassell's gloved hand as Mrs. Glassell looked daggers at him. I couldn't imagine why. He was merely behaving as any gentleman would. But then I remembered we widows were thought to be quite happy to turn the eyes of any man within reach. I could have reassured Mrs. Glassell that her husband held no attraction for me, but that would have left her just as miffed.

I was quite happy to see that my dress had suffered no lasting damage. A bit of trim here and there had torn but would be easily mended, and the horse muffin I'd landed on meant I'd have to change clothes before making any calls.

Sarah came running up.

"Oh, Maddie, how horrible! Are you all right?"

"Yes," I said, still breathing somewhat heavily. "I'm still a little shaken, perhaps, but perfectly well otherwise."

Shouting filled with foul language erupted behind us. Mr. Hewitt, a medium-sized man, dressed in a black suit and top hat, was fulminating quite loudly that his horse and buggy were gone, with Mrs. Hewitt hanging on his arm, begging him to be more discreet. Apparently, it had been his beast that had nearly run me over.

"What in tarnation could have gotten into her?" Mr. Hewitt raged. "She's as calm as a spring day. She never panics, even when a mouse comes by."

"Please, Mr. Hewitt," Mrs. Hewitt said. "Be mindful of your language."

"Dagnabbit! I'll mind what I want! And I'll find out who spooked my horse, come hell or high water!"

The crowd around me slowly parted as Policeman Ernest Navarro rode up with his horse at a walk, leading the runaway horse and buggy.

"Looks like this one got away," Mr. Navarro said. He was a young Mexican man, with dark, shining eyes and a happy demeanor that had entranced more than one young maid. The young rascal winked at me.

Mr. Hewitt's mare shook her head but looked quite calm in spite of her run. I realized I'd seen her and the buggy around town and I had to agree with Mr. Hewitt, she was among the calmer horses I'd seen.

Sarah insisted on walking me home. We didn't say much. She had the wan look of someone who had spent her night trying to bring her husband home, and given what I'd seen in Mr. Mahoney's saloon the night before, I didn't doubt she'd been doing just that. I was still feeling very shaken, first by Reverend Elmwood's sermon and then by the horse incident.

Sarah yawned loudly. "Oh, excuse me, Maddie"

"You were out again last night?"

"I'm afraid so. I found Mr. Worthington at Mrs. Medina's house. Fortunately, some of the men there were kind enough to drag him home for me."

"Hm," I muttered and we fell into silence again.

I couldn't help but worry, once again, that Sarah was out around saloons and the like late at night. I didn't think much of her derringers. Such small guns were scant protection in a world where much larger guns sent bullets flying all over the place at frequent intervals. Still, I supposed her derringers were better than nothing and I suddenly found myself wondering if I should carry one or two, myself. After all, I'd almost been killed just that morning.

Which caused me to wonder what had caused the mare to rear like that? I hadn't immediately associated the accident with malicious intent. Runaway horses were not all that common, but the newspapers usually had a report of at least one almost every day. Still, there was something about the timing of it, besides that very uncomfortable sermon, that troubled me deeply. I was glad to have Sarah there so that I could clarify my thoughts.

"What could possibly have caused that poor horse to rear?" I began as we came up to the gate to my rancho.

"It's a horse," snorted Sarah. "They all rear and spook at the least little thing. But I'm glad to see you haven't taken any hurt from the accident. Perhaps you'd best rest and leave off trying to find Mr. Rivers' killer."

"That is, indeed, excellent advice," I said. "Perhaps I shall. It is Sunday, after all."

"Then I'll leave you to your rest. Besides, I'd better make sure Hannah has Mr. Worthington's dinner ready on time."

"Thank you for walking me home," I said.

I watched for a minute as she turned back along the road, my head buzzing with my very uncomfortable thoughts. All of a sudden, I was glad Sarah had chosen to hurry home. I couldn't say for certain, but I was beginning to fear that Mr. Hewitt's mare had been spooked on purpose with the intent of causing me harm. There was no point in burdening poor Sarah with that thought. She had enough to worry about what with Mr. Worthington's excessive drinking and staying out all hours of the night. And I had no reason to believe that my misgivings had any founding in fact.

I turned and went back to my adobe, where Juanita scolded me about the state of my dress. I took it without explaining what had happened, except in the most general terms. There was no point in worrying Juanita, either. I changed to my brown riding habit, which had been freshly brushed and aired, and the plaster bits from Jacob Lomax's cast picked off. I waited to put on my hat, as it was time for dinner. The Ortiz families and the others had all returned from their services and were quite hungry. Being Catholics, they did not break their nightly fast before going to church, which is why we usually ate our Sunday dinner even earlier than the usual mid-day meal.

I chose not to linger. I did have the Lomax boy's condition to check on and I wanted to call on Mrs. Rivers and see if she would admit me. Given that such a call was considered rather scandalous, I did not want to make it too late in the day, thus interrupting a meal, perchance, or even an early bedtime, and adding to the scandal.

The ride out to the Lomax farm was quite pleasant. I was not sure what I'd find, as I didn't know if there was a Mormon church in the area. The Lomaxes were hardly alone in their faith, but Mormons were still relatively few and quite literally scattered far between among the different towns in the county.

However, the family was home and together and had just finished their Sunday worship. Young Jacob seemed quite cheerful, although I could tell his leg pained him quite a bit. But he appeared to be making a decent recovery and, better yet, had no fever nor other sign that he would take sick from his injury. His mother, Sabrina, thanked me quite effusively and insisted I take home a very nice seed cake as a token of her gratitude. As seed cake is my favorite, I said so, and set off another round of gratitude such that I feared I should never be allowed to leave the place.

I find such displays of gratitude most unseemly and deeply embarrassing. It is, after all, but another day's work for me. But a very wise soul once told me that it is shockingly unkind to deny people their chance to thank me. And I suppose, had I produced any children and had any one of them been grievously injured and possibly crippled by it, I would feel quite profoundly grateful to the person who had helped him and would want to express it. So I bore Sabrina's thoroughly undeserved accolades with as much good grace as I could muster (which, sad to say, was not very much), and the very instant I could leave, I did so.

Mr. Lomax was waiting for me on the porch of his house as Ruth shut the door after me.

"Your son is doing quite well," I told him.

"So I heard," he said, with that odd quirked smile. "Mind if we walk a bit?"

I untethered Daisy's reins. "I'd be happy to."

I braced myself for another fulsome display of gratitude, though why I should have thought Mr. Lomax, of all people, would give in to fulsome displays, I have no idea. He certainly didn't.

"I do appreciate your kindness to Jacob," he said.

"As I said, I would have done it for anyone, and in fact, do," I replied.

"So I've heard." He paused and looked out over the rolling hillsides above his farm. "You know my other job is to keep the peace around here, don't you?"

"I am well aware of that, Mr. Lomax."

He nodded. "It's got me wondering how you know Mrs. Medina is innocent."

"I was engaging in Christian charity that night," I said. "I won't say where. I think we can both deduce that. It's just that not everyone is going to understand. In fact, I'm not sure I'd expect you to, either."

He shrugged. "Got no right to complain."

"That, alas, does not mean you won't," I replied. "There are a great many people who complain about a great many things, never mind that they have no right to. However, I do have a question for you. Apparently, two men died last night in a fight at a brothel. What, if anything, have you heard about that?"

"I was there." Mr. Lomax frowned. "It was the usual. A couple of the teamsters that came in with the port wagon train got drunk at the Alessandro place. Started some fight over a card game. Lost one of the teamsters and one of the ranch hands."

I thought this over. "Does Mr. Alessandro keep, eh, you know, women?"

"He might. I didn't see any last night."

"And no one else died."

"Not that I know of."

"Hm. Reverend Elmwood was very specific in his sermon that the men died at a brothel, fighting over a wanton woman."

Mr. Lomax actually laughed. "Sounds like a man of the cloth to me. Why let what really happened get in the way of a good sermon?"

"You surprise me, Mr. Lomax." I looked at him, quite curious. Although I had to agree with his sentiment about the clergy, I wouldn't have expected such from him.

He shrugged yet again. "About as much as you surprise me, Mrs. Wilcox." He looked me over. "Been finding anything out?"

I sighed. "Not much, I'm afraid. Apparently, Mr. Rivers was so universally loathed, even you probably had a reason to kill him."

Mr. Lomax's entire demeanor became wary and watchful again.

"I wasn't accusing you," I said quickly.

He relaxed. "No. I expect not. But I do have a reason to have killed him."

"You do?"

"Nothing I would call cause, but some folks might." He looked down at his boots. "I've, eh, been known to take a nip or two of an evening. One of the reasons folks don't always guess we're Latter Day Saints. I can't abide drunkenness. I see every night what that does. Problem is, if Ruth catches it on my breath, well, she will give me grief."

"That explains why Hannah was so worried about me giving Jacob spirits. I'd wondered about that."

Mr. Lomax smiled and looked back at the house, then became serious. "The Friday before Mr. Rivers was killed, I'd stopped at Mr. Mahoney's place and Mr. Rivers stood me to a drink and I accepted. Then he kept pushing me to take another, and I thanked him and said I'd had enough. I even stood him to a drink, as well. He kept saying he wanted to see me drunk. Even threatened to tell my wife if I didn't go along with him."

"What did you do?" I asked.

"I left the saloon. Like I said, Ruth can always smell it on me, so I figured I wouldn't be in any worse trouble. I tell folks my wife and my, eh, 'sister' are Temperance followers so that usually gets me by. But as I left, Mr. Rivers threatened to tell Marshal Warren my secret. Very loudly, so several folks heard him."

"And does the Marshal know?"

Mr. Lomax nodded. "Marshal Warren guessed,

like you did. Said he didn't care what I believed and how many wives I had. He just wanted someone he could count on to be sober on a Saturday night. I don't think Mr. Rivers knew about my wives, though. He would have said something sooner. He liked having power over people,"

"He never bothered me."

"There were a few people he wouldn't bother, like his city council friends. Maybe he didn't bother you because you were part of the society wives."

"Who are all married to his council friends," I pointed out.

"Yep. Although, I would have thought a lonely widow would have been prime fodder for him."

"I have no idea." I began to fidget with my riding glove. "I was going to ask you if you knew anything about any other men in town who might have had reason to kill Mr. Rivers. It might be a little hard for me to enquire."

"I can ask around."

"Perhaps somebody saw something."

"There wasn't much to see. I went by Mr. Mahoney's saloon maybe around ten-thirty that night. I didn't see anyone, but now that I think about it, I did see Mr. Rivers on the ground. At least, I think it was him. I was paying more attention to something I saw in the alley next to the saloon. There was somebody there, but I never saw who it was. Ran off before I could see more."

"Well, that's interesting," I said. "Could you tell if it was a man or a woman?"

"Don't think it was either," Mr. Lomax said with a frown. "More like a boy. Pretty sure it wasn't a dog but could have been."

I sighed. "Well, that's something, at least." I frowned at my hand. "Oh, dear. Another hole. I fear I shall have to visit Mr. Montero again."

Mr. Montero was principally a tanner, but his wife made the most exquisite gloves. They even rivaled gloves made back East. Not everyone saw their value, but I did and would not purchase gloves from anyone else. Or have them mended elsewhere.

"Tanners need plenty of water," Mr. Lomax said quietly.

"Oh, for Heaven's sakes!" I groaned. "Was there nobody in the pueblo who liked Mr. Rivers besides me?"

It is no small measure of the discomfiture that I was feeling that such an outburst escaped me.

"I have heard tell there was one woman," Mr. Lomax said slowly. "He may even have loved her. I have no idea. But he often raised a toast. It went 'To all the ladies we love, and may our wives never find out.' And when he was particularly drunk, he would weep about the one woman he truly loved and how he could not have her."

"I wonder if Mrs. Rivers knew about her," I said.

Mr. Lomax offered his usual shrug.

"Well, I must go and pay her a condolence call," I said. "Thank you for talking with me, Mr. Lomax."

"Thank you again for helping my boy."

He helped me into my saddle, then touched the brim of his hat as I nudged Daisy into a walk.

I made my way to the Rivers' home, fully expecting to be turned back at the door.

As I tethered my horse to the hitching post outside the Rivers' home, I saw George, the third of the four Rivers boys coming from around the back of the house. He didn't look that much older than the youngest boy, Will. Indeed, he had all the rangy awkwardness of a boy in the process of turning into a man. I found out later that he was fifteen.

He was also wearing a rather nice suit that fit him, something I had never seen on any of the Rivers boys. Like his brothers, George was quite fair, with skin tanned by the relentless sun in our area. I sighed. I had mostly managed to keep my own skin as milky white as when I'd been dragged from Boston. But I feared it would ultimately be a losing battle.

The young lad saw me, looked frightened for a

moment, then gathered himself together.

"How do you do, Mrs. Wilcox?" he asked, forcing himself to smile pleasantly.

"How do you do, Master Rivers? Is your mother receiving?" I asked.

George gulped but nodded. "Yes, ma'am. Can I show you in?"

"Thank you."

George got me settled in the front parlor, then went to fetch his mother from upstairs. It seemed to take several minutes, but I began to suspect Mrs. Rivers was rapidly changing her dress. Susannah, the maid who always reminded me of Sarah's maid Hannah, brought in a tray with tea and slices of cake.

When Mrs. Rivers finally appeared, she looked a bit flustered and the bodice to her black poplin dress was not perfectly straight. She was followed by James, her eldest son who was twenty-one. George and Steven, the second son who was eighteen at the time, crowded into the room. The only one of Mrs. Rivers' sons who was missing was Will, which I thought odd. James and Steven took after their father's size, being tall and broad-shouldered, and as I looked at George, I noted that he would soon have the same stature.

"Good day, Mrs. Wilcox," Mrs. Rivers said, sitting down. "How kind of you to come by."

"Thank you for receiving me in your time of bereavement," I replied.

Mrs. Rivers barely repressed a small snort. "It is very kind of you to call. I know that most women prefer to be left alone at such a time. I confess I'm finding it rather lonely."

I debated sharing my own experience. "I understand. I found it so, myself. I trust all is going well with Mr. Rivers' business?"

James smiled and nodded. "Judge Sepulveda won't be back until Wednesday, so we won't be able to start the probate until then. But my father's lawyer, Mr. Higgins, assures me that everything is in order."

Which I did not doubt. However, I also caught the slight frown on George's face.

"That is good to hear," I said. "Pray forgive me for intruding on such a personal matter, and I'm sure it's simply a misunderstanding. However, I have heard from a family in the city who had gotten on the wrong side of one of Mr. Rivers' business dealings."

"Not another one!" Steven groaned.

"Hush, Steven," Mrs. Rivers said, then smiled at me.

"Ma..?" James began.

Mrs. Rivers shook her head. "Now, James, I understand, but we agreed we would do what we could to right any wrongs done." She turned to me. "It has sadly come to our attention that my late husband was not entirely honest in his dealings. I strongly suspect it has also come to your attention, as well."

"I'm afraid so, Mrs. Rivers," I said. "I've spoken with the Samples family."

"Samples? I don't believe I know them," Mrs. Rivers said.

"Negro farmers up north of town," James said. "Near the Lomax place, I believe."

"Yes. That's them," I said. "Apparently, the late Mr. Rivers forced them to raise sheep for the mill without paying them for the wool."

Mrs. Rivers looked at her eldest son, who nodded.

"How much do they say Pa owed them?" James asked with resignation.

"They didn't," I said. "Sadly, they seemed to expect to be used so badly."

"Well, they are just Negroes," Steven said.

I felt my ire rise, but before I could admonish the young man, Mrs. Rivers spoke up.

"That does not matter, Steven," she said. "Honest people do not cheat their lessers. James, have you made a note?"

"Yes, Ma." James had, indeed, already pulled out a small pocket journal and a pencil and was busily scribbling in it.

"Mrs. Wilcox," Mrs. Rivers said. "Please reassure the Samples family that they may keep the sheep and that we will buy their wool from now on."

"It shouldn't be affected by the probate," James said, with a small sigh. "There isn't any mention of them anywhere in Pa's books or inventories. I was trying to figure out how he was getting wool so cheaply, though."

"Pray forgive me for asking, but were there many irregularities among Mr. Rivers accounts?" I asked. "As you probably know, I was given the task of finding out who killed him."

That set off a series of shocked looks around the room, but Mrs. Rivers recovered first.

"No," she said quietly. "At least, none among his books."

James nodded. "That's been the problem. It's like the Samples' sheep. Pa bought wool from several farmers in the county, and I couldn't figure out why he was paying so little money for it. I know what the price of fleece is. But if Samples was giving him wool in addition to what he bought, then what Pa had to have been doing was recording an accurate number for the amount of wool he had so that he could account for the extra, then pretending he'd paid less by spreading out the price per pound between the paid and unpaid wool."

"So while his books and inventories appear to be completely in order," Mrs. Rivers continued. "It only appears so and we fear there may be many more claims on his property. We may, indeed, be ruined."

"Ma, they have to prove a claim, and that won't be easy the way Pa did things," James reminded her.

"How terrible," I said. "And to find out at such a sad time."

George snorted loudly. "It's not sad for us."

"George!" Mrs. Rivers gasped.

"Well, it isn't," George said, the anger flashing in

his eyes. "Mrs. Wilcox, you may as well know. We're glad Pa is dead."

"George, enough!" Mrs. Rivers snapped, then turned. "Dear Mrs. Wilcox, I am so sorry you had to witness this display of temper. But I am afraid George is right. However, ill you may think of us, it is true that Mr. Rivers was not kind to us and his death is something of a relief."

"I had heard that he used you quite badly, Mrs. Rivers," I said quietly.

Mrs. Rivers sniffed into her handkerchief. It was plain cambric and lacked the black edge of a mourning handkerchief.

"I should never have married him," she said softly. "But at the time, I was young and he was so very charming and dashing."

"I've been told he stole you away from Mr. Worthington."

"The man I should have married," she sighed. "But then I shouldn't have my boys, so perhaps it was all for the best. Nonetheless, I had been quite fond of Mr. Worthington but wasn't sure of his affections for me. He was a quiet man, even then. So when his charming cousin began courting me, I listened to my father who thought Mr. Rivers a better prospect as a husband. We had no idea what his true nature was. I didn't even find out until our two daughters were born. Sadly, they did not live long, but Mr. Rivers became quite angry to find he had girls after I'd produced such a fine son."

"Not that he'd ever let me know he thought me a fine son," grumbled James.

"James, darling, we mustn't let ourselves give in to bitterness." Mrs. Rivers reached over and patted his hand tenderly. "It will only eat away at us and make us into the dark person that was your father."

"I know, Ma," James said with a rueful smile.

I almost felt embarrassed by the intimacy of the moment, and yet I could see that although Mrs. Rivers and her sons had suffered greatly at Mr. Rivers' hands, she was determined that her boys would not follow in their father's footsteps.

"In any case, Mr. Rivers kept us quite nicely until we buried my second daughter," Mrs. Rivers continued. "Then he began to keep us in parsimony and began to beat both me and James. He said James needed toughening up."

"What brought you to Los Angeles?" I asked.

"Caleb Worthington," Mrs. Rivers said, with a soft chuckle. "His mother and Mr. Rivers' mother were sisters. We came from Philadelphia society. Mr. Worthington and Mr. Rivers both have older brothers and thus could never have expected to do more than work under their brothers in the family businesses. After I spurned Mr. Worthington's suit, he left to make his own way in the world and we later heard that he'd gone to the gold fields and actually did very well for himself. Mr. Rivers chose to work in the family business. However, he and his two brothers were always at each other's throats. It was very acrimonious. Finally, Mr. Rivers' father, a very angry, unpleasant person, as well, decided that my husband should leave the business." Here, Mrs. Rivers and her three sons all shivered. "It was a terrible night when it happened. But my mother-in-law reminded us that Mr. Worthington had moved to Los Angeles and was doing well, so she encouraged us to come here, which we did. Mr. Worthington was kind enough to help Mr. Rivers get established, which I suspect made my husband even angrier at his cousin."

"Angrier?" I asked.

"For some reason, Mr. Rivers envied his cousin beyond all reckoning," Mrs. Rivers said. "I never found out why. But whatever Mr. Worthington had, Mr. Rivers had to have and better. So when Mr. Rivers had to rely on Mr. Worthington's kindness, he made it even more his mission to torture his cousin. I wondered that Mr. Worthington put up with it for so long."

"Perhaps he didn't," I said. I quickly mulled over my interview with Mr. Mahoney the afternoon before, and suddenly something struck me. "Mr. Mahoney said that Mr. Rivers left at nine o'clock the night he died, after he and Mr. Worthington had come to blows. But Mr. Rivers wasn't seen again until just after ten o'clock when Mrs. Aguilar saw him from her window. So, where was Mr. Rivers between the time he left and the time he was seen again in front of Mr. Mahoney's saloon?"

There was a quick round of frightened looks, but Mrs. Rivers again recovered first.

"We should tell the truth," she told her sons, then looked at me. "Mr. Rivers had come home for a short while. He was... not well."

"You mean he was drunk," I said. I was, perhaps, unkind in being so blunt. However, I needed information and Mrs. Rivers seemed up to it.

"As drunk as a Virginia fence," she replied and shivered at the thought. "That was when he was at his absolute worst. When he was drunk and angry. If he were sober and angry, there would be blows struck, but nothing too terrible. If he were merely drunk, he would yell, but not hit anyone. But if he was drunk and angry..." She shuddered again.

James put his hand on his mother's shoulder. "It's all right, Ma. He's not ever going to do that again."

She nodded gratefully at her son. "It was not an easy life, Mrs. Wilcox. But it is at an end."

"What happened when he got home that Sunday?" I asked.

She paused and looked at her hands. "He simply left again. He'd do that sometimes, too."

I looked at her, feeling rather curious. Her words seemed perfectly reasonable but there was something not quite right about them. I brushed it aside and tried to think what else I should be asking Mrs. Rivers.

"Could you tell me who else has brought a claim against Mr. Rivers' estate?" I finally said.

She looked at James, who shrugged.

"Mr. Vasquez asked for some back wages, which

he was able to prove," James said. He got out his journal and opened it. "A few of the farmers said they'd been shorted on water, but can't really prove it. And Mr. Judson. He said he loaned Pa a hundred dollars, but I can't find a note and Mr. Judson hasn't been able to show me one."

"A hundred dollars?" I almost gasped. That was a great deal of money.

James nodded and I made a mental note to find a way to speak to Mr. Judson as soon as possible. I also decided that I had little more to learn from the family at that time. It was true that something seemed... not quite right, although I was at a complete loss to say exactly what it was. So I again offered Mrs. Rivers my condolences. I suspect she understood that my sympathies were for the sad years she'd spent being hurt by Mr. Rivers. George showed me out.

As we stepped onto the porch, George stopped me.

"Mrs. Wilcox, is it bad that I'm happy my pa is dead?" he asked with a worried frown.

I sighed. "It's not good to want someone to die, George. But if someone's death ends your suffering and pain, then I would say it's not bad to feel relieved. Have you tried talking to your minister?"

George made a face. "I once tried to tell him about how Pa beat my ma, and he told me a man had a right to beat his wife if she was disobedient and that I shouldn't say such terrible things about a fine upstanding man like my father."

I shook my head. When I was a young girl, most of the ministers I had known were kindly compassionate souls. So it always disturbed me when I came across a man of the cloth whose interests seemed to be more in hellfire and brimstone than in Christian love. And as the years have passed, I have come to the conclusion that the kindly souls are the exception rather than the rule. However, I had not yet become so disillusioned, and so found myself unable to reply to George's question.

"Well, the Bible tells us we should love one another," I said finally. "You didn't wish for your father to die, did you?"

"No, ma'am."

"Then I expect the Good Lord understands your relief at his passing."

"Thank you, ma'am."

He helped me up onto Daisy, and I rode back to my rancho, uncomfortably aware that George might not have only been happy at his father's death but might have helped him to it.

I did not have much time to brood about it, however. There was supper with the families and lessons to hear. Then, just after the sun had sunk below the horizon, and the western sky had turned a light lavender fading into indigo, we someone pounding on the door of the adobe.

"Mrs. Wilcox! Help!" cried a female voice.

I opened the door to find a young woman. She was russet-haired and missing her hat, her tresses falling about her shoulders. She wore a day dress that had been buttoned-on hurriedly and askew. I recognized her as one of the women employed by Regina.

"Mrs. Wilcox," she sobbed, falling into my arms. "You've got to come quickly. They're going to lynch Mrs. Medina!"

CHAPTER NINE

A crowd, bearing all manner of lanterns and torches, had gathered near where Aliso Road met Alameda Street. There was a corral there with a good high gate. Reverend Elmwood sat in his buggy next to the gate, a brightly shining lantern hung from the post on the buggy's side. A hastily erected cage of wooden fence rails sat nearby and in it, Regina sat on the ground trembling, her best blue walking suit billowing around her. I was surprised that the noose wasn't already around her neck, but profoundly grateful, nonetheless. I slipped through the crowd to the bars, Sebastiano and Enrique following as best they could.

"Maddie!" she hissed.

"We're getting you out of here," I declared.

Behind me, Sebastiano and Enrique stood with their rifles at the ready.

"No!" Regina cried. "Maddie, I don't want that. You know why. Just please make sure you're the only one who sees my body."

"It will not come to that," I said with far more conviction than I felt. I paused, then added, "However, I will be the only one who sees you if it does."

Tears streamed down Regina's face, but she offered me a wan smile.

A roar went up from the crowd. The marshal's deputy, Joseph Dye, strode up, the rope in his hands. I literally flung myself, back-first, against the bars to bare his way.

"You cannot hang Mrs. Medina!" I cried. "She did not kill Bertram Rivers!"

I presume it was the sight of an otherwise utterly respectable woman barring his path that flummoxed the deputy.

"The whore of Babylon must meet her fate!" Reverend Elmwood intoned to the cheers of the crowd.

"Then those among you who have never visited a whore's house may come and get her!" I screamed.

The crowd quieted, which did not surprise me. The men, and the crowd was almost completely men, shuffled their feet, looking at one another. I saw one of the few women push her husband forward quite hard, then gasp as he demurred.

"Well, go on!" Reverend Elmwood shouted.

The men looked at him, then looked at me.

"If you do, you are hanging an innocent person," I declared.

"And why are you so certain she's innocent?" the reverend demanded.

I looked out at the crowd and took a deep breath. "I was with her all the night that Mr. Rivers was killed." There were murmurs from the crowd and Regina sobbed behind me. "I was doing an act of Christian charity by delivering one of the young women in the house of a baby boy. I didn't leave until close to dawn, well after Mr. Rivers was thrown into the zanja."

"Since when are you a midwife?" Deputy Dye asked, bewildered.

"I'm not a midwife. I'm a medical doctor!"

The crowd fell silent. I gulped. My secret, the reason my father had sent me from his home and forced me to marry Albert Wilcox, was now public.

You must understand that we doctors were not held in very high regard in those days. There were few medical schools. Almost anyone who cared to could claim he was a doctor, and perhaps he had some skill and remedies. More often, he was as hamstrung by a lack of knowledge and science as the rest of us who were educated. I will say this, however. Back then a woman doctor, while rare and curious, was not as soundly disregarded as we are today. Since women were the guardians of health and sanitation in the home, it didn't seem quite so... masculine, I suppose, to engage in the art of healing. But now that the practice of medicine has become entirely the province of the sciences (which I firmly believe is a very good thing), we women have been shuffled off to the sidelines and denied our opportunity to practice as doctors.

So that night, as I listened to the sound of Regina quietly sobbing behind me and the crackling of the burning torches, I quaked at the revelation.

"In any case," I told the crowd. "I am a reliable witness that Mrs. Medina did not commit the crime for which you are all too willing to hang her. Now, go back to your homes. I will find the person who did kill Mr. Rivers and you can arrest that person and try him in a court of law. Until then, Deputy Dye, will you please see to dispersing this crowd so that I and my ranch foremen can help Mrs. Medina back to her home?"

Dye made a motion with his hand and the crowd began, one by one, to slide away.

"Ay, Maddie, que tu eres loca," Sebastiano whispered to me as we opened the cage where Regina was kept.

"No me importa, Basto," I said, even though I was very afraid that an attack of insanity had overcome me.

Sebastiano and Enrique walked me and Regina back to her house on New High Street. Once there, I was admitted for the first time to her parlor. Sebastiano and Enrique declined to enter and I could hardly blame them. But they did insist on waiting at the door.

"Oh, Maddie, what were you thinking of?" Regina turned on me, her eyes still flowing with tears.

I sniffed back a few tears, myself. "Justice and your safety."

"You're going to leave Los Angeles now, aren't you?"

"And where will I go?" I asked her. "As much as I'd love to be shut of this miserable, desolate place, where would I go? Anyplace there is decent society is not going to let me practice medicine. At least here I get to do that and make and sell wine and be a woman of property and respect."

"Well, you ruined that last part for yourself. Did I not make it clear that my miserable life was not worth that?"

"For Heaven's sakes, Regina, you are a creature of God—

"I am a monster!"

I paused. "I do not know what you are, Regina. But you are my friend. And even if you weren't, you did not kill Bertram Rivers, and that is the salient point here."

"By God, you are stubborn!" Regina swept over to me and pulled me into a close embrace.

I hugged her back and the two of us cried for some minutes. As I finally began wiping my eyes, I looked around me at the room. I'm not sure what I had expected, but it was not nearly as exotic as I would have imagined. It was rich enough, with rose-figured wallpaper and chaises and sofas with red velvet upholstery. But the kerosene lamps were very simple, and what few engravings there were on the wall were quite tasteful and not even suggestive. Even the small piano in the corner was draped with a modest shawl.

"Well," I said, finally. "I must be on my way home. Have you any men you can call on just in case the mob comes back?"

Regina slipped a hand between the lush rose-colored draperies on her front window and peaked out.

"They're already here," she said, returning the drapes to their place. "I do not envy Deputy Dye. I suspect he will receive quite a chastising from certain men in this town."

"And speaking of that," I said. "Have you heard of anything regarding Mr. Rivers' death?"

"Nothing I would put any stock in, except that Mr. Judson was no friend of the zanjero."

"Yes." I nodded thoughtfully. "I was told Mr.

Rivers had borrowed one hundred dollars from Mr. Judson and had yet to pay it back."

"A hundred dollars?" Regina's eyebrows raised in shock. "That is a lot of money."

"Indeed," I said. "Good night, Regina."

"Good night, Maddie." She swept me into another embrace. "Thank you for my life. Thank you so much."

When I got home, I endured quite the lecture from Olivia and Magdalena Ortiz. Then Juanita added her opinion. In fact, it was another hour before I could shake off the women of my household so that I could go to bed. I felt quite sad that I had made them so angry and was immensely grateful that they did not consider me so thoroughly disgraced that they could no longer work for me. As I later learned, they were rather proud that I had stood up for Regina, especially since it meant that I was just as likely, indeed, more likely to stand up for one of them. They were merely worried about me and my position in the town's society. And there was the wine business, as well.

I must confess, there were somewhat fewer orders that spring. But the Pico Hotel and my agents in San Francisco were far less interested in my reputation as a woman of society than they were in the reputation of my wine, which remained excellent. So I was, ultimately, not hurt at all in that realm of my world.

However, that was only to be borne out later that year, and that night, I was worried about my winery. I was worried about my position in the pueblo's society. I was worried about even being able to stay in the pueblo. My reassurance to Regina notwithstanding, I had truly believed it when I told her there was no place else I could go.

It had taken years before people would seek me out for my healing ability. Perhaps in some other wild outpost, the people would be grateful enough to have any kind of medical person at all. But I did not want to live in some wild outpost. I wanted to live in a real city, where people did not shoot at each other every night, where one could go to plays and concerts put on by people who actually knew how to perform and play instruments well, where one didn't have to wait for months on end for the latest fashion books to come out and could find seamstresses who could make anything one liked. But one couldn't afford concerts or plays if one practiced medicine. And given how long it had taken the people of Los Angeles to accept my services, I would likely starve before I could build up a practice in Boston, or some such place.

I do not often give in to self-pity or spend time bemoaning my lot in life. And on those rare occasions when I do, I usually remember that much of my situation has been of my own making. After all, I had known my father would not approve of my going to medical school. That's why my mother and I had agreed that we shouldn't tell him other than that I was staying with my mother's sister for a couple of years to keep her company. My aunt and my mother both had small inheritances, which was how they were able to pay my way for those two years.

Admittedly, we couldn't have foreseen both my aunt and my mother passing away within weeks of each other and right before I received my degree. We couldn't have foreseen my uncle taking over my aunt's property and sending me back home the second I graduated. And while I suppose I couldn't have foreseen my father giving me a choice between being thrown out on the streets and marrying Albert Wilcox, I could have guessed he would do something quite drastic.

So I had made my choice and married Mr. Wilcox, and no matter how much I rued it, I was bound to live by it. And on my better days, I would often acknowledge that things had worked out rather well.

But that night was not one of my better ones, and I tossed and turned, alternately worrying about what would become of me, wondering how I was going to find Bertram Rivers' killer, and worrying about the dead man's sons, of all things.

Perhaps it wasn't so odd that I'd worry about the boys. I knew how it felt to bear a father's shame and disgust. At least, I knew I had given my father cause. The boys had done nothing to deserve their father's rancor. Well, that I knew of. I was beginning to see that there was a world of difference between how people presented themselves to the world and how they truly were.

It was a bitter lesson, indeed, and one that would make my life in the pueblo even more careworn. After all, I had no idea who was being honest with me and who was lying. I had thought myself a good judge of character. Bertram Rivers had proved me otherwise and it was with no little chagrin that I recalled that.

As I lay awake, I tried to think if there had been little hints that he wasn't the fine man I'd supposed him to be, and the more I thought about it, I saw that there were. There was the way he kept his family close to penury. And many times, while waiting for Mr. Mahoney in the back office of his saloon, I had heard the men talk about this fellow or that as being congenial, or that fellow as being too upright (usually Mr. Judson). I realized I had never heard anyone speak favorably of Mr. Rivers. In fact, I'd even heard vague complaints about him, but nothing that on the surface of it should have caused me to believe he was anything than what I saw him as. In fact, I couldn't think of anybody who'd had a good word to say about Mr. Rivers except the other society wives.

He'd always been very pleasant to them when he saw them on the street. When there were parties, he was always very charming, even deigning to listen to the prattle of Mrs. Glassell and Mrs. Carson. He'd been more than civil to me every month when I went to his office to pay my water subscription. He'd been very friendly and asked about how things were going on the rancho in a way that made me believe he was genuinely interested. But ultimately, that's what had fooled me. Mr. Rivers had shown me a courtesy and consideration

I received from far too few men in the pueblo.

As I began to comb through all the people I had considered good neighbors and even friends, I realized that not only would I never fall asleep, but I would also never be able to offer a civil word to any of them, and it didn't make sense that they were all as duplicitous as Mr. Rivers had been. However cautious I might feel in the future, it did not do to dwell on such things.

I could hear the clock in the parlor striking the half hour, although I'd lost track of which hour it was. With a deep and profound sigh, I sank back into my pillows and tried to redirect my thinking toward something more useful than worrying about which of my neighbors were pretending they were my friends. Fortunately, my musings over Mr. Rivers yielded some bounty.

I remembered that Mrs. Rivers had said that Baldo Vasquez had been cheated by Mr. Rivers. And it was only upon Mr. Rivers' death that the farmer had been able to recover the wages he'd been due. Then there was the tanner, Mr. Montero. He had worked for the zanjero, Perhaps he had also been cheated. I made up my mind then and there that as soon as it was light enough, I would talk to both Mr. Vasquez and Mr. Montero. I would also visit Mr. Judson at his bank. There was no reason I shouldn't. I had an account there, after all, mostly to facilitate payments to the various shipping and merchant agents who saw to selling my wine to places in San Francisco and Santa Barbara and elsewhere. And somehow, pondering all these things, I fell asleep.

But later that morning, right after breakfast, fate played into my hands in the form of a visit from Mr. George Oliver, a farmer who lived not far from Mr. Vasquez on the south side of the pueblo. He and his wife attended the same church with me. He was a jolly sort, and his wife had been equally jolly until a few years before. I'd heard that she now suffered from melancholy and had wondered if she'd become dependent on laudanum, as it was all too commonly given for melancholy. I had Magdalena show Mr. Oliver into the parlor and joined him there a moment later.

He was of average size and dressed in his Sunday suit, his dark hair slicked down, and his skin still pink from a good scrubbing or, perhaps, from working all day in the sun. He bounced up off the sofa as I entered.

"Mrs. Wilcox, so good of you to see me," he said quickly.

"I'm happy to," I said. "Please, be seated."

I took the chair across from him.

He fidgeted with his hat, a dusty black felt with a wide brim.

"It's my wife," he began slowly. "As you may have noticed, she hasn't been herself in, well, several years now. We've seen several doctors, but none seem to know what is causing her melancholy. Then this morning, well, it's all over the pueblo about you being a medical doctor, after all. So I thought maybe a lady doctor could help Josephine. Could you please see her?"

Fortunately, I was already wearing my second-best riding habit, in anticipation of riding to speak with Mr. Vasquez and Mr. Montero. The habit was a blue wool and linen that I usually found too warm to wear. But that morning, storm clouds had built up to the west and there was a distinct chill in the air as the breeze blew in from the ocean. There were the others that I had hoped to speak to, but this was a patient. That had to come first.

"Of course," I said and got up. "I was just going out in any case, and it will be no trouble to visit your wife."

Mr. Oliver bounced up with me. "Oh, thank you! I didn't expect you would be able to come immediately, but it is so wonderful that you will."

I merely nodded, then fetched my bag as Sebastiano saddled up Daisy and the mule. He didn't say anything, but I knew his rifle was hanging off the mule's saddle and that I was going nowhere by myself that day.

It didn't take long to get to the Oliver farm. He mostly raised grapes, as did most farmers in the area. I often bought some of his for my own wines, and barley and hops. I could also see some of his beef cattle grazing on one of the nearby slopes that faded into the flat land south of the pueblo. The family lived in an adobe, with a large barn next to it. A huge chicken coop had been built onto the side of the rather ramshackle barn, its fenced yard bursting with chickens. The Oliver children were scattered about the garden and dirt space in front of the small adobe. There were eight of them at the time, or there had to have been. I remember delivering the ninth, and that was after these events.

Mrs. Oliver was inside the indoor kitchen, kneading bread. She was a good-sized woman, and well-rounded, with brown hair and a lackluster air about her. She smiled softly at her husband, then looked at me curiously.

"I've been told you've been suffering from melancholy," I said.

She looked over at Mr. Oliver

"Maybe she can help, Josephine," Mr. Oliver said.

"I'm feeling better," she said, a little defiantly.

I had to give her the truth of it. She was not as jolly as she had been, and I could understand why her husband was still concerned for her well-being. Still, she was clearly less anxious and nervous since the last time I'd seen her.

"You are," I said. "You do look better than you have of late. What's changed?"

She snorted, but focused, instead, on her bread.

"Any aches or pains?" I asked.

She again looked at her husband, then smiled. "I am quite well, thank you. It is kind of you to call."

She returned to her kneading.

I looked at Mr. Oliver and nodded toward the yard. He followed me outside.

"She does seem better," I said. "Has she been taking laudanum or perhaps some other tonic?"

"No tonics now." Mr. Oliver frowned. "No. The children would have seen it. She can't hide from them all. She's already tried hiding some bottles."

"Perhaps she got better after you stopped the laudanum."

"Oh, no. She didn't get better until last week. Right after we heard Mr. Rivers had died. But she's still quite melancholy." Mr. Oliver sighed, then flushed as red as a beet. "She's better, but not... well, we..."

I nodded. I suspected I knew what he was trying to say. "I see. Well, I'm glad to see that she is getting better. Perhaps if we just wait a while longer to see if she continues to improve. I'll make a point of visiting her every week or so. Would that help?"

"Oh, Mrs. Wilcox, I'd so grateful." Mr. Oliver took my hand and squeezed it. "It's the kindest thing anyone's offered yet. We tried tonics and laudanum and all they did is make her sleepy and even sadder."

"They frequently can. You were wise to stop them," I said. I looked back at the kitchen. "I'm afraid I must be on my way, but do not hesitate to call me if anything changes, for better or ill."

"I will, Mrs. Wilcox," Mr. Oliver said. "I will. I'll send one of the children over with a chicken."

"That's not necessary, Mr. Oliver."

"I can pay my own way. We've chickens, plenty of them. I'll do right by you."

I smiled. "Why don't you wait until I've actually done something for your wife?"

"You have. You are coming by to check on her. You're listening to her."

"Very well, then. Thank you, Mr. Oliver."

I collected Sebastiano, who had waited outside, and the two of us made our way to the Vasquez farm.

Baldo Vasquez was well over sixty years old, with white hair and a brown face filled with wrinkles. He may have been at least part Indian because he had that squat, broad build to his shoulders and a broader face. He greeted us warmly and beckoned both Sebastiano and me into the adobe, which was surrounded by groves of orange, walnut and olive trees. Mrs. Vasquez brought in tea and pan dulces, or small sweet breads decorated with honey. I remembered that Mrs. Vasquez kept bees and was justly quite proud of her honey.

"So, you've come to ask me about Mr. Rivers," Mr. Vasquez said as Mrs. Vasquez poured.

She hissed at him, but he laughed and shrugged.

"I've been told that he cheated you out of your wages," I said.

"Yes. He cheated me like he cheated everybody. But I could not have killed him."

"The first time your drinking has saved you," snorted Mrs. Vasquez, shaking a finger at him. She turned to me. "He was drunk that night. Came home from one of the saloons near the Plaza. I made him sleep in the barn."

"It was my brother's birthday," Mr. Vasquez explained.

Mrs. Vasquez snorted again. "Yes, you only drink when someone has a birthday. But your family is as big as mine. We have a lot of birthdays."

"I understand you were able to get some of your back wages from Mrs. Rivers," I said.

"She is a kind lady," Mr. Vasquez said.

I pressed my lips together, then took a deep breath. "I've been told that Mr. Rivers was prone to imposing himself on farmers' wives with the threat of withholding water to the farm."

Mrs. Vasquez laughed loudly. "Of course, he tried. I wished him eternal damnation. He said he would keep us from getting water. I told him he could for all I cared."

"My wife is a strong woman," Mr. Vasquez said with pride.

"Did he try to stop your water?"

"Of course," Mr. Vasquez said. "But it didn't matter. My trees are well-rooted. They don't need as much. And..."

"We have a well," said Mrs. Vasquez.

"Sh!" Mr. Vasquez hissed, looking quickly at Sebastiano and me.

"They're not going to say anything," Mrs. Vasquez said. "And it's not a big well. If we were trying to grow wheat or barley, we might have been in trouble. But there's enough water when we need it."

"I see."

We stayed just long enough to finish our tea and sweet breads, then Sebastiano and I moved on to our next stop.

The reality of a tannery is that you smell it long before you get there, which was why the Montero place was well on the outskirts of the pueblo, and I suppose why so few people knew about Mrs. Montero's ability with gloves. I had the pair of mine that needed mending in my bag and pulled them out the second Sebastiano helped me down from my horse.

Mr. Montero was a Negro, though his skin was almost as light as a Mexican's. His wife, though, was as darkly complexioned as if she'd newly arrived from Africa. The two were in their yard when I arrived. Mrs. Montero clucked over my torn riding gloves and immediately took them into the house.

"Mr. Montero," I asked. "As you probably know, I am trying to find the person who killed Mr. Rivers."

"I know," he said. His accent was more Mexican than colored, although he spoke English as if it were his native tongue.

"We've been hearing tale after tale of how Mr. Rivers cheated people," I said.

"He never cheated me," Mr. Montero replied very quickly. "I liked him. He was a good man."

I suppose I would have been more gratified to hear someone speaking up for Mr. Rivers if I hadn't gotten the feeling that Mr. Montero was lying.

I tried pressing him on a couple points but could not get him to say anything except that he thought Mr. Rivers was honest and kind and a capital fellow.

"What a liar," Sebastiano said to me as we left the tannery.

"I fear so. He's obviously afraid that we might think he's guilty. However, how are we to get anyone to believe that?"

Sebastiano shrugged. "I hope no one decides to hang Mrs. Medina again."

"I should hope not," I said with a shudder. "I would like to think I made it perfectly clear that she is innocent of that crime. But that does remind me, do you recall my saying that Reverend Elmwood had preached a sermon against her that morning?"

"I remember," Sebastiano said.

He was showing considerable forbearance. I believe I had mentioned that sermon many times over the day before and later that night.

"I think we should pay a call on the good reverend," I said.

"Maybe we shouldn't, Maddie," Sebastiano said, a little nervously. "He is a man of God."

"With clay feet and I fear I must remind him of that." I kicked Daisy into a trot and headed for the center of the pueblo.

Sebastiano, may God bless him, knew that mood and knew very well that it was much better to let me go my way than try to convince me otherwise. Kind fellow that he was, he seldom pointed out that he had warned me when my headstrong actions ended up the worse for us. Occasionally, he'd get angry enough, but not often and probably not nearly as often as he should have.

Fortunately, the reverend was at home when we arrived. If I must be honest, he was almost always there. He had the rather deplorable, to my way of thinking, habit of letting his flock come to him with their troubles as opposed to going to them. I was admitted to his office and invited Sebastiano to come with me, but he elected to stay outside.

Reverend Elmwood was not in any kind mood that morning, nor did I expect him to be. However, his greeting was gracious, if a bit stiff, and he invited me to sit on the sofa in his spacious office while he took a nearby chair.

"Now, how might I help you, Mrs. Wilcox?" he asked.

"You could tell me what on earth inspired you to make that wretched sermon yesterday and then fire up the populace to lynch Mrs. Medina," I said, coldly.

He sat up righteously. "I had every reason to believe that Mrs. Medina had killed poor Mr. Rivers."

"Name one."

"What do you mean?"

"Tell me one reason, any reason, you had to believe that Mrs. Medina had killed Mr. Rivers."

He shifted, suddenly uncomfortable. "Well, the marshal had arrested her."

"And almost immediately released her when it was proved she couldn't have done it." I tried not to, but my eyes rolled in exasperation.

"I am called to root out sin in our community."

"But not to advocate for the lynching of innocent people."

He snuffled. "Mrs. Medina is hardly an innocent person."

"She is innocent of murder." I almost snorted, myself. How obstinate he was. "And what good will it do to hang even one whore in this city? Even if you could hang all of them, the men in the pueblo would find others to satisfy their wretched desires. And why is it we always condemn the adulteress and never the men who seek her services? Are they not as guilty?"

"Those wicked women use their wiles to tempt our poor men," the reverend said.

"What utter nonsense!" I answered. "Shouldn't men be the masters of their passions, especially if you are going to insist that we women are the weaker sex?" As I warmed to my theme, I remembered what Regina had told me about why her women and others like them did what they did. "And may I point out, that most of these young women are pushed into their profession because they have been thrown onto the streets by their fathers or brothers who did not want to keep them. They have no other choice but to ply their noxious trade because men will not hire them to do honest work. And yet you would have them bear the brunt of the blame. In what way is that Christian charity? In what way does that emulate our beloved Lord and Savior, who, you may remember, forgave and cared for many an adulteress? How will hanging these poor women encourage them to reform their lives?"

"They will fear the Lord and His vengeance."

"Hah!" I could not believe I was behaving as I was, but I was undone. "How little you know of human nature. Trust me, Reverend Elmwood, these women fear starving more. We should be showing them kindness and love. We should find good honest work for them, and I do not mean in service, as there are many in this community who use the servants in their household as their personal whores. I know. I've delivered their babies and treated their diseases."

Again, the reverend shifted himself. "You should show more discretion in your charity, Mrs. Wilcox."

"And if I don't take care of them, who will? None of your so-called Godly people, I'll warrant. I dare say that if Jesus waited for people to reform before He healed them, we would not now be Christians."

That flummoxed the good reverend. As he sat, his mouth opening and closing, I was somewhat embarrassed by my speech, but I could not help myself. I had been burdened with these thoughts for a good many years and it was such a relief, at long last, to give voice to them.

"Now," I said, having run my course. "Coming back to the matter of your insisting that Mrs. Medina be hanged for the murder of Mr. Rivers. I am curious why you were so vehement about it. Indeed, you even led the lynching party."

"I know my duty to the good people of this

community," the reverend replied, trying to recover his self-righteous staunchness.

"Again, utter nonsense," I said. "One would almost think you were trying to deflect suspicion from someone by focusing it elsewhere."

He gasped, and my eyes narrowed.

"Good Heavens, you were," I said.

"I certainly did not kill Mr. Rivers," he snapped. "And if Mrs. Medina didn't, then I have no idea who did."

"But you must have had some reason to fear that someone you like or care about would be suspected. Or maybe even yourself. I have heard that you and your wife were not terribly complimentary toward Mr. Rivers."

His eyes darted frantically around the room. "Mr. Rivers was a fine, upstanding man. A credit to this community. Those who speak ill of him are lying. And if you want someone to suspect, you might consider Caleb Worthington. They were not known to like each other."

"I am well aware of their relationship," I said, even as I began to consider once again that Mr. Worthington appeared to have good reason for doing away with his cousin. I glared at Reverend Elmwood. "Far be it from me to tell you what to preach, but I firmly believe that a sermon on confessing our sins and forgiving others would not be amiss." I got up. "Good day, Reverend."

Outside, Sebastiano chuckled and shook his head. "I would not like to have been the Reverend. You look like you were not kind to him."

"He got quite the tongue lashing, I'm afraid," I said. I looked around. "I believe we should leave our mounts tied up here and walk for a bit. We need to pay a call at the lumber mill."

"Very good."

As we walked down the Calle Principal toward Mr. Worthington's mill, I saw Sarah and Mrs. Fletcher walking toward us from the Calle Primavera. I paused to greet them, but Mrs. Fletcher swept her skirt to the side and crossed the street. Sarah swiftly followed suit, and the two continued their walk ahead of us along the Calle Principal.

"I've been snubbed," I gasped.

"And by Mrs. Worthington, too," said Sebastiano. He sighed. "I think maybe that your reputation is in question."

"Hmph!" I replied.

But I had been stung quite deeply by Sarah's snub. How was it possible that my dearest of friends no longer valued our friendship? I had always known that Sarah placed a high value on her position in the pueblo's society. But to snub me, even after what had happened the previous night, that seemed unduly harsh. Especially as it appeared that she had done it because Mrs. Fletcher had, a woman Sarah had often disparaged when we were alone.

I shook my head to clear the unwelcome musings. But as Sebastiano and I made our way along the Calle Principal to the mill, more than one woman of the pueblo turned away from me. Most of these women I had never called my friends, but still, it stung. In many ways, it was everything I had ever feared about losing my reputation, everything my Grandmother Franklin had warned me about and despaired that I should come to.

There was, however, only one response to such behavior. I held my head high and walked straight on. I had not done anything wrong. Indeed, I had saved a life by my actions and if that made me a disreputable person, that certainly spoke more about the people who judged me so than it did about me. Once again, I thanked my beloved mother for such lessons. I hadn't actually scoffed as a young girl, but I hadn't entirely understood what she had been trying to teach me. Now, I was learning those lessons all over again and they were not pleasant ones at all.

I had walked by the lumber mill owned by Mr.

Worthington many times, however, I had never been into the yard. I looked around, hoping that Sarah was about, as she sometimes visited and had been headed toward the mill when she snubbed me. However, I could not see her. Huge mountains of logs were neatly stacked along the edges of the yard. At one end, piles of shavings and sawdust stood like the pyramids of Egypt. A tall building ran along the other side of the yard. If it had been a standard edifice, it would have been two stories. However, it only had the one floor that I could see. A great cable was strung from the top of the building across the yard to a post near a smaller cabin near the front of the yard's gate. Along the cable, two huge pulleys hung from wheels that rolled back and forth.

I could hear the shriek of the saw coming from inside the building and watched as four large men rolled a log into place under the pulleys. Mr. Worthington stood nearby, watching the progress. Sitting next to him was a blue-gray dog, about medium-sized, with a broad skull and a patch of white on its chest.

I thought about how to proceed, as I did not want to walk up to Mr. Worthington unannounced. However, the noise in the yard was such that I could not hail him without raising my voice, something a well-bred lady would never do. Perhaps because my reputation was now torn to shreds, I felt it even more imperative to behave as a lady ought.

Sebastiano, however, saved me by calling out quite loudly. Mr. Worthington turned and I approached him. The dog met me halfway and began sniffing at the hem of my skirt.

"Spot! Get back here," Mr. Worthington snarled.

Spot ignored him and continued sniffing as I moved toward his master.

"And what do you want?" Mr. Worthington demanded of me.

I decided to be blunt. "I have been told that you and Mr. Rivers were in a fight the night he died."

Mr. Worthington spat, sending the stream of tobacco juice toward where the log was being lifted onto a sling.

"We were always fighting," he said. "What difference does that make?"

"He was murdered, Mr. Worthington."

"I didn't kill him. Last I saw him—" He suddenly swore and jumped at me.

Before I could get out of the way, I had fallen flat on my back with Mr. Worthington on top of me.

"Mr. Worthington!" I gasped and tried to get up.

He pushed my head down and looked up. I started to struggle, then realized that something very strange was happening. Finally, Mr. Worthington rolled off of me, then stepped aside so that Sebastiano could help me up.

"Mr. Worthington!" I gasped again, as the dog danced around us and barked furiously.

He simply pointed up. I looked and saw a huge pulley swinging low above us. If I am honest, I do not truly know what happened. However, I do know that if Mr. Worthington had not fallen upon me, one or both of us would have been killed or grievously injured.

"Beg your pardon," he mumbled, once we were both standing.

I glanced up at the still swinging pulley. "I dare say, Mr. Worthington, I have nothing but thanks to offer you. I apologize for my outburst. I should have assumed you did not wish me ill by your actions."

"Obliged, ma'am."

I adjusted the bodice on my riding habit, trying to cover up just how hard my heart was beating over our near miss. I looked over at Mr. Worthington. He was behaving admirably but one could still see that he had been deeply shaken. And it was, perhaps, for that reason that I declined to press him further regarding Mr. Rivers.

I have often wondered whether if I had pressed him about his fight with Mr. Rivers that fatal night it

would have saved the life that was later lost. I don't
know that it would have, and, indeed, such speculation
serves little purpose. But still, even to this day, I can't
help but wonder.

CHAPTER TEN

Unfortunately, the state of my riding habit was such that I was forced to return to my rancho to change clothes, which also involved listening to yet another lecture from Juanita, who should have expected such things by that time. Or perhaps she had the expectation that my clothes would often take a great deal of punishment but it did little to ease the frustration and extra work such punishment caused. In any case, I was soon attired in my third best riding habit, which was also blue, but made of a cotton and wool that had faded considerably. Still, it was clean and in good repair, so I was perfectly happy to put it on.

I walked back into town, Sebastiano by my side, no more eased of mind, but more determined than ever to find out who had killed Bertram Rivers. On the surface of it, there was no reason to believe that the accident at the lumber yard had been anything but an accident. Still, I began to believe that it had, in fact, been no accident, but an attempt on my very life. There had been the incident of the horse spooking the day before, which, by itself, was easily disregarded as an accident. But after the incident at the mill, it seemed odd that there should be two such convenient accidents so close together. It seemed quite possible that my continued efforts to unveil the killer of Mr. Rivers had, in turn, caused that killer, who obviously did not wish to be unveiled, to look my way and try to find ways to eliminate me as a threat.

I suppose that should have been encouragement enough to leave well enough alone. Alas, it had the opposite effect on me, as such things usually did. Grandmother Franklin often complained that I was as stubborn as an old goat. My beloved mother, however, wisely counseled me that perseverance was a virtue albeit a dangerous one. Like most virtues, she said, it could be taken too far, and it took wisdom to know when one was fighting for what was just and true and when one was simply fighting to keep fighting.

That thought gave me pause as Sebastiano and I entered the Calle Principal. After all, horses spooked all the time, even very calm ones. As for the mill, I recalled Mr. Worthington's complaints the previous Saturday evening. He'd nearly been killed twice that week by accidents at the lumberyard. Perhaps this had been simply one more. Heaven knows, accidents were not uncommon and I'd been summoned to the bedside of many a laborer.

One might call me naive for my thinking, and I probably was. However, there was no such thing as crime investigation back then. We didn't have detectives who looked for clues and produced evidence, especially not in a little backwater such as Los Angeles was in those days. Unless a felon was seen actively engaged in his felony, there was no established way to find out who had committed the crime. It made no sense that Mr. Rivers' killer would want to compound his crime and further risk discovery by trying to kill me when all he had to do was stay silent and the odds were in his favor that my search would come to nothing.

"Sebastiano," I asked. "What do you think of today's accident at the mill?"

"I don't think it was an accident," Sebastiano said. "The pulley that came down, it came from the loft of the saw house."

"Oh, dear." I quailed.

"But I think it was aimed at Mr. Worthington. That's where he stands when he's watching the workers. And you've never even been to the lumber yard before. Why would someone think to hurt you there?"

"That's an excellent point," I said, recovering myself. "But why would someone want to harm Mr. Worthington? He's not the most pleasant of fellows, but that's hardly a reason to kill or hurt someone."

Sebastiano shrugged. "Don't know. Maybe the person wants his mill."

"Perhaps." I thought it over. "That would seem to be the most logical reason, especially since the accidents have all happened at the mill. However, there are far easier means of achieving that objective, and ultimately, it is of little consequence to us."

"Unless it hurts your friend, Mrs. Worthington."

"She only visits the mill occasionally. I see no reason for her to be hurt there. On the other hand, losing her husband would probably only add to her troubles, so I suppose we could spare a few minutes to ask a question or two. I only hope that we do not find out that the pueblo is secretly aligned against him, as we have with Mr. Rivers."

Sebastiano grinned. "That, I know will not happen. Mr. Worthington has a good reputation."

"He does?" I looked at Sebastiano. "He is not a kind husband."

"That is something only you would know."

I saw that the bank owned and run by Mr. Judson was nearby. "Well, we can at least ascertain whether there has been any undue interest in the mill. Mr. Judson should be in."

The bank looked very much like any other bank. The building was newly built of brick and decorated with white columns. Two attorneys and some mercantile agents had the offices on the floor above. The main room of the bank held a high cabinet with various bits of paper, pens, and inkwells so that customers could write drafts and the like. There was a long counter with bars on it, that ran the length of the room and that we generally referred to as the cage. The vault had been built onto the back wall and in front of it, the clerks had their desks. There was a door to Mr.

Judson's office, as well, and it was open.

The young clerk behind the cage tried to tell me that Mr. Judson was not in. I knew very well that meant that Mr. Judson did not wish to see me, however, and I chose to point out that I could plainly see Mr. Judson over by the vault. The clerk then tried to explain that Mr. Judson was very busy at the moment. I then said that I would wait for him to see me. I did have an account there, which I pointed out to the clerk, one that usually did not require Mr. Judson to offer credit on my behalf. Indeed, he mostly accepted payments for me from the various agents and buyers who sold my wines. The clerk spoke quietly with Mr. Judson, and then I was admitted into the office.

"Mrs. Wilcox," Mr. Judson said as he settled himself into the chair behind his huge oaken desk. It was littered with papers and account books and held a very nice inkwell with holders for two pens. "How might I help you today?"

He had the padded look of a very prosperous man, which he was. He wore a bristly mustache that was as gray as the hair on his head, which was neatly combed and pomaded down.

"I wish to know if there has been any interest in purchasing the Worthington lumber mill."

Mr. Judson's eyebrows raised. "No, madam. None whatsoever. Why do you ask?"

"It would appear that someone wishes Mr. Worthington ill. There have been several accidents there and on behalf of Mrs. Worthington's welfare, I thought I should ask."

"Oh." Mr. Judson looked over his desk. "This is very interesting. It's the first I've heard of it."

I bit my lip. "I wouldn't want you to deny Mr. Worthington a line of credit on the basis of this appearance."

"Of course I wouldn't, Mrs. Wilcox. He is an excellent customer." Mr. Judson suddenly sighed. "If I am nonplussed by your visit, madam, it is merely because I did not expect you to be asking after Mr. Worthington."

"Oh?" I asked, then remembered the money that Mr. Judson had tried to recover from the Rivers family. "Ah. You expected me to ask you about the one hundred dollars you have claimed to have loaned Mr. Rivers."

Mr. Judson's jowls almost seemed to quiver. "You heard about that, eh? Unfortunately, it was no loan. Mr. Rivers had cheated me out of it. I only called it a loan to ease Mrs. Rivers' suffering. No need to call attention to the kind of man her husband really was."

"She is already well aware of it," I said.

"So I gathered." He sighed deeply. "Her sons insisted on seeing a note, and I can hardly blame them for that."

"They wish to make reparations, but fear being ruined."

Mr. Judson nodded. "As well they should. Mr. Rivers was always a disreputable fellow. When he arrived and bought the wool mill, there was some shady dealing going on. As a result, I objected to his appointment as zanjero, quite vociferously, as I recall. But the rest of the council claimed he had been duly elected in the election that winter. And it turned out he wasn't on the ballot at all. I went back and checked the records."

"Perhaps your colleagues on the council were offered some consideration in exchange for the honor?"

Mr. Judson huffed and squirmed. "As much as I hate to admit it, I am afraid we see far too much corruption in our little town. And, alas, Mr. Rivers took advantage of it, as I predicted he would. I was about to suggest that he be removed from his position of trust on the grounds that he was not trustworthy when he met his demise."

I nodded thoughtfully. "But there remains the question of how he cheated you. If it was not a loan that he failed to pay back, how did he cheat you out of one hundred dollars?"

"He had a small vineyard out near Anaheim. You know, the German colony?"

"I have heard of it."

"It is located next to one of my properties and I wanted to purchase it. Mr. Rivers said I could and requested the one hundred dollars as good faith. So I looked over the titles and the grants and gave him the money. He claimed that I never gave it to him and sold the property to someone else."

"You didn't get a receipt for the money?"

"He was going to have a messenger bring it to me." Mr. Judson shook his head. "We were at Mr. Mahoney's saloon. I was certain someone would have heard the transaction, but no one did. So there were no witnesses. I should have been more wary but wasn't."

I sighed. "Do you know anyone else he might have similarly cheated?"

"No." Mr. Judson shook his head. "He seemed to be friends with the rest of the council. They were willing to look the other way. I, on the other hand, prefer the straight and narrow path of righteousness and Mr. Rivers delighted in challenging that. Hence, his cheating me."

"So I must ask, did you kill Mr. Rivers?"

The man paled and sputtered but answered directly. "Never! I did not kill him. I was most disappointed in him and in losing my money, but I would never have resorted to such ends. And, as it stands, it would have done me little good, as I cannot recover the money. Now, Mrs. Wilcox, unless you have other business to conduct, I shall have to end this conversation."

I stood and he bounced up, as well.

"I do appreciate your candor, Mr. Judson," I said and turned toward the front of the bank.

"Eh, Mrs. Wilcox, would you mind terribly?" He gestured at a back door.

"Excuse me?" I asked, beginning to feel a bit offended.

"I would not have you believe that I have anything but the highest respect for you, Mrs. Wilcox," he said, pulling himself upright. "But a bank runs on the trust of its customers. As your most admirable search for Mr. Rivers' killer is well known, I would not want someone in the community to see you here and draw the conclusion that you suspected me, never mind that you do not."

I debated asking him if he was sure I didn't. However, it was true that I did not find him or his behavior terribly suspicious. And as we have all seen banks fail over the slightest rumor, I decided, in spite of my umbrage, that he had a point. So I left through the back door, after checking both ways down the alley behind the bank building.

When I came around to the front, I found Sebastiano talking to Sarah's house boy, a Mexican lad of uncommon beauty. Not even 10 years old, Miguel had dark, lustrous eyes and long eyelashes, and a sweet, round face.

He had come to find me and handed me a note. I read it over with many misgivings but told Miguel to run ahead and tell his mistress that Sebastiano and I would be there shortly.

"You are going to see her?" Sebastiano asked, almost incredulously. "After she snubbed you?"

"Yes," I sighed. "It is only Christian charity to turn the other cheek and to forgive. At least, that is what I hope will transpire."

"You would do better to let her be. If she is not going to be a true friend, then why should you go to her?"

"I appreciate your loyalty, Sebastiano, but I should at least give her a chance to explain herself and I really don't feel like going home to receive her there."

I'm fairly certain that he did not approve, but he had the grace not to say so. So we walked the short way to Sarah's home. Sebastiano again decided to wait for me outside and made himself comfortable on the porch.

Sarah was waiting for me in her front parlor, still wearing her walking dress. I thought it somewhat odd, as she was usually careful to change to inside wear once home and receiving, and she'd certainly had time to do so.

"Why is your man going about with you today?" she asked as I came in.

She was watching through the front window, the lace of the curtain in her hand.

It was hardly the greeting I expected. As I tried to find something appropriate to say, Sarah sniffed back a sob and dropped the curtain lace.

"Maddie, I am the most horrible person who ever drew breath. I do not deserve the name of friend."

Her tears flowed freely and I must confess, my heart softened toward her. Not completely, mind you. I was still quite hurt by her behavior, but I was a great deal closer to forgiving her than when I'd arrived.

"I had the feeling you were following Mrs. Fletcher's example," I said softly.

"Oh, that horrid old thing," Sarah took her handkerchief from her pocket and dabbed her eyes. "Yes, I was taking her example. I was terribly afraid she'd snub me if I didn't. She is so cruel, you know. Oh, Maddie, I'm so close to finally being a member of polite society!"

"And if Mrs. Fletcher is so cruel and horrid, why would you want to be?" I asked.

Sarah waved me to a seat, and I took it. She, herself, sank onto the sofa, dabbing at her eyes with her handkerchief.

"Because it's all I've ever wanted, as you well know." She sighed again. "Or maybe you don't. You know my mother was part of society in our hometown of Providence. In Rhode Island."

"Yes, I know."

I had heard many times Sarah's tale of how her father had dragged the family out to the gold fields back in 1849 in search of a ready source of gold for the family's jewelry business. He had done rather well, initially, but had eventually lost everything to a combination of drink and general bad management. By that time, her mother had perished and her older brothers had run off to seek their fortunes elsewhere.

"I suppose that's why I fell in love with Mr. Worthington," Sarah continued. "He was from a good family in Philadelphia and everyone around me was so common. And that's why, when you arrived here, it was such a miracle to me. You are a real society lady. You're everything my mother hoped I would be. And will be, at least, if Mr. Worthington stops dragging his feet."

"How do you mean?"

"They asked Mr. Worthington to be the new zanjero. It's his due, after all the years he's served as deputy to Mr. Rivers."

"It most certainly would be."

"Yes. And I'll be the wife of the zanjero, and I will be one of them. They can't turn their backs on me then. I'll be part of polite society, such as it is in this town." Sarah beamed with joy. "That's why I can't afford to have Mrs. Fletcher snub me now. You must see that. That's the only reason it happened and I am devastated that it came to this. I assure you, Maddie, once I am established, I will be your benefactor once again. We will have such capital times together, won't we? It will be perfectly splendid."

I took a deep breath. "Yes, I'm sure it will."

If the truth is told, I was not sure what I made of Sarah's speech. That she hungered to be included among the higher echelons of society in the pueblo, I knew well. But that she would favor their good opinion rather than stand up for me, who had been her confidante and close friend for so long, that stung far worse than I could have anticipated. Still, I knew she meant well, even though I seriously doubted that Mr. Worthington had been offered the zanjero position. I was reasonably confident that I would have heard that he had before that time.

Nevertheless, my musings did not end in my saying anything to Sarah. Hannah, the maid, came into the room.

"I'm sorry for interrupting," she said. "But, Miz Wilcox, you man said he need you right now."

I rather loathed the way everyone referred to Sebastiano as my man, as if I owned him. He was more of a friend and a partner than a servant. In fact, shortly after these events, I did make him and Enrique partners in the winery. But that is getting considerably further ahead of myself than need be. At that moment, I merely swallowed my hurt and irritation, made my goodbyes to Sarah and hurried outside.

"It's Mr. Lomax," Sebastiano told me, as he pulled me toward the Clocktower Courthouse. "He asked me to bring you to the jail."

"What?" I gasped.

"No, no," Sebastiano said. "He has somebody there he wants you to talk to."

I was thoroughly puzzled and worried, and so hurried along even more quickly than Sebastiano. As we passed Mrs. Judson's house, I was not entirely surprised to see a group of ladies having tea on the veranda, which meant that Mrs. Judson was having another tea party. And I had not been invited. Having just left Sarah in her walking suit, I suspected she hadn't been invited, either, which boded ill for her much-wanted advancement in polite society. Still, I felt even more nettled and forced myself to focus on Mr. Lomax's odd summons.

When we got to the jail, Mr. Lomax was behind the counter, sitting at the desk. He smiled grimly and stood as he saw me come in.

"What is it?" I asked, not even trying to mask the worry in my voice.

"This."

He led me back to the jail. In the cell at the far end sat young Will Rivers. He had on a decent shirt and pants, but somehow still looked as though the least breeze would cause his shirt to billow out around him. The lad had sunk into himself. I looked at Lomax, utterly confused.

"Will, tell Mrs. Wilcox here what you told me," Mr. Lomax said.

Will looked up at me, then mumbled something.

"Mr. Lomax, let me into the cell with the boy," I said.

Mr. Lomax fetched the keys, and let me in. I settled myself on the other end of the sleeping pallet from where Will was sitting.

"Now, young man, what does Mr. Lomax want you to tell me?" I said.

Will swallowed. "I killed my pa."

I didn't quite gape, or at least I hope I visibly kept my composure. Will didn't seem to notice.

"What happened?" I finally asked.

"When Pa came home that night, he was awful drunk and mean." Will squeezed his eyes shut. "He was going to hurt my ma again. And I just couldn't let him. So I pushed him and he fell backward into the stove. He was knocked out cold, so Ma said we should lay him out in front of the saloon and maybe he wouldn't remember I'd pushed him. He'd sometimes forget stuff like that when he sobered up. So Steven and me took him and laid him out in the street, like Ma said. Steven went home, but Ma said I'd better stay away as long as I could so if Pa did remember, I wouldn't get a beating. So I stayed and watched until Mr. Lomax came along. At least, I guess it was him. I was in the alley, see, and I ran away for a while when he came by. But then I came back, and when I did, uh, Pa was coming to." Will's eyes darted all over the cell, then he took a deep breath and looked straight at me. "He saw me and came after me, so I took his gun and shot him."

It took all of what I had in me not to act as horrified and shocked as I felt. So I took a deep breath.

"What happened next?" I asked.

"I went and got Steven and James and they helped me put Pa in the Zanja Madre." Will looked up at me. "We didn't know he'd come to the surface in your zanja, Mrs. Wilcox. We wouldn't have wanted to do that to you. Honest."

"I believe you, Will," I said, then got up. "I will have to talk this over with Mr. Lomax, and we'll see how best to proceed."

Mr. Lomax let me out of the cell and we went back to the front office.

"Where is the marshal?" I asked, still trying to make sense of what I'd just heard.

"Gone to Riverside, chasing down a runaway prostitute," Mr. Lomax said.

"And Deputy Dye?"

"Chasing after Marshal Warren. It looks like the marshal is going to beat him out of another bounty." Mr. Lomax shook his head.

I wasn't sure what Mr. Lomax meant by all that, although I knew that the entire police force, such as it was, was paid in large part by commissions on the fines and bounties they collected.

"And what about Will?" I asked, sinking into the desk chair.

"What about him? He says he killed his pa." Mr. Lomax sat on the edge of the desk.

"I know, but you aren't going to string up a thirteen-year-old lad for trying to protect his mother, are you?"

Mr. Lomax frowned. "I might, except..."

As I looked at him, it hit me. "I think he's lying."

"I don't know why, but I think he is, too." Mr. Lomax looked around helplessly.

I stood up. "We need to talk to Mrs. Sutton. And do you know what kind of gun Mr. Rivers carried?"

It may seem odd now, but men in our pueblo generally carried a gun as a matter of course. It would be a good many years before the place became respectable enough to make that not a necessity.

"Same old six shooter as the rest of us," Mr. Lomax said.

"Did he carry a derringer?" I asked.

"Not so far as I know."

I went back to the cell. "Will, when you got your father's gun, what kind was it?"

"A six-shooter, ma'am."

"Are you sure?"

"That's the gun my pa carried. Didn't want any of them small ones. Said they were for girls and maiden aunts."

"Have you told anyone that your pa was shot?"

"No, ma'am. Just you and Mr. Lomax."

"Do not tell anyone else," I ordered.

I returned to the office. "That settles it, Mr. Lomax. We must pay a call on Mrs. Sutton immediately."

Sebastiano joined us and the three of us walked quickly to the Suttons' funeral parlor. We crowded into the back room where Mrs. Sutton was preparing the bodies of two Mexican laborers for burial.

"Another fight in a saloon," she said sadly as she pulled a drape over one. "Now, how can I help you?"

"Mrs. Sutton," I said. "You have seen a great many gunshot wounds, have you not?"

"Far too many," she replied.

Mr. Lomax started to say something, but I cut him off with an apologetic glance. Sebastiano merely hung in the doorway and watched with great interest.

"Can you tell what kind of gun made a wound?" I asked.

"Sometimes. Why do you ask?"

"The wound that killed Mr. Rivers, could you tell what kind of gun made that one?"

Mr. Lomax smiled, suddenly understanding why I had gone about my questions the way I had. Mrs. Sutton and Sebastiano both looked surprised.

"I told you I thought it was a derringer the night I prepared him. Don't you remember?"

"Actually, I did," I said. "But I have a good reason

for asking you the way I did. I wanted the testimony and your witness to be absolutely certain."

Mrs. Sutton looked at both me and Mr. Lomax with a puzzled frown. "But why?"

Mr. Lomax and I looked at each other and he nodded.

"Because Will Rivers has just now confessed to killing his pa," I said.

Sebastiano hissed.

"Oh, Jesus Santo!" Mrs. Sutton gasped. "Why would he do that? Was his father as cruel to him as to everyone else?"

"Mr. Rivers was cruel to his sons, and especially so to their mother, apparently," I said. "But Will was lying. Mr. Lomax and I both heard him say he took his father's gun and shot him and his father did not carry a derringer."

"No. It was a big six-shooter," Mrs. Sutton said. "I've had some of his victims come through."

"Still," I said. "He did know that Mr. Rivers was shot and I have not told anyone that."

"You didn't even tell me," Sebastiano said.

"And you can't tell anyone," I said.

"I only told the marshal," Mr. Lomax said.

"I have not told anyone, even Mr. Sutton," Mrs. Sutton said.

"Nor have I heard it bandied about, and I surely would have if the fact had been made known," I said. "Therefore, the boy knows something we do not. The question is why would he confess when he clearly did not do it?"

"That's easy," said Mrs. Sutton. "He thinks you know more than you do and he knows who really did the killing and wants to protect him."

"Oh, dear." I found myself leaning against an empty table alongside the wall. "Now what do we do? Asking Will is not likely to produce the truth. He has every reason not to tell it. And we can't hang a young lad, especially when he's innocent and simply trying to protect someone else." I looked at Mr. Lomax. "When is the marshal due back?"

"Hard to say," he said. "He left this morning and it's a good day's ride just to get out there. I can't imagine he'll be back before tomorrow night."

"Then I will have to find the true killer within that time," I said, feeling especially weary.

Sebastiano stepped up and put his hand on my shoulder. "We will find the killer, Maddie. Nosotros juntos."

"Sí," said Mrs. Sutton. "Nosotros juntos."

Mr. Lomax lifted an eyebrow. I looked at him with a wan smile.

"We, together," I translated.

He nodded and offered his odd half smile. "Then nosotros juntos, it is."

I am not easily overcome, but all of a sudden, I began to shiver. Mrs. Sutton saw it and pulled me into her back parlor. It was a small room with a low table and comfortable chairs and a sofa upholstered in brown velvet. She sat me there, and I do not know why, but I burst into tears. It was true I'd had very little sleep the night before and that can have the most deleterious effect on one's composure. But I fear I have little other excuse.

Mrs. Sutton did not seem to mind. She put her arms around me and rocked me gently. It wasn't long before my tears were spent. I got a handkerchief from my bag, which was still, as always, slung across my shoulder.

"I apologize for that miserable outburst," I said, sniffing and wiping my eyes.

"It looks to me like you needed it," Mrs. Sutton said. "You Americans with your ridiculous ideas about pretending you have no feelings."

"One does need to keep one's passions under control."

Mrs. Sutton laughed and gave me a quick hug. "And that is why I am happy to be Mexican. Passions can make a great deal of mess, but it is a lot easier to clean our little messes up than when one of you Americans finally blows up."

I sighed. Mrs. Sutton had made an excellent point. And my feelings were rather raw that day. In addition to the lack of sleep, there had been that accident and being snubbed and Sarah's ridiculous apology, then Will's confession. It was no wonder I was overwrought. I had no idea, at that moment, that it was soon to get worse and that my resolve and composure would be stretched beyond all measure.

CHAPTER ELEVEN

For the moment, Mrs. Sutton brought me a soft cloth that she had wet with cold water and allowed me a few moments to wipe my face and remove all traces of my outburst.

"I am so glad that the men didn't see this," I said, handing the cloth back to her. "They are always so ready to assume that we women cannot face the least dilemma without an attack of the vapors."

"And we see far more misery and trials than they do," said Mrs. Sutton.

She slipped out of the room for a moment, then returned to admit Sebastiano and Mr. Lomax.

"Now, we must make a plan," she announced, pulling around a small desk from the back of the room so that she could write on it while seated in one of the more comfortable chairs. She opened the lid to the desk and removed paper and a pen and inkwell. "Mrs. Wilcox, you must share with us everything you have learned."

I sighed. "I can't say that I have learned much, beyond that almost everyone in the pueblo had a reason to kill Mr. Rivers."

"You've talked to a lot of people, Maddie," Sebastiano pointed out.

"Yes. I talked to the Samples family. They are the colored farmers north of town. Mr. Rivers used them quite badly, but they seemed to expect it and bore no grudge toward him." I thought about the previous few days. "The Vasquez family had been cheated by Mr. Rivers. We talked to them this morning. They seem to bear him no ill will and had even gotten around some of Mr. Rivers' ill behavior. Reverend and Mrs. Elmwood seem to be behaving strangely. Mrs. Elmwood made a point of visiting me even before the marshal tried to arrest Mrs. Medina to tell me that she was not one of the women that had been seen walking away from Mr. Rivers body. She said she was out but helping Mrs. Ontiveras with her mother."

"I heard about the reverend's sermon, too," said Mrs. Sutton, who was writing furiously and did not even look up.

"Mrs. Hewitt was probably one of the two women that Mrs. Aguilar saw," I said, closing my eyes. "At least, she admitted seeing Mr. Rivers on the ground. She was quite furious with me for asking her about it and said that Mrs. Carson was not as innocent as she seemed."

"Have you talked to Mrs. Carson?" Mr. Lomax asked.

I shook my head. "Not without Mrs. Glassell nearby. The two made sure that I knew everyone else's secrets, not that they were much use. As for Mrs. Hewitt, she's far too small to have fired the shot."

"Yes. It was at close range and direct to the heart," Mrs. Sutton said. She looked up from her writing and slowly dipped her pen as she thought. "You're right. Mrs. Hewitt could not have fired the shot. Nor could have Will Rivers. He's not tall enough, either."

"There is also Mr. Worthington," Sebastiano said. "He is tall enough and wanted to kill Mr. Rivers, at least according to Mr. Mahoney."

"But why would he use a derringer?" Mr. Lomax asked.

"That is an excellent question," I said. "I was going to ask him about the fight he'd had with Mr. Rivers the night he died, but then there was that dreadful accident at the mill. Mr. Mahoney didn't want to tell me what the fight was about. And that was rather odd, as well. He'd been speaking perfectly easily, then suddenly decided he didn't know what the fight was about."

"Is it possible he didn't really know?" Mrs. Sutton asked.

"Possibly. But you know how he's normally quite verbose. When I asked about the fight, all of a sudden he was speaking in one-word answers." I racked my brains over and over again. "The Monteros said that they liked Mr. Rivers, but I'm fairly certain they were lying. I have no idea how to verify that. Mr. Judson had a reason to kill Mr. Rivers, but claimed he didn't and, truth be told, seems quite sincere."

"And then there's Will," said Mr. Lomax.

The four of us sat in silence.

"I did talk to his mother," I finally said slowly. "Mrs. Rivers was quite open, although she seemed nervous when talking about the night her husband died."

"But she would be somebody that Will would sacrifice himself for," Mr. Lomax said.

"Is she tall enough to have shot Mr. Rivers?" Mrs. Sutton asked.

"Possibly. One thing is for certain," I said. "I must talk to her again. Do you think she's aware of what Will has done?"

Mr. Lomax shrugged. "Hard to say."

"She had plenty of good reason to kill her husband," said Mrs. Sutton. "If the rumors are true."

"It depends on which rumors," I said. "But it appears he was beating her quite cruelly. And the boys, as well."

"And there was his mistress. The woman he supposedly loved," said Mr. Lomax.

"That." I thought. "I wonder if Mr. Mahoney would know who she is. It would account for him going silent so quickly."

"Does anyone else have a reason to kill Mr. Rivers?" Mrs. Sutton asked.

Mr. Lomax looked wary again, but I smiled. "We

all do, apparently. Except me."

"Maybe even you," said Sebastiano with a grin.

"What?" I asked.

"A rumor I heard this afternoon while waiting for you at Mrs. Worthington's," said Sebastiano. "The reason Mr. Rivers was so nice to you is that he wanted to marry you off to his oldest, once he achieved his majority. That way, Mr. Rivers could get control of your property."

I almost choked, my shock was so great.

Mrs. Sutton laughed merrily. "For all the good it would have done him."

I frowned as something else occurred to me. "Mrs. Medina mentioned something to me last Friday when she visited the rancho to thank me for letting her out of jail. She pointed out that so many in the pueblo are corrupt, one almost expects to be cheated by certain officials. So if someone was merely cheated by Mr. Rivers, it's not likely that person would consider it a reason to kill him. So while Mrs. Samples was used quite badly by Mr. Rivers, she expected to be used so, sadly, and thus was not enraged by the ill-use. Nor was Mr. Samples. The same could be said of Mr. Vasquez. And Mrs. Vasquez said that he had been to a family birthday party and was stone drunk that night and could not have killed Mr. Rivers."

"Then we must make a plan," said Mrs. Sutton. "Each of us should look at the various people who have the most reason to kill Mr. Rivers."

"I shall have to speak to Mrs. Rivers," I said. "And quickly, before Will is released from the jail."

"I can talk to some of the men and see if I can find out if Mr. Rivers had cheated any of them," Mr. Lomax said. "And I can also talk to Mr. Worthington."

"I'll talk to the Vasquez family relatives," said Mrs. Sutton, again writing everything down. "I know them and can find out if Mr. Vasquez was, in fact, drunk that night."

"I can go to some of the other Mexican farmers,"

Sebastiano said. "They might know if anyone wanted to harm Mr. Rivers."

I nodded. "And I will also speak to Mr. Mahoney. It seems unlikely, as he was probably serving the men at the time Mr. Rivers died, but it did happen right outside his saloon. He either saw something or can tell us what Mr. Worthington and Mr. Rivers were fighting about."

Thus agreed, we left the Sutton home. Sebastiano was reluctant to go, but I sent him off on his mission. Mr. Lomax and I went back to the jail to consider when we should let Will go. I prevailed, however, and we agreed to wait until I'd spoken with Mrs. Rivers.

As I got ready to leave, Mr. Lomax gave me a strange look.

"A medical doctor," he said.

"Yes."

"Why didn't you say so?"

I sighed. "My family was deeply ashamed of me. And I suppose I assumed anyone else who knew would snub me, as well. I could still practice medicine without anyone knowing."

"There's plenty of folk who call themselves doctors who haven't even been to school."

"I know." I looked at him. "And now you know my great secret."

"And you know mine."

I nodded, then frowned. "You don't seem terribly religious, Mr. Lomax. Not like some of the other Mormons I've met."

"I've little use for the Latter Day Saints," Mr. Lomax said. He looked out past me to the window overlooking the street. "I was born in upstate New York, but my family moved us to Southern Utah when I was a lad. We were in good standing with the elders, and I thought little of it when they told me to marry Ruth and then Sabrina. But Southern Utah is hard land to farm, and like everyone else, I was barely able to support my family."

"Is that what brought you to California?"

"No." He winced. "We're all elders, but the chief elders in my village were like most men of God. Vain, self-righteous, and generally hypocrites. The other, younger men in the village had begun to notice and then the chief elders started noticing that the younger men would come to me for advice and guidance."

"I take it that did not sit well with those elders," I said.

"It never does," Mr. Lomax said, offering me his half-smile. "So the chief elders decided to take their revenge by ordering me to take another wife, knowing I could not support one. Abby was a young girl, barely fourteen, who had run away from the village because she did not want to be some old man's wife. They gave her to me. I did not marry her, though. I did pack up my family and Abby and we left. Abby died on the trip, as did one of my boys. But the rest of us made it. I will not put Sabrina or Ruth aside, but I do not entirely consider myself a Latter Day Saint. We worship that way, me out of habit, and my wives because that's what they believe and have always believed."

He sighed and I looked back at the doorway to the cells.

"It does seem sometimes that folks mostly get in the way of the practice of religion," I said. "And now, I must take my leave."

I must say that my coming interview with Mrs. Rivers filled me with dismay. It did seem likely that she was the person that Will was protecting, but how to get her to confess to the crime? As it turned out, she confessed almost immediately after we were seated in her front parlor. The boys, fortunately, were absent, but somehow Mrs. Rivers had already heard that Will had confessed.

"He didn't kill his pa," Mrs. Rivers said, her eyes filled with tears. "You must know. I will tell you quite plainly, Mrs. Wilcox, he did not do it."

"Then what happened, Mrs. Rivers?"

"I killed my husband," Mrs. Rivers said slowly. "As I had told you, he had come home very drunk and angry. And he took a swipe at Will. It welled up in my breast and I simply could not take any more of his vile behavior. So I waited until he turned his back and hit him with a frying pan."

"You did," I said, blandly.

"That's what killed him, isn't it?" Mrs. Rivers said. "I did it. We were in the kitchen when it happened. I had Will and the boys put Mr. Rivers out by the saloon. I don't think they knew their father was dead, but they did as I asked and Will stayed behind to see that somebody would find him before too long."

"A pretty story, Mrs. Rivers," I said.

"It's the truth!" Her tears spilled onto her cheeks. "You must believe me."

"I would, except that I know you are lying," I said.

"No!" she cried. "Will is the one who is lying. I swear it!"

"You're both lying!" I said, my voice rising most unbecomingly.

Mrs. Rivers sank back in her chair. "What?"

I could no longer sit still, so I rose and began pacing. "You are quite obviously and understandably trying to protect your son. And Will is also trying to protect you, presumably because he believes you did, in fact, kill his father."

"But I did. I hit him with a frying pan."

"Neither of you killed him," I said, my irritation growing.

"But... How..?"

"Mrs. Rivers, you did not kill your husband with a frying pan," I said. I had no idea how much I should tell her of what I knew, but finally decided that while I had to let her know some of it, the less she knew, the better. I paced for a minute more, while formulating my words. "Mrs. Sutton asked me to come examine your husband's body the night after we found him in the zanja. I saw the wound on his head, and it was not made by a frying pan. It was something hot, but the shape was completely wrong." I turned on the stricken woman, feeling quite cruel, but also knowing it was my best chance to get the truth out of her. "So what happened the night of your husband's death? What really happened? I want the truth this time. I cannot protect you or Will without it."

Mrs. Rivers sank back into her chair and sobbed for some minutes. When the sobs finally abated, she slowly pulled herself up straight and wiped her eyes with her handkerchief.

"I don't know what you will think of me," she said, softly. "It was true that Mr. Rivers came home that night shortly after nine. And he was drunk and angry. George was upstairs studying. He wants to be an engineer, I think they call it. Someone who builds things like railroads and bridges. Mr. Rivers didn't think much of what George wanted, but then he didn't think much of any of our children and only grudgingly let James join him in the business because he had to. James was out with his friends and Steven was drawing, another thing Mr. Rivers frowned upon. In any case, I and Will were alone in the kitchen when Mr. Rivers came home. He started yelling and cursing, for no reason that I could see, and swore that he would kill me so that he could marry his mistress." Here, she choked, quite understandably.

"You knew he had a mistress?"

"Yes. I do not know who she was, but he regularly compared me to her to show how I was wanting." Mrs. Rivers drew another breath. "He also threatened to kill me quite frequently, so I didn't really take him at his word on that. But as he came toward me to strike me, Will rushed forward. The poor thing, he simply could not bear his father's cruelty to me any longer. He caught his father in the middle and pushed him back. Mr. Rivers fell and struck his head on the stove. When he fell down, both Will and I thought he was dead. But I checked and he had merely been knocked out cold. I don't know if I was relieved or not, but I did not want Will to get a beating when Mr. Rivers came to. So I called Steven and had the two of them drop their father in front of the saloon. We had done it before when Mr. Rivers came home drunk and caused himself some harm. In one instance he had blamed James for his injury and beaten the boy nearly senseless. From then on, we would leave him near the saloon and he would forget to blame the boys."

"Only this time, one of the boys was the cause of his injury," I said.

"That was why I told Will to stay away from the house," Mrs. Rivers said. "Only the boy came home some time after the clock had struck eleven. Actually, it may have been closer to midnight. I was dozing fitfully, as you might imagine. Anyway, he told me that his father was dead. So again, I sent Steven and George with him to hide the body. I did not want Will hung for trying to protect me, especially since it was an accident that his father had been killed."

"Had Mr. Rivers been killed by the blow to his head, I think a good attorney could make a case for self-defense," I said. "I cannot say more, and please trust me that it is for the best. But Will did not kill his father. Mr. Rivers died by other means."

Mrs. Rivers looked even more shocked and afraid. "He didn't drown, did he?"

"No. But again, I cannot say more and am counting on your discretion for your own and your son's safety. No one else can know that your husband did not die of a blow to the head." I sat down next to her. "The problem is, Will does know how he died. I have counseled him not to say how. But he clearly saw something. What, I do not know. He apparently believed it to have been you or perhaps one of his brothers who was responsible. At this time, he does not know that I am aware that he is also lying about how it happened."

"I don't understand," Mrs. Rivers said.

"The story he told me matches the one you told

me now in most particulars. But he made up certain details that I know did not happen because of what Mrs. Sutton and I found on your husband's corpus." I patted her hand. "I am so sorry about how all this has fallen out. But I will get to the bottom of it one way or another."

"Does it really matter? My husband is dead and no one else will be falsely accused of his murder."

"That is my hope." And here my heart stopped. It had again become imperative that I find the killer. "But the person who did kill your husband appears to have decided that I now know too much and has already made at least one attempt on my life. If your story were to come out and this person is not caught, I fear that you, too, will become a target for this person's wrath."

Her face grew pale. "We must hide Will."

"Indeed, you must. And now, I must get Will from the jail."

"I will send James and Steven with you."

With the two young men in tow, I hurried back to the jail. It was getting rather late in the afternoon, and I feared I would again miss supper and get another lecture, this time from Olivia, who often took my absences personally. With Mr. Lomax looking on, I restored Will to his brothers, after first lecturing Will on the vital importance of not saying how his father had died.

I was able to reassure Will that his mother was, indeed, innocent, but in my haste to speak with Mr. Mahoney, I neglected to question him about what he had actually seen. It wouldn't have necessarily brought out the truth, as it was possible he had seen one of his brothers doing the deed. And if the person he thought he'd seen was not one of them or his mother, he obviously hadn't seen that much if he was confusing them. Still, I would regret that failure deeply.

I hurried on to Mr. Mahoney's saloon and was admitted, as usual, through the back. As was usual by that time of day, Mr. Mahoney's beard was starting to grow and his hair looked lighter and flew about his head. He wore a vest over his shirt but had neglected to put on his jacket. It was his usual appearance.

"So, what can I do for you, Mrs. Wilcox?" he asked, leaning his desk chair back on its hindmost legs.

"I do not mean to be so abrupt, but fear I must," I explained. "I need to know what Mr. Worthington and Mr. Rivers were fighting about the night he died. It is of the utmost urgency."

Mr. Mahoney leaned forward, setting his chair on all fours. "I'm not sure as I can say, Mrs. Wilcox."

"He's dead. Whatever reason you had to fear him, it is no longer an issue," I said, my fear and urgency tearing away at my normal patience.

"What?"

"I'm assuming you had a reason to hate Mr. Rivers," I said. "Heaven knows, everyone else in this pueblo did."

Mr. Mahoney cursed under his breath. "Begging your pardon, ma'am." He looked at me and finally shrugged. "He was my landlord. He owned this building, and he used that to extort free drinks from me."

"Why didn't you simply move your saloon?"

"Because I would have lost all of my custom." Mr. Mahoney sighed. "It was one of the reasons Mr. Rivers caused me so much grief. The reason the city councilmen and others come here is because it's so close to the Clocktower Courthouse. They meet there, you know."

"Yes, I know."

"If I moved elsewhere in the city, I would have lost all of that business, and Mr. Rivers knew it. In fact, he coveted it and was hoping I would move so that he could take my business over. Only he had to be careful how he did it to stay in good with the rest of the city council. They did not entirely trust him, you know."

"I am not surprised."

Mr. Mahoney sighed. "If I had lost all my business, I would have had to leave Los Angeles, and I can't do that."

"Why not?"

He swallowed and toyed with the papers on his desk. "Because there is someone here in the city that I need to be close to. To protect." He looked me in the eye. "You are probably the only person I can say this to, who might understand."

"I would hope so, Mr. Mahoney."

"I probably shouldn't tell you, because I did not kill Bert Rivers, and there are plenty of men who can tell you I was in the saloon all night, pouring drinks."

"I had thought as much."

"But since you might find out anyway, better you hear it from me." He looked away. "I am Regina Medina's brother."

"Oh," I said. "Did Mr. Rivers know?"

"No, he didn't, and thanks be to God for that." Mr. Mahoney shuddered. "It terrifies me to think what he would have done with that information. He hated Regina."

"I understand she'd banned Mr. Rivers from her house because he was so rough on her girls."

"That's right. You are in Regina's confidence."

"Completely," I said, looking him in the eye.

His eyes opened wide. "Do you know..?"

"I observed and made a few guesses, but, yes, she confirmed them."

"And you still call Regina a friend?"

"She has served me well in that capacity."

"You have certainly served Regina well."

"How could I not? She was, in fact, innocent."

Mr. Mahoney sighed. "Perhaps, but Regina could have sent one of the girls to do the deed."

I frowned. "No. I do not think so. As I have said, I was with her the entire night. I don't think she had the opportunity to do so. Besides, how would she have known that Mr. Rivers was..."

I bit my lip. I had almost revealed the most damning evidence we had.

"There is that," said Mr. Mahoney.

"I must agree with you, Mr. Mahoney," I said, finally. "However, if I am to find out who killed Mr. Rivers, I must assume that anything could have happened."

"I don't think Regina sent one of the girls," Mr. Mahoney said. "As you pointed out, how would have Regina known that Mr. Rivers was passed out in front of the saloon? Besides, that threat had already been dealt with."

"Indeed, it had, if I am to believe her," I said.

"You generally can," said Mr. Mahoney with a great deal of chagrin. He sighed deeply. "How is it that you've been able to be friends with Regina? You seem like quite the upstanding Christian lady."

"I would hope that I am," I said. "Which is why I have counted her among my friends."

I winced as did Mr. Mahoney. He shook his head.

"Do you know what it is like to have a freak in your family?" he asked, his face creased with worry and hurt.

I closed my eyes. "No, Mr. Mahoney, I do not. However, I do know what it is like to be the freak in the family."

"How..?"

"I am a doctor and a lady."

"But how is that the same as..."

"It's not," I said. "But one might extrapolate the feelings and I have certainly been in a position to hear how Regina has felt about it."

Mr. Mahoney looked over his desk and sighed deeply. "I think I understand. When I came here, I encouraged Regina to come, as well. It was Regina's idea to keep our relationship a secret. When I saw... I must confess I was happy to agree. Still, I feel responsible."

"I understand, Mr. Mahoney. I don't doubt you would have raised appropriate legal counsel when Regina was first arrested."

"I was going to bust her out of jail," Mr. Mahoney said. "Which would mean I was going to have to leave Los Angeles, as well." He sighed. "I did not want to leave. I've done rather well here."

"Indeed, you have, Mr. Mahoney."

"But when the lynching began..."

"Mr. Mahoney, neither of us could have seen that transpiring. And, in fact, there was no lynching this time."

"Thanks to you."

"Perhaps. It could easily have gone the other way."

He shrugged. "Thanks be to God, it didn't this time. And, may I add, that I do appreciate you being friends with Regina. There aren't many who can be, as you know."

"Her girls would be, but for their business. That is, however, neither here nor there."

Somewhere in the house behind us, a clock loudly struck the hour of five o'clock. Mr. Mahoney sighed and looked back toward the kitchen.

"I'd best look after my business," he sighed. "After last night, I suspect there will be quite a group of men here to debate the event."

"I don't doubt it," I said, getting up. "Thank you for taking me into your confidence, Mr. Mahoney. I will treat it with the utmost discretion."

"You already have, Mrs. Wilcox, and I thank you for it."

I left quickly but once I landed on the Calle Principal, I suddenly felt at loose ends I still didn't know what Mr. Rivers and Mr. Worthington had been fighting about and it didn't seem like I would find out any too soon. I decided to return home and eat supper with my household. It had been a most unsettling day and perhaps the comfort of routine would help me regain my composure.

The children did not join us for dinner. Because it had started to rain by then, we had to eat in the dining room and there simply wasn't enough space for them. So they'd eaten in the ranch house. Talk at the table inside centered on the killing of Mr. Rivers. True to his word, Sebastiano hadn't told even his wife and brother what he now knew about the cause of Mr. Rivers' death, and I was profoundly grateful for that. But there was little more information. Maria Mendoza and Enrique had both had the opportunity to go to the markets and other places in the pueblo, and while the attempted lynching of Mrs. Medina was quite the topic of discussion, there was little to be heard about who else might have killed the zanjero.

"My cousins are all very proud of you," Maria said while gathering the dishes on the table. "A real medical doctor. And we thought you were simply a very good bruja."

I couldn't help but laugh. Bruja, in English, means witch, and of course, to we Americans, a witch is someone who has sold her soul to the Devil. However, if someone is Mexican or even Negro, a witch is someone who is also a very wise or healing woman. When I first arrived in Los Angeles and started my charity, as I called it, my patients were largely the Mexican laborers and their families who could not afford a real doctor. They were the ones who first called me "La Bruja." I was quite offended, at first, until Magdalena explained what they had actually been saying. But then, I also began to wonder if I had, indeed, sold my soul to the Devil by marrying Albert Wilcox. I hated Los Angeles. It was barren, hot, violent, the people largely uncultured and uneducated. I eventually acquired a few wealthier patients, first among the Californios, then even a few Americans. However, most of my American patients were whores. I'm afraid the shocking truth is that I could have built quite a successful practice among them alone, there were so many in the pueblo at that time.

I seldom considered it, probably because I lived there, but it occurred to me that one of the reasons I found the pueblo such an uninviting place to be was that most of the people there did not, in fact, live there.

While we had a good many families, which meant women and society and the like, the vast majority of the people in the pueblo were not only men but transient ones. They came as teamsters and manufacturers' agents and miners and cattlemen and all manner of laborers looking for a quick job before going off to their next destination. Few of the people who did live there had been there longer than twenty years, and even among the Californios, many had only gotten their lands within the previous generation or so.

Which made it possible that someone had shot Mr. Rivers simply because they stumbled across him in the street. It was entirely possible that Mr. Rivers' killer was long gone from the pueblo and living in Santa Barbara or even San Diego or San Francisco. After all, it was not only possible but presumably likely that what I had seen as attempts on my life were the perception of a fevered imagination.

"Maddie," Juanita suddenly asked. "Are you all right? You are looking as though you were undone."

"I may be," I sighed, then explained what I had just been thinking, of course, not mentioning that Mr. Rivers had been shot. "We could be looking at this from the wrong perspective completely."

Sebastiano looked thoughtful. "It might be, except for the accident in the lumber yard."

"That could have easily been a real accident," said Rodolfo. "I'm there almost every week or so and pulleys and things fall all the time. I'd say Mr. Worthington is lucky he hasn't been killed already."

Comment on this conjecture was forestalled, whoever, by another frantic banging on the adobe's door. I assure you, it did my nerves no good at all, and sadly, my worries about more bad news were fulfilled.

This time it was Steven Rivers who had come. The rain dripped off his hat, but he was much too upset to remember to take it off once inside.

"Mrs. Wilcox," he begged. "Please, can you come? Someone shot my brother Will."

CHAPTER TWELVE

It would be hard to imagine a situation any worse than what I faced as I arrived at the Rivers home. They had brought Will up to his bed and as I entered, his mother sat next to her youngest son, her eyes flowing with tears.

Will was conscious, but that only made things worse, in my estimation. His face was pasty white in the lamplight and he was sweating. When I saw the wound, I knew he would soon burn with fever and had a long night of pain before he would die.

He'd been shot in the gut, and there was no other end that could transpire.

I almost collapsed with the knowledge of it, but seeing Mrs, Rivers and hearing her weep forced me to steel myself.

"Is there anything you can do?" she whispered as I replaced the bandage over the wound.

I shook my head. "Nothing. Once the bullet has pierced the intestines, the contagion spreads. There is no way to stop it. I could try a poultice, but I fear it will only prolong the inevitable and it will not be easy. The best I can do is try to ease his pain as much as possible."

"Mrs. Wilcox," the boy sighed from the bed. "Gotta tell you."

"Easy, Will," I said, laying my hand on his forehead. It was just starting to warm with fever.

"I didn't kill my Pa," he gasped.

"I know. You don't have to trouble yourself."

"But I gotta tell you."

"It's all right, Will. You can rest,"

"No!" he all but shrieked. "I thought it was Ma that shot him. But you said it wasn't."

"No. It wasn't." I bit my lip. I did not want to press him, but he seemed very anxious. "Why did you think it was your mother?"

"I saw a woman," Will gasped, his breathing a little easier. "Pa was still out on his back. She bent over him and shot him. I could hear the shot. She looked up in my direction, but I couldn't see who it was under her bonnet. I didn't know she'd seen me until she came to the shed where I was hiding. She said I wouldn't tell anyone now, and then the gun..."

His breathing quickened and his face grimaced in pain.

"Did you see who she was?" his mother asked quickly.

Will shook his head. "Too dark."

His face tightened again with his hurt.

"There, there," I said. "You're a brave young man to tell me all this. Now, I'm going to give you something that should help you sleep and maybe ease the pain."

I did have some ether and thanked the Heavens I'd gotten my order of supplies that weekend. But first, I thought I would give him some morphine to relieve his pain. It was another potion that I used very sparingly as it was hard to get good morphine in the pueblo.

Mrs. Rivers gasped as I pulled out my hypodermic syringe and filled it from the morphine bottle.

"This is for the pain," I explained to her, and bent to inject the drug into Will's all too thin arm. "The medicine will work faster this way."

Will looked a little frightened when he saw the needle but didn't cry or whimper. The morphine did its work well, and he was soon breathing softly and had fallen asleep.

"Is there any hope?" Mrs. Rivers asked again.

I shut my eyes against the tears and shook my head. There are few things worse than having to tell someone that a loved one is not going to survive, especially if it's a child. I'd had to do it many times and have done it many times since, and it never got any easier. Will's case was even worse because the infection from the gut shot would take time and cause him great pain as it did.

I can call it an infection now, but we didn't know what the contagion was then. We didn't know about bacteria and germs. Dr. Pasteur's work had just been done and it would take even longer to get to our benighted little corner of the world. And in looking back, that knowledge wouldn't have helped, in any case. Even today, in the early part of the new Twentieth Century, with better surgeries and sterilization and hospitals, gut shots are almost always fatal. Once the intestines are pierced, the abdominal cavity becomes infected and the infection cannot be stopped. Perhaps someday we will find a drug that can stop an infection once it has taken root. One can but hope.

It was a very long night. I alternated between holding Mrs. Rivers' hand and bathing Will's forehead as the fever took hold. He would be restless in fits and then would settle down. It was sometime after the clock had struck twelve when Mrs. Rivers motioned me away from the bed.

"Yes?" I asked softly.

"Will said Mr. Rivers was shot," she said with a frown on her face.

"Yes. Mrs. Sutton found the gunshot wound in his chest."

"So, that's how you knew I was lying." She looked over at her son who was, for the moment, sleeping peacefully. "And he saw it and was afraid it was me."

"That's why he confessed to the murder," I said. "He knew I was looking for the killer and when I'd come to visit you, he became afraid that I would find out."

"Such a brave lad," she said, her voice almost strangled by a sob.

"He is," I said, putting my hand on her shoulder.

"You have every reason to be proud of him."

"I am," Mrs. Rivers said, then pressed her lips together. "What vile, unnatural woman could have done this? Mrs. Medina, perhaps?"

"It's very unlikely," I said. "Based on Will's testimony, I would think that the same woman who shot your husband also shot your son. He certainly believes so. And Mrs. Medina and I were together the entire night of your husband's death. If she had sent someone, I would have probably heard her do so. Besides, she had no way of knowing your husband was lying outside the saloon."

"Then you must find this evil woman, Mrs. Wilcox," Mrs. Rivers said. "I don't care much that she killed my husband, but she's taken my precious son away from me, and I want her hung for that."

"I will do my best, Mrs. Rivers. But you mustn't tell anyone else about your husband being shot, and make sure your other sons don't. It's the only way I have of knowing who's lying and who isn't."

As we watched and waited, I tried to stay focused on Will's breathing and agitation, looking for hints of when to give him some more morphine or ether. Still, I couldn't help wondering about what he had told me he'd seen. A woman, bending over the man sleeping, presumably, on the ground and shooting him. A woman would account for the derringer as the weapon. It was certainly not unusual for a woman to carry one in the pueblo, although most of us did not.

But if Mr. Rivers had been on his back on the ground, then it wouldn't matter how tall the woman was.

There was nothing to be done about it for that time. I had a patient and his mother to care for, and it was something of a relief to finally be able to talk like the doctor I am, as opposed to a healing woman. Or it would have been had not the prognosis not been so grim.

Will's breathing grew more and more shallow

as the hours wore on. I kept thinking it couldn't be much longer, but he was a tougher little man than I'd thought. It was about an hour or so before dawn when he woke briefly and asked for some water. I fetched it quickly and his mother gave it to him. And still he hung on, the fever making his face red as it raged.

Then, just as the first rays of the dawning sun slid in over the window sill, Will became agitated, his breathing ragged. He struggled, and then finally, finally slid into that blessed sleep from which no one will awake until the last trump.

I held Mrs. Rivers as she cried, all the while longing to shed tears of my own. Fortunately, Mrs. Sutton was already in the front parlor when I came down. For the second time in as many days, she held me close as I sobbed. When I was able to stop crying, I held Mrs. Sutton back.

"I know you must go to Mrs. Rivers," I told her, wiping my eyes. "But we must talk at your earliest convenience. Will was able to tell me something vital and we need to discuss it."

"I've learned a little, too," Mrs. Sutton said. "But you need to go to your bed and get some rest, or you will be no good to the rest of us."

I nodded and left the house. How I got home, I have no idea. My heart was utterly broken, my spirit equally so, and it felt as though I had exhausted every last ounce of my strength. Juanita, for once, refused to scold. Instead, she brought me some coffee with cream, chocolate, cinnamon, and a large dose of sugar, and a warm sweet bread, then sat with me as I ate and drank. There were no words. Then she helped me get undressed and into bed. I couldn't imagine sleeping but fell asleep almost instantly.

It only lasted for a couple hours, however. Juanita brought more coffee, this time, with nothing added, and another sweet bread and some bacon for my breakfast. She did insist that I eat in bed, then helped me wash up and get dressed. I did feel somewhat better, but my heart was so very heavy, I felt as though I should burst into tears at the least provocation. However, I am a strong woman, fully in control of my passions. I drank another cup of coffee, although I generally prefer tea, and had Sebastiano saddle up Daisy.

Sebastiano was ready, as well, and had his youngest son, Damiano, a bright-eyed lad of twelve, and Enrique's son Juan, also twelve, sharing another mule.

"You will not be alone today," he said. "If I must send for Enrique or someone else, I have the boys. And I have made sure they have guns, too."

And, indeed, each boy had a six-shooter stashed in the belt of his pants. I did not doubt that they could use them well. Aside from the violence of the pueblo, there were hazards aplenty on the rancho, including snakes, coyotes, and bears. Both Enrique and Sebastiano felt that the best way to keep the children from hurting themselves was to teach them how to shoot as soon as they could fire and stay standing.

My first stop was my intended call on Mrs. Sutton. She insisted that I join her in her little back parlor and admitted Sebastiano, as well. I did not look at the work table where a small form was laid out and fully covered by a sheet, but my heart clenched, nonetheless.

"This is a sad day," Mrs. Sutton said.

"It is," I said. "But we have little time to lose if this madwoman is to be stopped before someone else is killed."

"Madwoman?" Mrs. Sutton's eyes opened wide.

"Will saw the killer shoot his father," I said. "It was a woman, who he could not see. He initially thought it was his mother."

"That's why he confessed," Sebastiano said.

I nodded. "But then the woman apparently found him in the shed where he'd been hiding and told him he wouldn't be saying anything to anyone right before she shot him. He seemed certain it was the same woman as shot his father, but did not see her well enough to know who she was."

"But who else would it be?" Mrs. Sutton asked.

I sighed. "Perhaps someone trying to protect Mr. Rivers' killer. But that seems unlikely."

"It does," Mrs. Sutton said. "And trying to find two killers? That's crazy."

"Crazy, indeed," I said. "But not only are we now looking for a woman, it doesn't matter how tall she was. Mr. Rivers was shot while lying on his back."

Mrs. Sutton went over to her desk and pulled up the list she had written the day before.

"That means Mrs. Hewitt could have killed him," she said, looking at the paper.

"Almost anyone could have," Sebastiano said.

I frowned, thinking. "Which means I should go back and call on every woman I've asked about this, and maybe a couple others."

"Even a couple of the men," Sebastiano said. "A man might not have killed Mr. Rivers, but if his wife did, he might make a mistake and say something he shouldn't. Especially if he knows something."

I sighed. "Which means I am right back to the place I started from." I mentally went over the names of all the people I had spoken with the day before. "I forgot the Olivers. I spoke with them yesterday morning. Remember, Sebastiano? We went there first because he had asked me to see his wife for her melancholy. And now that I think about it, he said she had begun to feel better right after Mr. Rivers died. I must speak to them again."

Mrs. Sutton already had a fresh piece of paper out and was again writing. "Mrs. Oliver. And could Mrs. Judson have been angry over her husband's loss of money?"

"No one has ever seen her abroad at night and she says she doesn't go," I said.

Mrs. Sutton sniffed. "Are you sure?"

"What do you mean?"

"I've seen Mrs. Judson out fairly late at night more

than once."

I gasped. "But she said she does not have to chase after a drunken husband." My mind slowly began working. "However, she did not say she doesn't go out at night."

"Like you, my dear Mrs. Wilcox, I am out very late a great many nights." Mrs. Sutton looked over her paper. "There isn't one woman on this list that I haven't seen walking one place or another. Even Mrs. Aguilar, although, she must not have killed Mr. Rivers or why would she have told everyone what she had seen? It would have been better to let everyone think it was an accident."

"That is true," I said. "Even Mrs. Worthington has been out late at night and I do know that she was out the night that Mr. Rivers was killed. But she had no reason to kill him. She, like many of the other women of society in the pueblo, actually liked Mr. Rivers."

"Perhaps Mrs. Worthington was Mr. Rivers' mistress?" Sebastiano asked. "Then she might have reason to kill him."

"She might," I said, my stomach twisting. "And Sarah is very anxious to be free of her husband. But if she was Mr. Rivers' mistress, why would she kill her... eh, paramour? It doesn't make sense. Besides, she would have had to seek a divorce from her husband to have married Mr. Rivers, and she would not do that because she would be banned from pueblo society. She wants to be fully accepted more than anything else in the world. If anything, she would have killed her husband and found a way to marry Mr. Rivers. No, that doesn't make sense, either, because that would also get her banned from society because Mr. Rivers would have had to divorce his wife to marry Mrs. Worthington. Can you imagine the scandal?"

"And the wrong people are dead," said Mrs. Sutton.

"But there was that accident in the lumber yard yesterday," Sebastiano said, then frowned. "No. Why would she kill her husband if her lover is dead?"

"True," said Mrs. Sutton. "She would have killed her husband and Mrs. Rivers first so that she could marry Mr. Rivers."

"Nor do I think she has the stomach for killing in any case," I said, wincing at the memory of her latest bout of weeping and whining. "As many murders as we see here, one might forget that it is no easy thing to take another life, unless one is hardened to it. Indeed, most murders here happen in the heat of a drunken fight. A woman of society might do something rash in a fit of rage or kill someone who was about to kill her. But to coldly shoot someone as he slept? That takes a great deal more grit than Sarah Worthington has."

Mrs. Sutton shrugged. "That would be true of most of these women."

"Except Mrs. Hewitt," I said. "She is known for her temper and even told me that she would be more likely to become enraged and hit Mr. Hewitt over the head with a frying pan than kill Mr. Rivers." I paused, thinking over the interview. "However, she did not refer to how Mr. Rivers died. It could be she did shoot him and was lying about it." I shook my head. "But, somehow, that doesn't make sense, either."

"I think we should add Mrs. Fletcher to the list," Mrs. Sutton said. "I've seen her walking about at night many times."

My sigh rose up from the very depths of my being. "I shall have to call on her, as well, then. I hope you do not consider my taking this in hand as a lack of respect for you, Mrs. Sutton, but I seriously doubt she will speak to you. I have little enough reason to believe she will talk to me."

Mrs. Sutton snorted merrily. "I am happy to leave it to you, Mrs. Wilcox. The less I have to do those gallinas, the happier I am. I almost didn't go to the tea party yesterday but thought I'd better because of Mr. Sutton's business."

"What happened there?" I asked, suddenly. "I saw the ladies on the veranda and realized I had not been invited. I suppose Mrs. Worthington hadn't been, either."

"Mrs. Warren told me that she wasn't at home when the invitation arrived." Mrs. Sutton looked away, then shrugged. "The party was held to talk about you. They were mostly shocked, of course. And appalled that you help the fallen women of the pueblo. I asked them who would if you didn't and said that it seemed to me that you were taking on a great deal of work that no one else would stoop to do, such as finding Mr. Rivers' killer. That sent them fluttering. I think someone must have heard inside the parlor because Mrs. Judson suddenly came out to visit with us. She did say that the ladies inside were all saying how shocked they were, as well, and how none of them would ever think to call on a lady doctor for their ailments. I did not say so, though I should have, that I can think of a few ailments I'd rather talk to a lady doctor about."

"It's a good thing I do not have to rely upon those ladies for my practice then," I said, with a small sigh.

"You do well enough with us Mexicans," Sebastiano said. "Like Maria told us last night, you are a very good bruja. Being a medical doctor doesn't change that."

I smiled wanly at the two of them, then got up from the sofa. "In any case, it seems as though I've a great many calls to make. I wonder how hard I should try to find Mr. Rivers' mistress."

Mrs. Sutton and Sebastiano both shrugged.

"If he wouldn't say who she was," Sebastiano said, "why would she? Mr. Lomax said he didn't know who she was, nor did he think anyone else knew. According to Mr. Lomax, Mr. Rivers only mentioned her when he was drunk."

"Mr. Lomax!" Mrs. Sutton suddenly said. "Where is my head? I should have thought to fetch him."

"As should I," I said. "Sebastiano, could you have one of the boys run home to fetch one of the good linen sheets, please? One of the soft ones from New York. Magdalena will know which ones I mean. And have him tell her I will procure another. I have to replace the one we used for the Lomax boy's cast. Then have him meet us at the Lomax place. I don't know if we'll find him home, but we do need to share all that we have learned."

We made our goodbyes and, with one last wrench at my heart, I passed by the table where poor young Will's body was waiting to be prepared and left the house.

As we approached the Lomax place, Damiano came running up. He had the sheet, and after handing it over to me, bent over gasping for air.

"That was well done, young Damiano," I said, smiling in spite of myself. "Now, the rest of you, I'll thank you to stay right where you are. You can see me from here and the Lomaxes have secrets that I would not betray even to you."

Sebastiano glared at me but chose to remain in place and signaled the boys to, as well. I dismounted and left Daisy with them.

The Lomax children had spotted me on the road and as I approached the farmhouse, came running out to greet me. Hannah gravely smiled and gave me a big hug, which went a long ways toward lightening the heaviness in my heart.

I was also cheered to see that young Jacob was doing equally well. Mr. Lomax had made a crutch for him, and he proudly hobbled about the house to show me how well he could manage.

"Are you hurting much?" I asked.

He shrugged. "Some. But Mama says I'm a big man now and mustn't cry over it."

"That you are, young man," I said. "But I've brought some more willow bark for the tea that will help you bear it."

Jacob made a face. "That stuff is worse than the hurt."

I chuckled. "Then you are certainly getting better. But it's going to be a long time before we can take that cast off. You might change your mind before then."

"How long?" Sabrina asked, her face suddenly growing anxious.

"About two months," I said. "And the leg may never be completely right after that. However, he still has it, and that's something."

"Yes, it is," sighed Sabrina. "It mostly seems to pain him at night."

"Then give him the willow bark tea right before bedtime. You might also want to give him a sweet or something alongside, if you can manage it. The tea can upset a boy's young stomach. And here is a sheet to replace the one I tore up for the cast."

Even the suspicious Ruth was agog. "But you saved Jacob's leg. You didn't need to bring us this."

"And yet it was your best sheet. My conscience would not let me rest until I had replaced it."

Ruth ran her hand over the smooth fabric. "With one that is much finer than ours. How can we ever thank you?"

"You can see to it that Jacob heals well," I said. I sighed. "We lost another young boy in the pueblo last night, you may have heard, and under the worst circumstances. There was nothing I could do." I looked over at Jacob, still hobbling about. "At least I can take some comfort in that I was able to help your son."

Sabrina's eyes filled with tears. "Of course, Mrs. Wilcox. Such kindness. And you being of such a tender disposition, no wonder you are distressed. If there is ever anything we can do, you have but to ask."

I smiled and nodded. "All I really need, at the moment, is to speak to your husband. Do you know where Mr. Lomax is?"

The two women shook their heads.

"He left a short while ago to fetch supplies from the market," Ruth said. "When he returns, we will tell him that you are looking for him."

"Thank you. Alas, I'm not sure where I will be or when but I should be about the pueblo most of the day,"

I said.

The children, including Jacob, all hurried over and gathered around me, offering me hugs and other sweet sentiments. Jacob even insisted that I bend down so that he could kiss my cheek. It was all I could do to keep the tears from spilling over. I thanked them, as well, and hurried from the house. Before I returned to the road where Sebastiano and the boys were waiting, I made a point of wiping my eyes. I fear my nose was red from all the wiping, but it could not be helped. At least, I had no angelica or other wine on my breath.

As we made our way to the Oliver farm, I asked Sebastiano if Mr. Oliver had, indeed, sent over a chicken and Sebastiano shrugged.

"He did," said Juan, excitedly. "A big fat hen. We had her for dinner. Tia roasted her over the coals and made the skin all crackly. It was really good."

Damiano nodded. "I love that crackly skin. And I got a leg. I love the leg."

Chicken was often on our table as we had quite a flock ourselves and usually too many roosters. Olivia frequently boiled them to go with the different moles that she made. Roasting chickens was time-consuming since she had to watch the birds lest they burn, so it was a treat when she did. I suddenly felt sad that I hadn't really noticed it the night before.

"She treated the children," Sebastiano said softly to me. "To make up for them having to eat in the barracks. I'm told Magdalena was furious with her for smoking up the kitchen with the coals."

"She couldn't have cooked it outside with the rain," I said.

I looked out over the barren landscape, quickly growing brown after the dry winter we'd had. The storm, as it usually did, had left the air bright and clean. The sky was brilliant, even with the few remaining clouds floating across, white and puffy. Even the hills, with their mantle of dark green trees, seemed to shine. Alas, below our feet, the roads were sticky with mud and pools of icy cold water. All of a sudden, I longed to be back home in Boston, where at least some of the streets were paved and where mysterious women didn't shoot young boys. Truth be told, I was not that naive, even then, and had seen ample evidence of the desperation that drove some women to do the unthinkable.

Which led me to ponder again at what Will had told me. I had no reason to doubt the accuracy of what he said he had heard. Indeed, if he had lied or confused it, wouldn't he have come up with words that were far more feminine? The words, "You won't tell anyone now," were so incredibly cold and harsh, they must have come from some madwoman. That, in turn, made me shudder, as my next interview was with a woman suffering from melancholy. Who was to say that she wasn't mad, as well?

As we approached the farm, I saw Mrs. Oliver under a sprawling oak tree washing clothes in a rough wooden trough next to the zanja on their property. She was alone and I insisted that Sebastiano and the boys keep their distance, the better to encourage a confidence on her part. I hoped her children would remain wherever they were.

Mrs. Oliver glanced up as I approached, but little more.

"Good day, Mrs. Oliver," I said brightly. "And how are you today?"

"Well enough," she said, turning back to scrubbing a spot on a shirt.

"Oh." I waited, then decided there was no easy way to go about asking what I needed to. "Mrs. Oliver, you may have heard that I am trying to find the person who killed Mr. Rivers."

She shrugged.

"I think you have cause to be glad he's dead," I said.

"We all do," Mrs. Oliver said.

"But not all of us are suffering from melancholy," I said and took a deep breath. "And you have been markedly better since he died."

Her lips barely tightened, but she said nothing.

"I know for a fact that Mr. Rivers treated many women in this community quite badly," I said and waited.

She continued scrubbing.

"Were you one of them?" I finally asked.

"Does it matter?"

"He did, then, didn't he?"

She glared at me. "If you know, why would you bother to ask? Why would you shame me again?"

"Because I have no reason to believe that it was your fault. He was known to use force."

Slowly then she began to crumple and as she slid to the ground, great, wailing sobs escaped her. I still do not know how we were not heard for miles around. I got down next to her, heedless that I was wearing my best riding suit, although I do recall thinking that Juanita was going to scold me again. Carefully, I put my arms around her quaking shoulders and rocked her gently as she cried. The sobs eventually abated, replaced by gasps, as if Mrs. Oliver could not recover her breath. I waited, knowing that she shortly would.

"It's my great shame," she finally whispered, wiping her eyes with her apron. "I know some willingly gave themselves to get their water. Me, I didn't. He got me, anyway. He forced me. And every time he did, I had to give myself to my husband in case I became pregnant, knowing I was soiled in the worst way by that... that... I fought him every time, but he always won. I don't know how the children missed him. They see everything else."

"Dear Mrs. Oliver, what a horror you've lived."

"I'm glad he's dead!" she cried. "Dagnabbit, I'm glad! But poor Mr. Oliver, how can I be a wife to him? I cringe every time he comes near me. He's been such a tender husband, always kind and gentle. I used to look forward to... to our time together. Now, all I can feel is that horrible man, pushing me into the dirt, grabbing at me. I feel so unclean, so worthless."

"Maybe you could try talking to your husband."

"And what man is going to understand, even my darling George? How would he feel, knowing that he couldn't protect me? He even liked Mr. Rivers. He might not even believe me."

I was at a complete loss. "Mrs. Oliver, did you take matters into your own hands, maybe acted in revenge against Mr. Rivers?"

Her face screwed up in silent rage.

"I would have loved to," she said, her voice cold and furious. "I would have dearly loved to have been the one who knocked him over the head. I would have happily taken a fireplace poker, a frying pan, whatever. Many's the night I dreamed of hitting him over the head over and over again, smashing him in the face. Smashing that evil grin of his." She crumpled again. "But I didn't. I should have. But I didn't. I was afraid of being hung and what that would do to my children. At least, suffering as I was, they would never know my shame."

"It's not your shame," I said, feeling quite angry and put out. "It was Mr. Rivers'. He alone bears the guilt for what happened to you and would even if you hadn't fought him. I grant you, most men wouldn't understand that. But if anyone would, it is your Mr. Oliver, who adores you and cares so deeply for you that he is almost as tortured as you are. Now, I will tell him to use you very gently and be patient and understanding, but not say more. That is up to you."

She nodded and slowly got up from the ground. "It's strange. Most of the time, I work desperately hard not to think about it. But just now, since I've told you, I feel as though a great burden has been lifted from me, as if I can breathe again."

"I can't think why that would be," I said, getting up and brushing dirt and dead leaves off my habit. "Although they do say confession is good for the soul, never mind that you have not sinned, but have been sinned against, and most fouly, too. I have never met a kinder woman, nor a jollier one before this happened. I am so sorry for what has happened to you, Mrs. Oliver."

She smiled softly. "Thank you. And thank you for hearing me. I have borne this for too long."

"Well," I said, wondering if I would come to rue what would come next. "If talking about it seems to help, then by all means, call on me as you need to and I will listen."

"I can't imagine why talking about it, reliving again and again, will help, but I will accept your offer."

"I must talk to Mr. Oliver. He is most anxious for you, and while I will not expose what you have shared with me, I think I can advise him to be good to you."

She smiled again and went back to her work. As I walked away, I thought I heard her humming. Some minutes later, I heard a full-throated song coming from the zanja.

Mr. Oliver appeared from the ramshackle barn, looking over at the zanja in wonder. He almost didn't see me approach.

"Is that my wife singing?" he gasped in joy.

"I do believe so," I said, feeling more weary than not. I did not look forward to my talk with him.

"She used to sing all the time before..." He paused and swallowed. "What have you done to restore her, you wonderful Mrs. Wilcox?"

"I have not restored her," I said pointedly. "She is obviously considerably better. But she has suffered very greatly. You must be extremely tender and gentle and patient. Especially patient. I cannot promise all will be as it was before. She may never be able to be a wife to you again. But she loves you with all her heart, and you must love her in turn."

"But... but..." He looked at me, both ecstatic and terrified at the same time.

I sighed. "I cannot say more. That is for her to do, when and if she chooses. If she does not, it is only to avoid hurting you that she keeps silent."

"Hurting me?" He gazed at his wife under the oak tree, then swore most vilely under his breath. "Begging your pardon, ma'am."

"Granted."

"It was him." Mr. Oliver grew quiet and angry, his face paling as he realized what had happened. "It was that dadblamed Rivers. I'd heard what he'd done to some of the other wives. I had no idea. I thought he had too high a regard for me to use my wife so. I liked him."

"He forced her," I said quickly. "She is blameless and you must hold her so."

"Of course, she is blameless!" Mr. Oliver snarled. "My darling Josephine. How she has suffered, never saying a word to me. If only I'd known, I would have killed him with my bare hands!" Tears leaked onto his face. "My poor, darling Josephine." He turned on me suddenly. "What must I do? Please, tell me. You seem to know what is best."

"I do not," I gasped. I thought furiously. "I only know that she has been used most ill. As I said, you must be gentle and tender and patient. Very patient. Whether you tell her what you have discovered, that it is up to you. Both of you. I have suggested that she tell you, and it might be better if she believes you did not know. But she feels as if she were at fault, so reminding her that she is without blame might be a very good idea. I think. I have never heard of such a case, so I don't know. I'm just guessing based on what she just told me. However, if you feel the need, please do not hesitate to call on me."

"Thank you, Mrs. Wilcox," he said, pulling a handkerchief from his pocket. "Thank you so much! This is terrible news, and yet, such good news. I... I..."

"I'll leave you to her, then," I said. "I do have other stops to make and cannot tarry, much though I'd like."

That last part was a lie, God forgive me for it. There was nothing I wanted more than to be away from there. I felt as though my heart had already been rubbed raw by Will Rivers' death, and now to hear of Mrs. Oliver's suffering. I tried to focus on what appeared to be her deliverance but fretted that there was more to be heard on the matter.

As it turned out, there was more. Mrs. Oliver would visit me several times over the course of that summer. However, the last time she came, it was to tell me that she was expecting her ninth child and that if things were not as they had been before, it was because they were even better.

CHAPTER THIRTEEN

However much better things seemed to be for the Oliver family, I was no closer to finding out who had killed Will Rivers. As I returned to Sebastiano and the boys, Sebastiano looked at me expectantly.

I sighed. "Mrs. Oliver had more motive than most, but I cannot believe she killed Mr. Rivers. I cannot say more. Where do we go next?"

"We went to the Monteros yesterday," Sebastiano said.

"Indeed. Mrs. Montero might even have my glove mended," I said. "Then let's be at it."

I found Mrs. Montero in her house. Sebastiano and the boys waited outside. While I hadn't told him what had happened to Mrs. Oliver, he'd seen us under the oak tree, and if he hadn't guessed what had happened to her, I expect he did not want to know entirely. Nor did he want his presence to discourage any confidences that a woman might share with another.

Mrs. Montero was happy to see me. "Are you here with another glove for me to repair? I declare, Mrs. Wilcox, you are uncommon hard on your gloves."

"I do a fair amount of riding," I said, haplessly. "You wouldn't happen to have the ones I brought yesterday, would you?"

"They're all ready." She picked up the gloves from a nearby table and showed one to me. "See? I'll bet even you can't find the mend."

There was more embroidery on the glove, but she was right. I couldn't find the spot where it had torn.

"This is a miracle," I said, smiling. Then I sighed.

"It grieves me to have to ask you, but you are not prone to wandering our pueblo's streets at night, are you?"

"No. I go to sleep early," she said, pleasantly. "I'm up with the sun and Mr. Montero every day, so it's hard to stay up late. I do a little glove work after dinner, then go to bed."

"I thought as much. Your husband said he liked Mr. Rivers."

She laughed. "I do not know why. He hated Mr. Rivers. Like everyone else here. He was a powerful bad man."

"I know," I said, trying not to sigh. "But in your husband's case, do you know why?"

She gaily shook her head. "I do not. But, look. Here he comes. You can ask him, yourself."

I debated leaving. Mrs. Montero seemed extremely unlikely to be the woman who had killed Mr. Rivers, and I was looking for someone who was most likely mad. However, Mr. Montero's entrance into the crowded front parlor left me with little opportunity to escape. He was not happy to see me.

"I have not changed my mind about Mr. Rivers," he said. "And I did not kill him."

"I have reason to believe you didn't," I said. "But I do not believe that you liked Mr. Rivers."

He glared at me, then saw his wife standing there with a smile on her face.

"He cheated me," Mr. Montero said, finally. "My family has owned this land for three generations. We were the first tanners in Los Angeles. My grandmother, Maria Paula Mesa, came here as a child with the Pobladores, who founded our pueblo. My grandfather bought his land when he married my grandmother. We are proud people. But Mr. Rivers did not care about that. He cheated me out of my rightful allotment of water. I worked for him day and night because of the law that says we must contribute to the upkeep of the zanjas. But that was not enough for him. So I did not get as much water as I needed. It's a good thing I have many friends in the pueblo and they helped me. But I almost lost my land, first because I had to pay so much for my water and then because I had to do so much work for the zanjero, it was hard to do my own." He paused. "My wife is right. Mr. Rivers was a powerful bad man. But I did not kill him."

"Did you, Mrs. Montero?"

She laughed and for a moment, I feared for her sanity. "I did not kill him. How would a tiny thing like me hit that big old man over the head?"

"How, indeed," I said. "Well, how much do I owe you for mending my gloves?"

She asked for twenty-five cents, but I ended up giving her fifty. The work was excellent and it had suddenly occurred to me that the more people, within reason, that I could prove innocent, the closer I would get to the one person that was, in fact, guilty. So, since it seemed as though the Monteros were very unlikely to have killed Mr. Rivers, that meant there were two fewer people to worry over.

I told this to Sebastiano as he and I and the boys rode back into the pueblo's center, and Sebastiano agreed there was cause, if not to rejoice, then to be grateful. It did not stop him from watching every corner and window as we rode down the Calle Principal.

It was a good thing he was watching, however. When the shots rang out, they actually came from Calle Segundo, which we had been about to cross. Daisy almost reared and the mules backed up quickly. Sebastiano had his rifle in hand, and the boys had their six-shooters ready. I quickly slid off of Daisy's back and the others dismounted, as well. They looked all around us and Sebastiano motioned at me to get to the cover of a nearby saloon. I thought it reasonably likely that the shots had come from there, but then I saw Mr. Worthington running from Calle Segundo onto the Calle Principal. The shots continued as he ran, and I could see tiny splashes of mud pop up where the bullets hit the street. As I watched, Mr. Worthington slipped around the corner in front of a house on Calle Principal for cover, then peeked around the corner to look up Calle Segundo, his six-shooter in his hand.

Sebastiano stood up against a shop building on the other side of Calle Segundo from Mr. Washington. After glancing at me, Sebastiano looked up Calle Segundo in the direction from which the shots had come. The shots stilled, and Sebastiano slipped up Calle Segundo, then returned a few minutes later, shaking his head.

"I couldn't find anybody," he said, as I crossed the Calle Principal to join him next to where Mr. Worthington was.

The boys followed closely behind.

Mr. Worthington shook his head. "I'll be blamed if I can figure out who was shooting. I was just going up Calle Segundo to go home for lunch when he started. I didn't stop to look too carefully."

"You can hardly be blamed for that," I said.

He spat a stream of tobacco juice into the street. "Nearly choked on my chaw. What in tarnation is going on?"

"I have no idea, Mr. Worthington," I said.

He looked startled for a second. "Begging your pardon, ma'am."

"Granted."

"Still, Mrs. Wilcox, when you get to finding Bert Rivers' killer, I'd be obliged if you would look into who is trying to kill me."

My eyes opened in surprise. "Mr. Worthington?"

He shrugged and spat again. "I don't know who else could do it. I'm at wit's end."

"I would imagine so," I said. "However, I do not think I am equipped to undertake something like that. Wouldn't you be better off going to the City Marshal?"

Mr. Worthington laughed bitterly. "I don't know if I could afford the bounty he'd charge."

"Too true." I sighed. "I suppose I should ask you if you have any enemies."

"None that I know of," Mr. Worthington said.

"Other than Bert Rivers, and he's dead. You think one of his boys could be after me?"

"Only if they wanted to reward you," said Sebastiano with a grim chuckle.

"That's what I thought," Mr. Worthington said.

"And yet, you and Mr. Rivers were involved in a nasty fight the night he died," I said. "What were you two fighting about?"

Mr. Worthington looked embarrassed. "Nothing I can talk about." He frowned. "I still can't figure what got him so riled, though. He must have just been in one of his moods. He'd get that way, you know. When he first came out here and my mother had asked me to help him, he hated me more than ever because I did. That's why I tried to keep my distance. Until they made him zanjero. I was already the deputy. I would have quit, but I didn't want to upset Mrs. Worthington. She sets great store by our position in town."

"That was kind of you," I said.

He shrugged.

"Were you aware he had a mistress?" I asked.

"Oh, yeah. Everyone knew. Don't know who it was, though. No one does. I'm guessing it was some Mexican girl because otherwise, he would've found some way to get rid of Mrs. Rivers and marry the mistress." Mr. Worthington frowned. "He sure liked flaunting that he had her, though. I guess he wanted me to know he had more than me when it came to women. Just like he did with everything else."

"I'm sorry, Mr. Worthington," I said. There was little else to say.

And, as it happened, that was just as well. A young Chinese boy came running up and gave me a note. I recognized him as Mrs. Judson's house boy, thanked him, then read the note. He stood waiting, so apparently, he'd been asked to wait for my response.

It was another summons to her house, technically a request to call on her at my earliest convenience. I debated leaving it go, then remembered that I needed to speak to her, as well. So I told the house boy that I would be along shortly, then nodded at Sebastiano and the boys. We made our goodbyes to Mr. Worthington and headed back down the Calle Principal. I turned back to say something to Sebastiano and noticed that Mr. Worthington had decided against going home, after all, as he appeared to be headed back to the lumber mill. Well, that made sense. The person trying to kill Mr. Worthington had obviously been waiting for him to go to his house.

Mrs. Judson admitted me immediately, herself, although she did look askance at Sebastiano and the boys and told them to wait on the veranda. Once we were in the front parlor, she offered me the sofa but remained standing.

"I am most unhappy with you," she said, finally. "How dare you accuse my poor husband of killing Mr. Rivers?"

"I did not accuse him. I merely asked him about a claim he'd made on the Rivers family." I thought about it for a second. "And I did ask if he had killed Mr. Rivers."

"And that's not an accusation? I am mortified. Not to mention distraught. I was under the impression I could trust you."

"If you could not trust me, I would not now be here." I got up, also, feeling quite nettled. "It's bad enough you avoided inviting me to your tea party yesterday."

"I thought I was sparing your feelings."

"I was being snubbed. Just like I am every time you seat me on the veranda, and so is every other woman there."

"I told you that is for your and everyone else's safety. The women of my parlor are vicious creatures. Why would I expose women I like to their intrigues unless it's necessary?"

"Why do you invite those vicious creatures in the first place?"

"I don't dare not. They have considerable influence

over their husbands. My darling Mr. Judson's position is precarious enough. You would think that people would appreciate a banker who is above corruption. That, I am afraid, is hardly the case." She turned on me again. "Which makes your visit to the bank all the more appalling. What those vicious tongues are saying, I shudder to think."

"I needed information. Your husband had made a claim. He, apparently, had a reason to kill Mr. Rivers. Don't you want the killer caught, especially since there's good reason to believe the same person killed poor Will Rivers?"

She paled and sank into a chair. "Oh no! Is there?"

"There is also good reason to believe that you were not completely honest with me when we last spoke."

"That's ridiculous."

"Then why did you fail to mention that you've also been abroad at night?"

Mrs. Judson swallowed. "You didn't exactly ask if I had. Only if I knew someone."

"And you implied that you did but did not want to cast the shadow of suspicion. Alas, Mrs. Judson, we are well beyond casting shadows and if there is any suspicion, I must have it out now. Lives are at stake. This person has killed more than once and may well strike again. So I am asking you now, Mrs. Judson. Do you go abroad at night? Were you out that night? And who else may you have seen?"

Mrs. Judson shuddered. "I wasn't out that night, although I do go abroad sometimes in the wee hours. I can't sleep sometimes and I take a short walk. I stay well away from the saloons and I do carry a pair of derringers, just in case. I've never had to use them. So I have seen one or two other ladies. One, of course, is Mrs. Hewitt. The other is…" She sighed. "Mrs. Glassell. Please, Mrs. Wilcox, do not let her know I told you. I do not think she has seen me. I've sometimes seen her coming from the Mexican part of town, although I do know that she has a daughter that lives there. It seems as though it is quite legitimate. She usually has her house boy with her."

"And how do I know that you did not kill Mr. Rivers? Your husband's claim was substantial. You could have easily sought revenge."

"By hitting him over the head?" Mrs. Judson asked. "What good would that do? I know Mrs. Rivers to be an honorable woman, but I can't imagine killing somebody for a few measly dollars."

"It was a hundred dollars."

Mrs. Judson gaped. "That much? Good Heavens. Right now, I think I am quite grateful that Mr. Judson does not bother me with his business matters. I should be in a state of constant anxiety. A hundred dollars. No wonder you suspected my poor husband. But he is such an upstanding man, he would hardly sneak up behind somebody and knock him over the head. He wouldn't hurt anybody unless he had to defend himself."

"I know how upstanding he is, Mrs. Judson. That is why I didn't really suspect him, but merely had to check. I also wanted to find out if he knew anything else about the matter. He didn't." I looked at her and took a deep breath. "I also have found out that he couldn't have killed Mr. Rivers."

Mrs. Judson's eyes lit up. "Do you know who did?"

"No." I shook my head and sat down again. "I do not. He had a mistress. Perhaps you'd heard."

"No. I hadn't heard a thing." Mrs. Judson's smile was a little perplexed.

I nodded. "I do hope you keep that to yourself. I do not know how important it will be to finding the killer and I must find that person soon. As you know, Will Rivers was killed last night and I believe it was because he saw something. What I do not know."

Again, my habit of rushing in and doing things without thinking had gotten the better of me. But as I thought about it, it was a worthwhile gamble for it would show me two things. The first would be whether I could trust Mrs. Judson or not. If I could, all to the better, as I had few people I could trust. If I couldn't, well, then I would be warned and that was also important. The second thing I might find out would be who the killer was. After all, if Mrs. Judson did let this bit of information out, it might force the killer into accidentally revealing herself. So, if I was not completely honest in not saying what Will had told me, it was probably the wisest choice I'd made all day.

"Poor Mrs. Wilcox," Mrs. Judson said with a deep sigh. "This has affected you deeply, hasn't it?"

"I'm afraid it has, Mrs. Judson," I said, again feeling the weight of the past few days upon me. "Sunday night was bad enough. But I watched last night with Mrs. Rivers. Such a good, brave little lad taken from us far too soon. I am very angry."

"Yes, I can see that you are." She glanced about the room and again sighed. "I fear the ladies are intent upon snubbing you and I wish my position were more secure. I have encouraged them to be kind. You do have the best of intentions. Indeed, we should all aspire to the Christianity of your deeds. But I fear I am not strong enough."

"I am assuming you do what you can, Mrs. Judson," I said. "I hope I may continue to call you a friend."

"Oh." She pursed her lips.

I laughed, trying not to sound bitter. "Perhaps in secret? I do have more than one friend I would not acknowledge as such in society to avoid being snubbed."

Mrs. Judson sniffed. "I would not go that far." She paused. "However, we might choose to be more discreet about calling on one another." She smiled. "I wouldn't want your friends to think less of you because of your association with me."

I genuinely laughed at that and Mrs. Judson joined me. We were, indeed, in rather precarious positions. Or I had been until my secret had been revealed. And I had never been fully accepted into the upper echelons of our pueblo's society. Mrs. Judson, whose husband depended on an excellent reputation, was in more danger. A loss to her reputation could very well mean a significant loss to her husband's bank, and as I had noted, banks do fail on the slightest of rumors.

It was quite sad, really, that we women were so consumed by our husbands' livings and yet so sheltered from knowing anything about their affairs. It has gotten somewhat easier these days, but it's still quite difficult for a woman alone. We are utterly dependent on our husbands for our lives and welfare, and yet, we have no way of knowing if they are doing well in their business or not. Even worse, should we fail to be good wives, or even be suspected of such, it could be to our husbands' undoing. It is one of the many reasons I chose never to marry again and, fortunately, never had to. Still, I ache often for my sisters who are trapped in their marriages and see few opportunities to escape.

But thinking about Mrs. Judson's awkward position did remind me that I had to call on another lady on whose reputation her husband's hung. Poor Sebastiano, he had condemned himself to several hours waiting on verandas while I spoke with someone inside. I began to suspect that he had brought the boys along to have someone to talk to, as well as run errands.

Nevertheless, we shortly arrived at the home of Reverend and Mrs. Elmwood. The Reverend was home, however, it seemed he was perfectly content to let his wife speak to me, rather than speak to me, himself.

"I apologize for my husband's absence," Mrs. Elmwood said as we made ourselves comfortable in the front parlor. "He is just finishing his dinner."

"Pray forgive me for interrupting," I said more to be polite than because I was distressed at interrupting them.

"Oh, you didn't interrupt us," she said with a brief smile that suggested I most certainly had. She even looked me in the eye briefly.

"In any case, it is you I came to speak to," I said. "It has occurred to me that you may not have been entirely concerned only with your reputation when you came to me the other day."

"I was concerned about your reputation." Mrs. Elmwood sniffed and drew herself erect in self-righteous indignation.

"Or maybe you had a reason to kill Mr. Rivers and wanted to know what I knew to better protect yourself," I said.

Mrs. Elmwood trembled. "I did not do that."

"But, Mrs. Elmwood, you came to me before there was even reason to think to suspect you. Not to mention the fact that your husband was more than eager to accuse Mrs. Medina of the killing, never mind the incontrovertible proof that she is innocent."

"He was trying to rid this town of a proven menace to the souls of the men here."

"Oh, for Heaven's sakes!" I am very afraid I did lose patience with her. "What an utterly ridiculous premise! There is nothing in a woman of ill-repute, or any other woman, that is so alluring that a man is forced to give in to her urging. That is only an excuse used by weak-minded men to absolve their lowest behaviors. Indeed, Mrs. Elmwood, it is the women of ill-repute who are the victims here. They are forced into their vile trade by men, often their very fathers and brothers. First, the men refuse to offer any help to women who are abandoned by their husbands or their fathers, usually by no fault of their own. They do not provide honest trades for women, so when a young woman is widowed and her husband was either too poor or too improvident to keep her, she has little recourse. And when one of these women manages to marry, do we welcome her into the fold of our society, rejoicing in a repentant sinner? No, we do not. She carries the stain of her former career, one she was forced to take up by circumstance, and we shun her. Is that any way for a Christian to act? And if a young woman loses her reputation by a man forcing himself on her, what do we do? Go after the man who harmed her? No. We blame her and force her into a life of sin."

Mrs. Elmwood trembled and her lips grew tight. She glanced up at me but said nothing.

"Well, it's true," I said, suddenly feeling as though I had said too much.

"Yes, I'm afraid it is," Mrs. Elmwood said, softly and sadly. "But what else is there to do? There are only two of us in this town against so many, and unlike you, I have my husband's reputation to maintain. He would be utterly ruined if it were not. And you know how easily one can lose a reputation here."

"I do, indeed," I said, sighing in spite of myself. "Perhaps I am trying to make the best of a bad situation, but I do believe that I would rather have a ruined reputation than be dishonest or fail to behave as a true Christian should."

"You are a braver woman than most of us, Mrs. Wilcox." Mrs. Elmwood gazed at her hands.

"Nonetheless, I have come to ask you a question or two and I absolutely need honest answers," I said. "I have been told that you have been very uncharitable regarding Mr. Rivers of late, in fact, shortly after your daughter married and went to Santa Barbara."

"And what of it?" Mrs. Elmwood's lips pressed thin and her eyes shifted their gaze even more quickly as she drew herself up.

"Why have you been so uncharitable toward him?" I said. I was beginning to guess why.

"He was a most despicable man!" she said.

"Not as far as we women of pueblo society were concerned. He was quite kind and charming to us."

"Not all of us." Mrs. Elmwood's gaze flickered to meet my eyes and she looked away as if startled. "If you are here to level an accusation, you might as well get it over with. I did not kill Mr. Rivers."

"But you had a reason to," I said, watching her carefully. "A very good reason to, and your husband knew it."

"He doesn't know all of it, I can assure you of that. And it doesn't matter whether I had a reason to kill

Mr. Rivers or not. I simply did not do it." Here, she did look at me.

"Then what was your reason?"

"I do not need to justify myself to you." Mrs. Elmwood sniffed. But she began wringing her hands.

"And I think I know why you wanted to kill Mr. Rivers," I said, suddenly realizing the truth and all but quailing with it. "Was it your daughter? Did he force himself on her?"

Mrs. Elmwood suddenly sank into herself and began crying softly.

"Oh, dear Lord," I sighed. I moved over next to her on the sofa and put my arms around her. "He did, didn't he?"

Mrs. Elmwood nodded. "My husband doesn't know how far it went. He thought it was merely a flirtation, which is how it started. And fortunately, Eduardo Navarro, the older brother of our deputy, was quite sweet on Victoria. It was very easy to convince them to marry, especially since Eduardo was being sent to his family's holdings up north. Victoria did not want to be married. She did not want a man to touch her after... after what Mr. Rivers had done. But she had to. She would have been ruined and forced... forced to..."

"I understand," I said.

"But I did not kill Mr. Rivers," Mrs. Elmwood said. "I couldn't have. I'm too short."

"I know," I said.

And it did seem unlikely.

"I wanted to," Mrs. Elmwood said. "But I am a Christian. I didn't want to put my soul in that kind of peril. So I held my bitterness close to me and tried to focus on doing works of charity." She took a deep breath and smiled wanly. "And I am to be a grandmother. Fortunately, we know it will not be one of his brats. She did not conceive until last month, well after his get would have started, if you'll pardon me for being so crude."

"Happily," I said.

Mrs. Elmwood pulled her handkerchief from her sleeve and wiped her eyes. "This has been such a terrible burden to carry. I can't imagine why, but it feels like such a relief to have finally told someone about it."

My heart froze but I decided to do the right thing. "Yes. I've heard that before. If you feel the need to unburden yourself, you have but to call on me."

"That is so kind of you, Mrs. Wilcox," Mrs. Elmwood sniffed as the tears started flowing again. "Especially since we have not been so kind to you. I will insist upon it from now on."

"Thank you, Mrs. Elmwood." I froze as another thought hit me. "But I have just now thought. On the night in question, you said you were abroad chasing down Mrs. Hemphill."

"Yes." Mrs. Elmwood wiped her eyes and moved away from me. "She had wandered off. It happens fairly often. She goes looking for her deceased husband, and for her sons. I'm not sure where they moved to, but they are not in the town any longer." She frowned. "Or one is, but he's unmarried and a manufacturer's agent and, thus, traveling quite a bit."

"Yes, she's quite mad," I said.

"I'm afraid so, poor thing. Her daughter is very devoted, but it is a terrible trial for her." Mrs. Elmwood straightened and looked at me oddly. "I know you meant well, but did you have to give her the laudanum? It is the Devil's own tonic."

"I agree," I said, which surprised her. "And I know you have very good cause to be suspicious of it, given what happened to your sister. However, there is a great deal of difference between a young vital woman being dosed unnecessarily for her vapors and an old woman at the end of her days receiving a dose or two to calm her."

"But she could become dependent!"

"For how long? She's very old."

"Almost seventy-one," Mrs. Elmwood said. "And

being mad already, it can't make her any madder, I suppose."

"That is my thinking, and I did counsel Mrs. Ontiveras to use it sparingly."

Mrs. Elmwood nodded. "It seems to have been helping. Mrs. Ontiveras couldn't say enough wonderful things about you. That you had calmed the old lady down just by talking to her."

"I have no idea how I did it, I must confess. However, I've just had another thought. Mrs. Hemphill was abroad that night, as well. If I remember correctly, it was after ten o'clock that you got her home."

Mrs. Elmwood thought. "No. I remember hearing the clock strike that hour while Mrs. Ontiveras and I were waiting for Mrs. Hemphill to fall asleep. I can't remember if the clock had struck the half hour by the time I left, but it must have been about to if it hadn't. We waited some time after ten o'clock, but before it was eleven."

"Oh," I said. "Well, I will ask Mrs. Ontiveras to be sure. It can't hurt."

As I rose to go, Mrs. Elmwood grasped my sleeve. "Mrs. Wilcox, I can trust your discretion, can't I?"

"Of course, Mrs. Elmwood," I said.

I let myself out and nodded at Sebastiano.

"Where to now?" he asked.

"We have the rest of las gallinas to consider," I said. "Who's closest to us?"

"That would be Mrs. Glassell, I think."

"Then that is where we will go."

I got back on my horse and we rode the short distance to the house on Calle Primavera. As we did, I pondered whether Mrs. Elmwood could have been the mysterious mistress. But like Mrs. Oliver, she had more reason to hate Mr. Rivers than love him.

At the Glassell home, I was told by the colored maid that Mrs. Glassell was not in. As I had seen movement in the front parlor window, I knew what that meant. I told the maid that I would wait on the veranda and very shortly, by some great miracle, Mrs. Glassell suddenly returned home and would see me.

She was wearing a day dress of green sprigged lawn and looked decidedly nonplussed. Her front parlor was cluttered with all manner of bibelots and paintings on green-striped wallpaper. I had not heard that she painted. But if she did, her talent was sorely lacking, if the paintings on her wall were any indication. Her husband was an attorney, in addition to serving regularly on the City Council. He also owned a great deal of land and raised all manner of fruits and vegetables, although he mostly raised cattle on his vast rancho near the Anaheim colony.

"Have you come to accuse me of murdering Mr. Rivers?" she demanded from her throne-like chair by the fireplace.

She had not invited me to sit, but nonetheless, I sat on the huge sofa, a ghastly monster covered in rose-figured chintz, and smiled.

"I appreciate your being so direct," I said. "However, I did not come to accuse you of anything, but to gather information."

"I've already told you everything I know," she said, coldly.

"But not everything you've done."

"I thought you said you were not here to accuse me."

My patience was, again, beginning to slip. "Mrs. Glassell. I am only here because a man was most foully murdered in this pueblo. Furthermore, his son was also murdered last night because, presumably, the killer thought he saw something. Which is why I must go among the living to find out who has seen what in order to bring the killer to justice."

"I was not abroad that night, so I did not see a thing," she said with a stuffy little sniff.

"But you do go abroad at night."

"I most certainly do not."

"Then you are lying, because you have been seen

coming from the Mexican side of the pueblo."

Mrs. Glassell all but rose out of her chair. "Who told you that?"

"I am not at liberty to say.

She snorted. "That is ridiculous. Now, out with it!"

"Mrs. Glassell, if you want me to keep what you say here in confidence, then you cannot expect me to betray anyone else's, beyond what is necessary to get the information I need to find this killer. It is very urgent that I do so."

"You keep confidences?"

"Yes. Of course." I would have added that one expects to keep things in confidence when asked to, but then realized that such an expectation would not have occurred to Mrs. Glassell.

She sat back with a bewildered sigh. "And you will not repeat what I tell you?"

"I stake my reputation, such as it is, on it."

"Oh." She thought for a moment. "Hm. It is true that you are known for keeping yourself to yourself. A rather annoying trait, I've always thought, but useful sometimes."

"And you go abroad at night?"

She sniffed and let out a deep sigh. "My daughter married into the Sepulveda family. Fine people, a fair amount of land, and, of course, you know the judge."

"I do."

"Her daughter is quite sickly, so I go to help and keep the young ones out of trouble."

"Young Maria Sepulveda? Is she your granddaughter?"

"Yes. How do you know her?"

"I've been taking care of the children for several years now. I had no idea Mrs. Sepulveda was your daughter."

Mrs. Glassell sighed deeply. "I suppose I wasn't as kind as I should have been when she decided to marry Juan. He's been very good to her and does quite well for himself and the family. Rather surprising when you consider how foolhardy most of those families have been, taking loans and then losing their land grants. In any case, she seldom mentions me to others. Nor I, her. It's only been in the past two or so years that I've taken to visiting to help out."

"When Maria got scarlet fever."

Maria had been thirteen when she'd gotten the dreaded disease and she had never fully recovered. But even though she was very weak, she was the darling of the family and a sweeter soul had never breathed. She never complained about her aches and pains and often worked at her various chores and bits of needlework far harder than she should have, given her condition.

"Yes, that's what brought us back together." Mrs. Glassell smiled softly. "I never minded having Mexican grandchildren, and my little ones are such a delight. But I did fear being snubbed by the other ladies. Perhaps I should have been a stronger woman. Nonetheless, I have been able to go and help Dorothy when she needs it and usually end up staying quite late. Maria is such a sweet young girl. And such a cheerful soul, even when she's doing poorly. She loves it when I read to her."

I smiled. "She did mention how kind her grandmother is to her, the last time I saw her. How she reads for hours on end."

"I wouldn't say hours." Mrs. Glassell looked away and I could see that she was blushing. "How kind of you to mention that. Isn't there any tonic you can give her?"

I sighed. "I'm afraid not. I don't know why, since among those children who do survive scarlet fever most are usually none the worse for it. But some remain sickly and weak for the rest of their lives. There is, sadly, nothing to be done but make sure she eats well. She is drinking her beef broth every day, isn't she?"

"Oh, yes."

I paused, remembering why I was there. "So if I am to understand you correctly, when you are abroad at night, you are going home after taking care of your granddaughter."

"Yes, exactly."

"And nothing else?"

"Why else would I go abroad?" Mrs. Glassell looked at me curiously.

"Aren't you afraid of going home so late?" I asked. "You must pass all manner of saloons and rough places."

"Bah!" Mrs. Glassell snorted happily. "I have nothing to be afraid of. If anyone wishes to tangle with me, then he will face this!"

From a carpet bag at the side of her chair, she quickly produced a very large six-shooter. I, alas, cannot tell one gun from another, so I cannot say what kind it was, just that it was huge. She proudly laid the gun on the whatnot table next to her.

"Oh, my goodness," I said, completely flummoxed. "How do you carry something so big and heavy?"

"As easily as you carry that monstrous bag of yours, I don't doubt," she said merrily. "And believe me, I know how to shoot it."

"Have you ever shot anybody?" I asked, still in awe.

"Not recently." She relaxed back into her chair. "Mr. Glassell was quite furious with me when I killed that cowhand last year. But he did concede that it was better than him killing me. Fortunately, the other cowhands thought that one or the other of them had shot the idiot and they all skedaddled after he was buried." She looked lovingly at the gun. "I would have loved to have shot Mr. Rivers, though. Alas, someone hit him over the head before I could."

"Indeed," I said. "And, uh, what was your reason for wanting him dead?"

Mrs. Glassell sat up straight, in indignation. "He cheated my husband! Poor Mr. Glassell. He had set up the council election to give Mr. Rivers the zanjero position and voted for him on the promise that Mr. Rivers would give him an extra allotment of water. We only got the extra for two years. Trying raising wheat with no water. It was impossible."

"But that was several years ago."

"Yes, but one cannot let people cheat without consequences. It only invites them to cheat you again."

"I see." I debated whether to ask her about Mr. Rivers' mistress. The problem was that if I did, I did not doubt the rest of the pueblo would know about it within hours. But then I thought of another avenue to pursue. "Still, you always seemed to hold Mr. Rivers in high regard"

"Oh, I suppose I did. He was quite congenial," she said, grudgingly, then sighed. "Actually, I didn't want anyone else to know."

"To know what?"

She sniffed and blinked her eyes. "That I was aware that he did not hold me in similar regard. He was quite flirtatious and charming with the other ladies, including you, I might add. But he mostly ignored me. I even heard that he'd called me an old bat behind my back."

"Oh, dear." It was highly indicative of the state of my nerves that I wanted to laugh. Such a small thing to be upset over, but the poor thing was obviously very hurt by it. So I kept my face sober. Besides, it seemed unlikely that she had killed him. "Was there a lady who seemed to return Mr. Rivers' flirtations?"

"We all did. It was part of the game. But we are good, married women and that is all it was, a game."

"And you were not abroad that night." I shifted and stifled a sigh.

"No, I wasn't," Mrs. Glassell said, quite easily.

I wasn't sure what to make of that. I was fairly certain she was not lying. Besides, I generally knew when Maria Sepulveda was doing poorly, as her mother almost always sent for me, and Maria had been in fine fettle for the past few weeks. So if Mrs. Glassell only visited when Maria was doing poorly, then she had not been about on the night Mr. Rivers was killed.

Feeling completely nettled, I made my goodbyes.

Once outside, Sebastiano and I decided to speak to Mrs. Fletcher next, although we waited long enough to quickly eat a couple bits of bread and cheese that Olivia had sent with the four of us. It wasn't much of a luncheon, but enough to keep me going.

The Fletcher home was on Calle Forfin, across from Sarah Worthington's house, as a matter of fact. It had been painted blue with dark blue trim and was among the grander in the pueblo, with three floors and a turret on the front corner. The yard overflowed with all manner of shrubs, grass, and flowers, which suddenly made me wonder if Mr. Rivers had also paid off Mr. Fletcher with additional allotments of water. Mr. Fletcher had been on the city council when Mr. Rivers was elected zanjero, but at that time, I think he was running for some state office. In any case, he was not at home, being a lawyer in addition to all his land holdings.

Like Mrs. Glassell, Mrs. Fletcher was not in when I arrived but suddenly arrived home and agreed to speak with me once I made it clear I would wait on the veranda until she did. I was seated in the front parlor and offered tea and cakes, which were excellent. The room was somewhat less cluttered than Mrs. Glassell's parlor, and the chairs and sofa were all covered in deep blue velvet upholstery. The paintings on the wall were quite good and I thought I spotted one by Rembrandt Peale or one of the other members of that most prolific family.

"You're looking at my art," Mrs. Fletcher said, crossly.

I started. She was wearing a red poplin day dress and standing behind me in the parlor doorway.

"Pray excuse me," I said. "I was admiring your paintings, actually. Is that still-life by one of the famous Peale brothers?"

"Yes, Raphaelle Peale," Mrs. Fletcher said. She was trying to keep her cross look. But she was clearly immensely proud of the small painting of a bowl of fruit and the fact that I had recognized it for what it was impressed her, even if it was against her will. "How do you come to know that art?"

"I studied in Philadelphia," I said. "And my aunt and uncle were part of society there. They had any number of works by the brothers."

"Studying?" Mrs. Fletcher asked, the disdain making her high-pitched voice sound even higher.

"The Women's Medical College of Pennsylvania."

"Did your aunt and uncle know where you were studying?"

I straightened my back. "My aunt did. In fact, she paid my tuition and boarded me. My uncle, her husband, was deceased by then."

"I thought you said she was part of society," Mrs. Fletcher said with a sniff.

"She was, but by that point, didn't really care that she was." I turned to her fully. "I take it you came from that same society?"

Mrs. Fletcher sniffed again. "I did. My father fell on hard times, you understand, which is why I was only able to marry Mr. Fletcher. But he has done very well for himself, and I did get a bequest or two, as well." She paused. "How odd that I should tell you, of all people, all of this."

I shrugged. "Perhaps I am better able to understand what you suffered by your father's hardship."

Mrs. Fletcher let out a short cough. "Perhaps. But that is not why you're here."

"No, I'm afraid not." I waited while she settled herself on the sofa, then took a nearby chair. "It has come to my attention that you are often abroad at night."

She stiffened. "I do not care to be accused."

"I am not accusing anyone," I said severely. "But I am sure you have heard there is a killer loose in this pueblo, one who must be stopped as soon as possible. And your taking umbrage before I've even had a chance to ask a simple question or two will not help."

"And why should I answer your questions?"

"As I said, there is a dangerous killer loose in the pueblo," I repeated, desperately trying to keep my patience.

Mrs. Fletcher let out a deep sigh. "Well, you can ask me anything you like, but it won't do you any good. I know nothing about these events and don't care to."

"You might have seen something and not even realized it," I pointed out.

"I don't see anything." Mrs. Fletcher coughed again, this time taking out her handkerchief. "Like any good Christian woman, I am in my bed by ten o'clock every night."

"As I understand it, that is not true."

"Of course, it is," she snapped. "Why would I lie?"

"I do not know, but I do know that you are not telling the truth. You have been seen walking abroad of an evening."

"I have not!" Her cough suddenly became more insistent. "Whoever told you that is a liar, himself. I am in bed at night, as all decent people should be."

She coughed again and then noticed that I was watching her. To be truthful, I hadn't noticed the smell when I'd first entered the parlor. It was relatively faint and not at all an indication that anything was amiss. After all, many men smoked in their front parlors, and the scent of tobacco was not at all unusual.

"It's not the consumption," Mrs. Fletcher said, fiercely, as she recovered herself.

"No, I do not think so," I said. "That is a somewhat different cough. And I do think I know why you are lying. You want to protect yourself from shame and embarrassment. Although I would think that if you stopped smoking that would protect you even better."

Mrs. Fletcher turned pale and gasped. "I do not smoke! The sheer effrontery to suggest that I do!"

"It's not a suggestion, Mrs. Fletcher. I can see the signs of it on you. The stains on your fingers and your teeth. That nasty cough. The tiny burns on your skirt. I can even smell the smoke upon you. You smoke cigarettes, don't you, Mrs. Fletcher?"

"No!" She cried, then suddenly crumpled and began sobbing. "It's so utterly shameful! But I can't help it. I have tried to stop but I become so nervous and upset every time I do, I have to take even more laudanum. And then I become so sleepy that I stumble about as if I were an idiot in an insane asylum." She slowly got control of herself. "I mostly smoke at night. That way the scent airs out before morning and Mr. Fletcher doesn't smell it. Of course, he smokes constantly, so it's no wonder he can't smell me. But I do go outside, usually into the back garden, and sometimes I'll walk a bit so that the smoke doesn't cling to me. But I never go further than the corner. I don't go anywhere near Mr. Mahoney's saloon. The only thing I saw the night Mr. Rivers was killed was Mr. Worthington stumbling back home."

"Do you remember what time it was?"

"After ten o'clock?" She shrugged. "It could have been after midnight. I do not know. I don't pay attention to the time. But I do go to bed around ten o'clock, as does Mr. Fletcher. I do not go out until I am sure he is asleep, and sometimes it takes him longer than other nights to go to sleep." She blinked back more tears. "You can't tell anyone. You simply mustn't."

I suppose that nowadays, it doesn't seem so shocking to see a lady smoking. Good heavens, the young ladies are puffing away with impunity on street corners. But back at the time of these events, women did not smoke. Even the women of ill-repute didn't, at least, not publicly. A woman who smoked was unheard of. Well, it wasn't unheard of, but no decent woman smoked unless she, like Mrs. Fletcher, had found a way to hide the filthy habit. So while perhaps there were more shocking secrets, it was understandable that Mrs. Fletcher would be very worried about people knowing hers.

"Mrs. Fletcher, I pride myself on my discretion,"

I said, trying to keep my voice as soothing as possible. "I will not say a word unless I must to prevent an injustice."

"Even then, you mustn't."

I sighed. "Now, I must be thorough, and, Heaven knows, everyone else had some reason to kill Mr. Rivers. What would be yours?"

"I did not kill him," she said, her voice rising again in indignation.

"I did not ask if you had, merely whether you had a reason to kill him, as most people do, it appears."

"I had no reason or interest in killing him. He was a fine man. I was quite grieved when he died." She took her handkerchief and dabbed at her eyes. "Such a charming man. I'd heard he beat his wife. But dear Mrs. Rivers is such a good woman. It pains one to consider what she must have done to earn a beating from such a delightful man."

"Yes, it's hard to imagine," I said, dryly. "Do you own a gun?"

"What?" she demanded.

"When you're walking at night. It's quite dangerous. I wondered if you carried some sort of gun," I asked.

"I do not go onto any streets where I would need one."

"That does not mean you do not own one."

"It does in this case."

I said goodbye after that. She did seem to have been very fond of Mr. Rivers. Still, I found it hard to imagine that her portly shape and grating, high-pitched voice would inspire any kind of devotion, much less the kind I'd heard described to me.

So I went on to Mrs. Carson's home, which was nearby and almost as grand. Mrs. Carson, fortunately, did not pretend that she was not in, but did arrange for me to come through the back of the house. She was wearing a gown of pink lawn, which did not complement her complexion or her stout stature. She was also quite agitated as she paced among the chairs and sofa in her front parlor.

"Everyone is saying that you're going about making the most unkind accusations," she complained.

"I am sorry that it has been interpreted that way, but what else am I to do?" I asked, seating myself on the sofa, never mind that I had not been invited. "I must ask questions if I am to find Mr. Rivers' killer, and it has become very urgent that I do so since it seems obvious that this same person also killed young Will Rivers. There's no way of knowing who will be next if I don't."

With a great sigh, Mrs. Carson flopped into a nearby chair. "Very well, then. Ask away."

I gathered my thoughts together. "What reason did you have to kill Mr. Rivers?"

Her eyebrow lifted. "Direct, aren't we? Well, I did and I didn't." She leaned forward conspiratorially. "He was trying to seduce me."

I doubted that but declined to say so.

"He was," Mrs. Carson insisted. "Made brazen overtures of all kinds. At first, I thought it was just in fun. But I do think he meant to seduce me."

"To what end?" I couldn't help but ask.

Mrs. Carson smirked. "I have no idea. Unless he wanted to rob my husband of his good name for some reason. Mr. Rivers could be a bit of a rascal, as you've no doubt discovered."

"I have. Did he succeed?"

"Succeed at what?"

"Seducing you."

"Oh, Heavens, no." Mrs. Carson smirked again. "I shouldn't have liked having my name linked to his, nor would I have liked being put out of my home, as Mr. Carson would most certainly have done, and with good reason."

"Do you go abroad alone at night?"

"Of course." Mrs. Carson smirked again. "We all do, and you shouldn't let anyone tell you she doesn't.

We all have our little secrets, you know. I see Mrs. Sutton all the time, for obvious reasons. I'm not sure what Mrs. Judson's secret is."

"What about yours?"

"Mine?"

"Your little secret."

Mrs. Carson sighed and shrugged. "I have headaches that force me to take to my bed in the afternoon. I take willow bark tea for them. The problem is, if I take to my bed in the afternoon, then I can't sleep at night. So I take a short walk. That usually does the trick."

"Aren't you afraid?" I asked although I doubted she was. I did not want to ask directly if she had a gun as I realized it might give too much away.

"Not really. I stay away from the saloons and keep to the shadows." Her eyebrow lifted, this time in amusement. "I see all manner of things that way. Including you."

"I don't doubt it. But to the point, did you see anything the night that Mr. Rivers was killed?"

She groaned slightly. "Of all the nights for me to keep to my bed. I was asleep. Missed everything. It is too aggravating, really."

I was trying to decide whether Mrs. Carson was telling the truth or whether she was an extremely clever liar, and if she was, how I could best get the truth out of her. But our conversation was cut short by the arrival home of Mr. Carson.

He was as round as his wife, with thick white hair and mustache, and a perpetual sneer on his face. I had wondered if he was dyspeptic, and, as it turned out, he was.

"My darling," Mrs. Carson said with mild pleasure as he filled the front parlor doorway.

He glared at me. "What's she doing here?"

"I'm consulting her regarding your dyspepsia," Mrs. Carson said without blinking.

"I don't need a lady doctor," he growled.

"Well, you haven't done very well with the men."

He harrumphed and disappeared into the house.

"He does have dyspepsia," Mrs. Carson said.

"I thought as much." I began digging through my bag. "Has he tried asafoetida?"

"I've never even heard of it."

I pulled out the small jar of tan powder. "It smells rank, but put a small spoonful of it into some broth at dinner and before supper. It tastes like leeks when cooked. You might also try getting him to drink some bitters before eating dinner or supper."

"We've tried the bitters," she said.

"Have you tried either of these?" I held up two small bottles and let her read the labels.

She took one of the bottles. "This one we haven't."

"Then try it. But I think the asafoetida should be quite helpful."

"I suppose it's worth trying." She opened the little jar and took a sniff. "You were right about the smell."

"That's why you put it in his broth."

She glanced at the hallway, then we both got up.

"Very kind of you to help, Mrs. Wilcox," she said.

"Please let me know how he does."

"I will." She rang a little bell and had her maid show me out through the front.

The asafoetida did help Mr. Carson and he became quite kindly disposed toward me as a result. Both he and Mrs. Carson became my patients, although, unlike the other people in the pueblo, they continued to act as if my medical work was an act of charity. It was some time before I had the nerve to suggest that it was also fast becoming my primary source of living, and if I were to continue providing my services as charity, it would be for those who could not pay, not those who could well afford me.

Having been let in through the back, that was where Sebastiano was waiting for me. He had left the boys in front, just in case something untoward happened there. I had to send young Juan after his uncle while

I waited with Damiano. Sebastiano laughed when he saw me in front of the house.

"So now you know what it feels like to be a servant," he said.

"I hope I never treat you that way," I said. "Still, I appear to have turned the table. She had the maid show me out, no less."

"Did you learn anything?"

"Not really. She is not unlike Mrs. Judson that way. Far more clever than she would have us believe," I said, briefly repeating our conversation. "I really don't know what to make of her."

Sebastiano shrugged. "I think we only have Mrs. Hewitt to visit next."

"I do hope she has something to tell us," I sighed.

But it was not to be.

Mr. Hewitt owned a carriage manufactory at the edge of town. After inquiring at their home, Sebastiano and I found Mrs. Hewitt in the manufactory's office, dictating a telegram about parts of some sort to a clerk. She looked up at me and Sebastiano with a guilty smile then dismissed the clerk.

"I have heard you've been busy ferreting out everyone's guilty secrets," she grumbled.

"I would be perfectly happy not to be doing so," I said. "But—"

She cut me off. "I know, I know. Poor Will Rivers."

"Where is Mr. Hewitt?" I asked.

"Him!" She snorted with deep disdain. "Dead drunk in the back of the warehouse. I'm forced to run this business if we are not to starve. As for Mr. Rivers, I would have liked to have hit him over the head, but I didn't."

"I know you're too small," I said.

"There is that," she said bustling to the huge oak wood desk and sorting through papers. "But I've been thinking about it. It would have made more sense to have smothered him, the way he was lying there like that. Sadly, I didn't think of it."

"And why did you want to kill him?"

"He was going to ruin our business! We were constantly late with our orders because Mr. Montero couldn't deliver our leather order, thanks to that scoundrel. He didn't know that I do all the work Mr. Hewitt should be doing, but he knew I did a lot of it and told me he was going to spread it about town. That would have finished us. Who is going to buy a buggy from a woman? I ask you, who? No one, that's who. Never mind that our buggies are the finest and most solid in this entire county."

"They are good carriages," I said. My buggy had been made by the Hewitt manufactory and I was very fond of it. "Have you heard anything about Mr. Rivers having a mistress?"

"Nonsense!" she snarled. "I've never heard anything so ridiculous."

"He was known to force himself on women," I pointed out.

"Not on me, he didn't." She glanced over at Sebastiano, then bent and spoke quietly to me. "I'm burdened enough with my husband. I'm not going to take on a second man, I don't care how charming he is. And after I found out what all that scoundrel had been up to, I certainly wasn't going to take up with Mr. Rivers." She straightened. "Now, Mrs. Wilcox, will you kindly take your leave of this place? I do not have time to dawdle in idle chatter. I've got a manufactory to run. I'm sure you understand."

"I'm sure I do," I said quietly.

Sebastiano gestured and we left rather quickly.

"That was strange," he said softly as we untied our mounts.

"Indeed." I looked back at the office. "I find it very interesting that she assumed I was speaking about a connection between her and Mr. Rivers when I asked if she'd heard about him having a mistress."

"And the way she talked about smothering him."

"That's right," I said. "That is interesting. I'm not

sure what to do about it, though. It's not as though we have solid proof that she killed him. And we'll need it, I'm afraid." I looked back over the pueblo. "I think our next visit should be Mrs. Ontiveras. I need to verify what Mrs. Elmwood told me."

Which Mrs. Ontiveras did, in between fulsome thanks for taking care of her mother. I disentangled myself as quickly as I could and hurried back to my horse.

One of the older Lomax children was waiting for us as we entered the Calle Principal. He told us that his father would be at home for the rest of the afternoon, so I had the boy join our little parade. Sebastiano put Damiano on his mule with him, then let Juan and the Lomax boy share the other mule. Mr. Lomax saw us coming and met us at the gate to his place. He sent his son back to the house.

"Well, Mrs. Wilcox, you've done it again," he said as I and Sebastiano dismounted.

"What?" I asked.

"The sheet," he said, with his odd half smile.

"Well, I needed to replace yours," I said.

"Still, we're much obliged."

"Stuff and nonsense," I replied with great irritation. "Have you spoken with Mrs. Sutton today?"

He nodded. "And you're sure a woman killed him?"

"Very sure," I said with a sigh. "Now, let me tell you what else we've found out."

Which I proceeded to do. Mr. Lomax, as always, was an excellent listener. He waited until I was done, asked a couple questions for clarification, then nodded.

"I think we'd better find out who this mistress is," he said.

"How?" I asked. "We asked the women, and they didn't say anything, nor would they."

"What if we asked Mr. Mahoney?" Sebastiano said. "Maybe he knows something and if the three of us go together, then maybe he'll be more likely to answer us."

"That is an excellent idea," I said. "What do you

think, Mr. Lomax?"

"Let's go," Mr. Lomax said.

He went and fetched his mule and the five of us rode back into the pueblo. We got the boys settled in the back kitchen with Mr. Mahoney's daughters, who doted on them, and then found Mr. Mahoney in the hallway into the saloon. He seemed a little nervous to see all three of us facing him, but smiled, nonetheless.

"This is quite the deputation," he said. "What's going on?"

"We need to take you into our confidence, Mr. Mahoney," I said. "As you know, the situation is growing more perilous by the day."

"You mean Mr. Rivers' killer?" he asked.

"And Will Rivers' killer, too," said Sebastiano.

"That's right. I've been hearing that it was probably the same man."

"The same woman," I said.

Mr. Mahoney gaped. "What?"

"I can't say how I found out," I said. "But we know that Mr. Rivers was killed by a woman. We think it was probably his mistress. Who else would have a reason to kill him that would be likely to be wandering about the pueblo after eleven o'clock at night?"

"That's still a good many women," Mr. Mahoney said.

"Perhaps," I said. "But what we're hoping is that you heard something, anything, that could give us an idea of how to find her."

Mr. Mahoney frowned in thought, then shook his head. "I haven't heard a thing about her."

"Mr. Worthington thought she might be a Mexican," Sebastiano said. "Else why wouldn't he marry her?"

"It isn't that," said Mr. Mahoney. His eyebrows rose as he thought of something. "She's married. To someone else, obviously. She could be a Mexican, but..." he frowned, thinking hard. "I don't know why, but I don't think so. If she were Mexican, I'd figure he'd simply use her like he used all the others."

I looked at Mr. Lomax and Sebastiano. We all agreed that it made sense.

"Is there any way you can ask some of the men who come in?" I asked. "Discreetly, of course."

Mr. Mahoney pulled a dirty handkerchief from his pants pocket and wiped his nose. "I could, indeed. You never know what I might find."

"And please be careful." I put my hand on his arm. "This killer probably killed Will because she thought he'd seen something."

Mr. Mahoney agreed and we left, collecting the boys, who had been stuffed with cakes and muffins.

After a quick conference on the street, we went over to see if Mrs. Sutton could spare us a few minutes so that we could let her know what all we had learned.

"I don't have long," she told us as she led us into her back parlor. "The viewing for poor Will is tonight and I'll have to make sure Mr. Sutton has his supper before I have the boys bring the casket over to the Rivers house."

Mrs. Sutton had her maid bring out sweet breads and tea to fortify us while I told her and the others everything I knew. She wrote quickly on her paper as I talked, shaking her head every few minutes.

"Well," she said after I had finished. "I think Mrs. Fletcher and Mrs. Hewitt are our best candidates. There's no reason to think either of them were telling the truth about Mr. Rivers and Mrs. Fletcher is almost the only person to admit that she liked him."

"That's true," I said.

Mr. Lomax groaned. "You know, what's worrying me is that Mr. Worthington is under attack. There have been those accidents at the lumber yard and he was shot at today."

"Yes, as he was going home to his dinner," Sebastiano said.

"What if the woman who shot Mr. Rivers was actually trying to kill Mr. Worthington?" Mr. Lomax said.

"I don't understand," I said.

"They were cousins and looked somewhat alike," Mr. Lomax said. "They were about the same stature. With it being so dark that night, they could have been confused. And someone is trying to kill Mr. Worthington. What if that woman is trying to kill him and only killed Mr. Rivers by accident?"

"Oh, dear Lord!" I groaned. "The only woman I can think of who might want to do that would be Sarah, but it doesn't make sense that she wouldn't be able to tell the difference between Mr. Rivers and her own husband. And she doesn't really have a reason to kill Mr. Worthington. She needs him and his position to fully enter pueblo society. As a widow, she'd be out on the fringes again. And that is assuming she had the stomach to do something that drastic. Which she doesn't."

"No, she doesn't," said Sebastiano.

"On the other hand," I continued. "It now occurs to me that she's been complaining that Mr. Worthington has been coming home smelling of perfume. Could it be that he's the one with the mistress and that the mistress is trying to kill him?"

Mrs. Sutton sighed. "And that puts us right back at the beginning, only now we have to start questioning everyone about Mr. Worthington."

"The problem is," said Mr. Lomax. "Mr. Worthington has a very solid reputation in town. It doesn't make sense that somebody would want to kill him."

"Unless they wanted the lumber mill," said Sebastiano. "Or wanted to be the zanjero or zanjero's deputy."

I closed my eyes, trying to think. "No. I don't know why, but I think the person trying to kill Mr. Worthington and the person who killed Mr. Rivers are two different people. And the only reason to think that someone is trying to kill Mr. Worthington is that he was shot at today. It's entirely possible that what happened at the lumber mill were actually accidents. And the person shooting at Mr. Worthington may not have been shooting at him, at all, but at someone else. I admit, it seems suspicious, but it could just as easily be a series of unfortunate occurrences."

Mr. Lomax nodded. "Probably so. We certainly have enough people with reason to kill Mr. Rivers and hardly any who would want to kill Mr. Worthington."

Somewhere in the house, a clock chimed five o'clock.

"Oh, dear," said Mrs. Sutton. "I'm afraid I've run out of time."

I got up immediately, and the men with me.

"We have intruded abominably," I told her.

"Not at all," she said, smiling. "We will find this person and before someone else dies. Will I see you at the viewing?"

"Of course," I said.

I knew that Sebastiano wasn't invited and doubted that Mr. Lomax was. However, he chose not to say anything, and we parted ways outside.

The sun was just starting to head toward the horizon, turning the western hills into dark shadows and giving the rest of the valley a soft glow. It seemed so peaceful. As I kicked Daisy into a trot, I regretted deeply that the pueblo was anything but.

CHAPTER FOURTEEN

Olivia had our supper ready early so that I would have time to change for the viewing. The mood at our table was somber and the conversation was mostly stilted. I was just going to hear the children's lessons when there was a knock on the door and Maria came to get me.

Regina was waiting for me in the front room.

"Forgive me, my darling, but you look horrible," she said. She looked quite refreshed and nice, in her best blue walking suit.

"I didn't get any sleep last night," I said, sinking into the chair across from where she sat on the sofa.

"So I hear," she said. She looked down at her hands. "I also hear you spoke with my brother."

"Yes, I did."

"Will you forgive me for not saying anything?"

"You had to honor his feelings," I said, then tried to smile. "And who's to say I've told you all my little secrets?"

Regina chuckled. "Never mind, my dear. You've had a most trying past few days, and I've come to do my part to ease some of your work."

"Oh?"

"I can't say how, but I have learned something interesting about our Mr. Rivers. You will have heard that he had a mistress in addition to all the poor women he coerced and otherwise forced himself on?"

"Yes. Someone he loved, apparently."

"Apparently, indeed. I don't know who she is, nor does the friend of mine who told me this. But it would seem that she is someone who is very much like Mr. Rivers. Always grasping, seeking to take advantage of any and all, scheming relentlessly and a complete liar."

"How would your friend know this?"

"He caught them in flagrante, as it were. He doesn't know who she is because he doesn't live here, and Mr. Rivers did not deign to introduce them. However, they apparently spoke long enough for him to form an opinion of her. So I don't know how many people you know like that, but I would imagine one or two of the town's gossipy hens would fit that category."

"They would, indeed. Thank you, Regina."

She reached over and touched my arm. "Are you going to be all right? You've suffered so much already on my behalf, and now poor Will Rivers. I was told you've been quite affected."

I took a deep breath. "It was a most terrible night. They warned us when I went to college that we would see the worst of human suffering and be powerless against it. One of the reasons some of the men teachers were worried that we women would suffer greatly if we were to become doctors. Yet, we suffer so much already. And, yes, I've been quite affected not only by Will's death but other secrets I have learned. As you know, Mr. Rivers was quite an evil man and I do not say that lightly. He hurt a great many women in the pueblo and beyond."

"Yes. I'm not surprised. But then, I've always had a much better grasp than you on just how cruel men can be. Sadly, I do see their worst sides all too often."

"I'm sure you do, Regina." I smiled wanly, then paused. "I do have one question for you, though. More because I have to be sure, you understand."

"Of course. Ask on."

"Did you send one of your girls to kill Mr. Rivers?"

Regina frowned. "I suppose you do have to ask that. But, no, I didn't. I'm fairly certain none of them left the house that night. We were rather busy, as I recall. I suppose it's possible one of them did leave and decided to knock him over the head while she was out. But that doesn't make sense. None of the girls I have now were working when I banned Mr. Rivers, so none of them really has a reason to have wanted him dead."

"And I don't recall you sending anybody off that night, and since we were both in the same room the whole night, I think I would have heard you do so." I tried not to sigh, but one escaped, anyway. "I am sorry, but I had to ask just to be sure."

"Naturally, my darling. I am not the least offended.

"I am glad you stopped by." I looked her over carefully. "How are you? Recovered, I hope?"

"Much better, thank you," she said, and her smile grew impish. "Business is back to normal, thank Heavens for that. There is nothing worse than playing faro with bored girls. And they cheat so relentlessly."

I found myself chuckling in spite of myself. Regina smiled.

"There's the thing, my darling," she said, warmly, as she got up. "Now you hurry back from that viewing and get yourself some rest. You won't be any good to anybody if you don't."

I let her out and went to get dressed in my brown visiting dress.

The dark cloud of grief had descended on the Rivers home, filling the very air with a deep sadness. Will was laid out in his newly acquired suit. I was one of the first to arrive, just in time to see that a photographer had set up his equipment. He took two pictures of Will in his coffin, then packed everything up. Mrs. Rivers sat near the coffin, dressed in her veils, and this time, I could see that she had been crying. Her head was bent low and her shoulders sagged under the weight of her grief. Her remaining sons stood nearby, all trying to look manly and brave, and yet it was plain that their hearts were breaking.

"So good of you to come, Mrs. Wilcox," Mrs. Rivers said softly as I greeted her.

"It was kind of you to invite me," I replied.

The phrases were the standard formula, what one always said. And yet the words were imbued with a sincerity I had seldom heard. I murmured my condolences again, then stepped aside so that Mrs. Judson, who had arrived just after me, could greet Mrs. Rivers.

The grand house was quickly filling with neighbors and well-wishers. Most funerals back home in Boston, the parlor would have been filled with relatives of all kinds. Here in Los Angeles, very few people had any extended family nearby. Indeed, it was a relatively rare occurrence when the deceased had anyone to attend his funeral, let alone family members. So our neighbors made up the difference whenever possible.

The front parlor had been emptied of furniture and the sliding doors between it and the dining room were open. The table had been pushed to the wall but was filled with tea things and any number of cakes and little sandwiches. Susannah, the maid, was pouring tea. Even she seemed to have lost some of her usual aplomb.

I had thought I would merely take one cup of tea and a cake and then leave. But before I could get my cup, Mrs. Warren slipped up to my side.

"Mrs. Wilcox, may I prevail upon you for a moment?" she asked softly.

I nodded and she led me to a corner next to the door to the kitchen.

"I'm not sure how to say this," she began, glancing around to be sure no one could hear us. "I, perhaps, should have come to you sooner. But yesterday morning, before my husband left for Riverside, he said something rather strange."

"Oh?" I smiled, trying not to show my desperate desire to get my cup of tea and go.

"He said that you will never find out who killed Mr. Rivers because you didn't know what he did about how Mr. Rivers died."

My heart sank. "Did he say what it was that he

knew?"

"Of course not, but he was quite happy about it."

"Well, thank you for telling me this," I said, not at all happy about what I was hearing.

Mrs. Warren excused herself, and to my relief, I saw Mrs. Sutton nearby, talking with Mr. Lomax, who had apparently been invited after all. I slipped up to both of them.

"We have a new problem," I said, then told them what Mrs. Warren had told me.

Mr. Lomax frowned. "He shouldn't know any more than what I told him. And keep in mind, I let him believe that Mr. Sutton had called attention to that bullet hole and didn't give a hint that either of you ladies were involved."

"So, in other words," said Mrs. Sutton. "Marshal Warren doesn't know that Maddie and I know what really killed Mr. Rivers."

"That's what I hope is the case," Mr. Lomax said.

"Let's just keep hoping," I said, looking over at Mrs. Rivers. "This miserable mess has been far too troublesome already."

I wasn't sure if it was that people in the pueblo were that sorry that Mrs. Rivers had lost her youngest child, or if they were merely curious, given how he had been murdered. Some may have even been both. Nonetheless, there was quite a crowd growing.

I managed to make my way over to the tea table where Sarah, Mrs. Judson, and Mrs. Aguilar were standing and talking to each other. Mrs. Carson and Mrs. Fletcher were carrying on their own conversation next to them. As I picked up my cup of tea, Mrs. Judson greeted me.

"Mrs. Rivers was most complimentary toward you, my dear," she said rather loudly.

"That is exceedingly kind of her," I said. I looked around for the sugar, as I don't really care for tea without it.

"Oh, Maddie, dearest," said Sarah. "You were too

wonderful, sitting the entire night with poor Will and his mother."

"I'm glad you think so," I said, trying to sound sincere and kind. Inside, I felt anything but wonderful. "It was a most difficult night."

"It must have been," said Mrs. Aguilar. "I remember when you sat with my Alicia the other week or so back. Such patience."

"It is what I do," I said quietly. "And it is to be expected."

"I don't know about that," said Mrs. Judson. "Doctor Clancy would dose my boys and leave as fast as he could. Granted, they never really had terribly serious fevers, although they all got scarlet fever at one point or another. And the ague."

"Oh, the ague, it's always around, isn't it?" said Sarah.

"It certainly seems to be," said Mrs. Aguilar.

Or she said something akin to that. If truth be told, I wasn't entirely listening. I kept hearing snatches of the conversation between Mrs. Fletcher and Mrs. Carson and across the room, I could see Mrs. Hewitt.

My gaze must have fallen on her once too often, because as I finally found the sugar bowl and put my spoonful of sugar into my tea, Mrs. Hewitt stormed across the room.

"You!" she screamed. "How dare you come here after accusing me of all manner of ill deeds."

"I didn't accuse you of anything," I stammered.

It didn't matter. Mrs. Hewitt continued haranguing me, coming quite close and almost spitting in my face as she looked up at me. Someone, I did not see who, saved my tea cup from disaster.

"Mrs. Hewitt!" screamed Mrs. Carson. "This is most unseemly. Kindly get control of yourself."

"I will not have her accusing me of murdering Mr. Rivers!" Mrs. Hewitt snapped.

"Mrs. Wilcox hasn't accused anybody of doing anything," said Mrs. Judson, gently shoving Mrs.

Hewitt back and handing me my tea cup. "Now, please, have some respect for the family in mourning."

Mrs. Hewitt snorted, turned on her heel and left.

I looked over at the Rivers family. The three boys had gathered around their mother and were watching intently as Mrs. Hewitt departed. James looked at me and I shrugged.

"Poor Mrs. Wilcox," said Mrs. Judson soothingly. "How trying this must be for you."

"Dear Maddie," said Sarah, touching my arm. "I hope you are all right."

"Yes, dear," Mrs. Judson said. "Now, take some tea. That will ease things, I'm sure."

I smiled weakly at both of them and thanked them, then moved off. I did take a couple sips of the tea, but it tasted unusually bitter and metallic. I did not want to embarrass Mrs. Rivers by calling attention to it, but I did not want to drink it, either. The night was cool and threatening rain again. However, it had become quite close inside the house, and someone had thought to open the windows. I found one overlooking the side garden and surreptitiously emptied my cup outside. As I replaced the cup on its saucer, I noticed that the grains inside were considerably larger than that of sugar. So, I slid the cup into my small and mostly empty ladies' bag that I was carrying instead of my usual large leather bag.

"Good evening, Mrs. Wilcox," purred a friendly voice.

I looked up and saw Mrs. Downey standing quite close by.

"Such a sad evening," she observed. "But I am glad to see you again."

"As am I," I said, and was happy to note that I was genuinely glad to see her. "How are your researches into astronomy going?"

"Well enough. Mr. Downey returned on Sunday and brought me my telescope. However, last night the rain made it impossible to see anything. I fear tonight will be no better. Still, we'll have clear skies soon enough. But I wanted to ask you about your medical training. Am I to understand you have a degree from a real college?"

"Yes, I do."

"Oh, I would have loved to go to college. How was it that you were able to go?"

I smiled at the memory. "My mother wanted me to go, along with all of my younger sisters. Mother was a transcendentalist and a suffragist, which suited me and my sisters quite well."

Mrs. Downey smiled, knowingly. "And your father and brothers?"

"I have one brother who ignores me. And my father was quite put out when he learned what I'd been doing while living with my aunt. My mother's sister. The two of them were quite determined that my sisters and I be fully educated, and when I showed an interest in the healing arts, my aunt made sure that I was able to go to the Women's Medical College."

"I do wish I'd had an aunt like that. That being said, I'm very grateful that Mr. Downey allows me my little hobby."

I smiled, but my stomach was suddenly feeling quite queer. I felt my throat go tight and knew that I had best leave the house at once if I were not to embarrass myself. I had a very good idea of what had happened but was more concerned about how it would appear should I be sick in front of everyone. So I excused myself and ran out through the kitchen, and then around the side of the house. I wanted to get to the street but did not get the chance before I emptied my stomach all over the flower beds. I made quite a mess but was eventually able to stumble around to the front of the house, where Sebastiano was waiting in the buggy. I thanked God I had thought to have him drive that evening. He immediately saw that I was sick and got me up onto the seat and home as quickly as possible.

It was, I'm afraid, not that quickly. I had to have him stop at least twice so that I could be sick again and again. I was fairly certain I knew what had caused my illness but was feeling far too poorly to say anything beyond indicating when I needed to stop. Once home, I was treated to a chorus of scolding from Juanita, Olivia, and Magdalena. The three of them rushed me to my bed, only to have me get up several more times to be sick. Young Elena helped hold my stomach as I heaved and then gave me water to rinse my mouth out with. I fear I was rather curt with her, but years later, she assured me that it was to be expected. I have never been a good patient and it has only gotten worse as I've grown old.

"I'm supposed to be sleeping," I grumbled as the clock struck one o'clock in the morning.

"You will be soon," whispered Elena. She fed me still more anti-emetic tea, and I was finally able to keep it down.

The next day, clouds filled the sky and delivered on the promised rain. I had slept fitfully and was not feeling entirely better when I finally awoke. I was also surprised to see my ranch hand Wang Fu standing by my bed.

"You doctor," he told me in his halting English. "I doctor, too. I have herb for stomach. You take."

He presented me with a cup of tea and bowed slightly. I looked at him, surprised.

"You take. Drink," he insisted.

To this day, I do not know what was in that tea, but it was as if a miracle had occurred. An hour later, I was busy getting dressed for Will's funeral. Wang Fu had disappeared back to the fields or vineyard.

"You should stay home and rest," Juanita said.

"I'm feeling much better," I told her. "And I want to see if anyone is surprised to see me there."

"They all saw you get sick. They'll all be surprised." Juanita gestured with my hairbrush.

"At least one person will be more than surprised,"

I said. "Go fetch the bag I was carrying last night."

"It's right here." Juanita handed it to me.

I pulled out the cup. "I can't say for sure, but look at the crystals in the bottom. Those are not sugar."

Juanita poked at one and was about to bring it to her lips when I stopped her.

"Don't taste it," I snapped. "They're probably arsenic salts."

"Poison?" Juanita gasped.

"Based on my symptoms, I would say so," I said.

"But who would try to poison you and at the viewing of all places?"

"Someone who is very desperately trying to keep me from finding out her identity," I said and sighed. I thought over who had been next to me when I'd gotten my cup of tea, and realized all of the women I thought might have killed Mr. Rivers had been within easy reach. "And I'd thought I was among friends at the viewing. Mrs. Judson was even kind to me."

"That's your problem, Maddie," Juanita said. "You know who your real friends are. But you keep trying to be friends with people who will never be your real friends, who only think of themselves and their reputations."

"Reputation is an important thing, Juanita."

"Yes, but those old gallinas, they are so terrified of being judged and found wanting because all they do is judge each other. Those are not real friends. And your real friends will understand if you are not at the funeral."

"You are utterly right, Juanita." I paused as something occurred to me. "Juanita, I think of you as my friend."

"Yes, and I think of you as a friend, too."

"And yet I am your mistress. Don't you find that awkward or unfair?"

She shrugged and went back to brushing my hair. "There are always servants. Even in the days of the Californios, my family were servants. It doesn't make any difference to me whether you are Americana or a California. I'm still a servant. But I like having my mistress be my friend. It makes it easier, especially when I have to tell you to be sensible and stay home this morning."

I was forced to smile but then sighed deeply. "I probably should stay home. Still, I think it's important that I go. Not for friendship, but to find an end to this terrible mystery."

Juanita tried, but she could not argue with that, and so off I went.

However, the funeral only brought me more heartache. As we left to go to the cemetery, James Rivers slipped up next to me and put a note into my hand. It was from his mother and as I read it, my heart froze. Suddenly, everything made sense. I could not stay for the graveside service. I was too worried that I would give something away before I could speak with Mrs. Sutton and Mr. Lomax. I was almost sure I knew who the murderer was and, as my heart broke, I realized I needed a plan that would hopefully prove me wrong.

I went home and then sent notes to both. They responded right away and approved of my plan. So, I sent still more notes around and made arrangements with Olivia for a tea party.

Mrs. Sutton arrived first, with Sarah Worthington close behind. I was surprised when Mrs. Hewitt agreed to come, but she did, as did Mrs. Judson and Mrs. Aguilar. Once we were all settled in the front parlor, Mrs. Judson asked if I was feeling better from the night before.

"Much better," I replied. "Thank you for asking."

"But what happened?" asked Mrs. Aguilar. "One minute you were speaking with Mrs. Downey and the next you were running from the room."

"I was poisoned," I said.

The women all gasped.

"Unfortunately, one of you here is the one who did

it. The rest of you are here as witnesses."

"What do you mean?" asked Sarah warily.

"I mean that you put arsenic in my tea, Sarah Worthington, and you killed both Mr. Rivers and young Will."

Mrs. Aguilar and Mrs. Judson both dropped their jaws in shock.

"I did no such thing," said Sarah, smiling as if no one could possibly believe my accusation.

"Oh? Then how is it that the only other person outside of the Rivers household who knew where young Will was hiding when he was shot was your maid Hannah."

"What has that got to do with me?" Sarah began toying nervously with the cuff of her sleeve.

I looked at her grimly. "Everything. This morning Mrs. Rivers sent me a note asking if it meant anything that her maid Susannah was sister to your maid Hannah. Apparently, Susannah had told Hannah where Will was. But no one else seemed to know he was hiding there except the woman who killed him."

"Then Hannah killed Will," Sarah said, glancing about the room, then standing up straight.

"No, she didn't," I said. "Hannah told you where Will was hiding and you killed him. You killed him because you thought he'd seen you as you killed his father."

"I did not shoot Bert Rivers!," Sarah's voice was getting desperate.

"Shoot?" asked Mrs. Judson. "Mr. Rivers was hit over the head."

Mrs. Sutton smiled. "That wasn't what killed him. He was also shot. I found the bullet hole when I prepared his body. I asked Mrs. Wilcox to stand as witness, along with Mr. Lomax. Together we decided that we should keep it a secret because the only other person who would know that Mr. Rivers was shot was the person who killed him."

"And, in fact, Sarah," I said. "I remember the

morning we found the body that you said that he'd been shot. I thought at the time that you'd made an assumption based on what you'd thought had happened. However, you said he'd been shot because you were the one who did it."

"But.. But..." Sarah's eyes filled with tears as her bravado rapidly faded. "I loved Bert Rivers. No one loved him like I did. Why would I kill him?"

"Perhaps you thought he was your husband, who you are still trying to kill," I said.

The tears abruptly stopped. "I can tell the difference between my husband and my lover," Sarah snorted. It was as though she was moving further and further away from sanity. "It didn't occur to me to try and kill Mr. Worthington until after you suggested I'd be all right as a widow. And I haven't succeeded, anyway. You have nothing to try me on."

"So, you are trying to kill Mr. Worthington," Mrs. Sutton said.

"And you killed Mr. Rivers," Mrs. Hewitt said, clearly amazed. "Why?" "

"He wouldn't marry me," screamed Sarah. "He could have divorced his wife. We could have gone to San Francisco, where there is real society, not the vain attempt you have here. But, no. He didn't want to leave Los Angeles. Not even for me. So when I saw him there..."

She paused and dug something out of her bag. It was one of her derringers. She pointed it at me and pulled the trigger.

Even a tiny gun like that still made a huge roar. I thought I'd been hit but realized that was only because I'd been knocked to the floor by Mrs. Sutton. Mrs. Judson had Sarah's hand firmly in hers even as Sarah struggled. Mrs. Hewitt groaned as blood seeped through the sleeve of her green poplin gown.

"My best visiting dress," she moaned and sank to the floor in a faint.

Seconds later, Sebastiano and Mr. Lomax rushed

into the room and grabbed Sarah. Sighing, I picked myself up and went to look at Mrs. Hewitt's arm. It was only a scratch, but a fairly deep one. I cleaned the wound and had it bandaged before she came out of her faint.

Sarah wailed loudly as Sebastiano and Mr. Lomax took her to the city jail. Mrs. Judson agreed to take Mrs. Hewitt home. My ears were still ringing when Juanita came in, bearing chamomile tea for both myself and Mrs. Sutton.

The two sat on either side of me as I drank it.

"We were bosom friends," I whispered. "When I first came here, she took me under her wing. I felt horrible that she had come to spend so much time complaining about her marriage."

"She was very good at hiding her true nature," Mrs. Sutton said. "I would never have guessed."

It did not make me feel better. Mrs. Sutton looked at Juanita, who nodded and put me to bed. I fell asleep almost immediately and did not wake until late the next morning.

I did have to go to Sarah's trial and testify, but I did not go to the hanging. I couldn't. That morning, my household, every one of them, made a point of greeting or even hugging me. Sebastiano came and sat by my side as the clock struck the hour of the hanging. Earlier, I had received a note from Mr. Lomax, asking after me and offering to come by and cheer me later that afternoon. Then Mr. Worthington came by. His tall, muscular frame was dressed in a fine suit, his dark blond hair was slicked down and he was freshly shaved.

"Did you go?" I asked as he seated himself in the front parlor.

"No. I couldn't any more than you could," he said. "She fooled us both, you know."

"I would never have thought she'd have been able to knock a bunch of logs down on you," I said.

"That was actually pretty easy," he said. He sighed. "I guess I owe you an apology."

"What for?" I asked.

"I believed what she said about you. That you thought I would never amount to much and that I just had to show you that I would. That you hated me and thought I was coarse and cruel."

I blushed. "I never said the first part, but that last bit, I'm afraid was true."

"But only because you naturally believed what she told you about me." He looked down at the floor in embarrassment. "I didn't get drunk that often, or not as often as she swore I did, anyway. And I never went to another woman. Never. Not even a lady of the evening."

"I'm not surprised," I said. "I had reason to believe you hadn't, so I was always puzzled by her insistence that you patronized our local houses quite regularly."

"I did love her." Mr. Worthington looked away and blinked. "I came here so that she could be part of society. I became deputy zanjero to please her. But it wasn't enough. The only thing that would satisfy her would be to become one of those crooks on the city council. I couldn't abide that. So when they asked if I wanted to be zanjero, I told them no."

"Oh, dear," I said. "Did Sarah know?"

He shook his head. "No. I hadn't told her, but I was going to divorce her. I had already decided to settle the lumber mill on her and then leave Los Angeles. The night Bert Rivers died, I had told him I was leaving the pueblo. I guess he thought I was taking Sarah with me and that's what made him so darned mad. I didn't tell him I was going to leave her here."

"So, you're leaving now?"

He shrugged. "I've sold the lumber mill to James Rivers and I've taken a job as a manufacturer's agent. I did talk to May Rivers. We were courting when we were young."

"I know. She told me."

"I don't think that we'll ever be able to go back to courting again. She isn't ready to get married again and I'm not either. I figure I'll do some traveling, which I've always loved doing, and then we'll see what happens in a year or two."

I nodded. "It appears I have misjudged you. I apologize, as well."

"Accepted." He smiled, then sighed. "And thank you, Mrs. Wilcox. If you hadn't exposed Sarah, who knows what other kind of mayhem she might have caused. I might not even be here now."

"You're welcome, Mr. Worthington."

He left shortly after that. I returned to my study where Regina and Angelina Sutton had been left waiting. They, too, had been with me when the clock struck the fateful hour.

"I'm sorry about that," I said, wearily sinking into my desk chair.

"Darling Maddie, you have nothing to apologize for," Regina said kindly. "We were able to hear every word and it was quite interesting."

"One's heart bleeds for poor Mr. Worthington," said Angelina, who had recently invited me to call her by her first name. "But he did choose to marry her."

"And I chose to be her friend," I said listlessly.

"She befriended you first." Regina smiled wickedly. "And you've certainly developed better taste in your associations since then."

Angelina looked at Regina and giggled. I was not entirely surprised that the two were getting on well. They both had a terribly wicked sense of humor. Angelina had also guessed the truth about Regina, but oddly, it didn't bother her. As Angelina had said, death reveals all manner of unpleasant truths, and she had certainly seen just as strange a thing before. If anything, she was quite curious about Regina and the two had been embarrassing me horribly with their intimacies.

Regina cleared her throat. "Now, we have this

fine decanter of your most excellent angelica. I propose that we keep Señorita Juanita busy refilling it and get ourselves quite unwell."

We didn't, of course. Regina could hold her liquor amazingly well, and I was shocked to find that Angelina could, too. I simply don't like the sensation, although it's appalling how much I can drink before I feel it. Even so, we did have a lovely day together, snug and cozy in my study, with the rain pouring down relentlessly outside. It turned out to be a very wet April. The Zanja Madre remained quite full for the larger part of the summer, which was a very good thing for my vineyards. And even as I knew the value of water in Los Angeles, what I had come to know was the value of real friendship.

SNEAK PEEK

Here's a look at the second in the Old Los Angeles series featuring Maddie Wilcox, **Death of the City Marshal**. *This one is based on a historical event.*

DEATH OF THE CITY MARSHAL

When the shooting stopped and the smoke cleared, there were five people bearing wounds from the bullets that had flown so fast and furiously. I had made a point of diving for cover the moment I'd seen City Marshal William Warren pull his derringer from behind his back. Most of the other women in front of the Clocktower Courthouse that fateful afternoon of October 31, the Year of Our Lord 1870, had quickly left the street for some safe indoor place the moment they'd heard Deputy Joe Dye screaming at Marshal Warren. The men and I stayed to see the show.

My father often said that I didn't have the sense that God gave a goose. However, in my defense, I must point out that the closest indoor cover was a saloon, from which those of my fair sex were barred, and that any effort to seek cover across the street in the market on the first floor of the courthouse would have been impeded by the crowd that was gathering. I was looking for some other safe haven when I saw the marshal's derringer and decided that down on the board walkway was safer than anywhere I could reach.

As I rose, I was not surprised to see the marshal and a Chinaman on the ground and bleeding. What did surprise me was that Mr. Dye was bleeding from his forehead and his leg, but so enraged was he that he had pounced upon Marshal Warren and was biting his ear. Two men, I did not see who, grabbed Mr. Dye by the throat, and pulled him off the Marshal. Deputy Jose Redona was easing onto the ground, a bullet hole in his upper right arm. Deputy Constable Robert Hester was bent over his bleeding right hand. The young Chinawoman Marshal Warren and Mr. Dye had been fighting over sat huddled near Mr. Hester, too frightened to move.

I went first to the Chinaman and saw that the bullet had struck his jaw. I grabbed some bandages from the huge bag I always wore and began to gently bind his head, but another Chinaman eased me away and took over. So I went over to Marshal Warren.

"I'm killed," he groaned.

"Not if I have anything to say about it," I told him.

I began to bandage the nether region above his limbs in spite of his embarrassment. I did not like doing so in public, but he was bleeding and the bandage was necessary.

Perhaps I should explain. My name is Madeline Franklin Wilcox, called Maddie by my intimate friends, and I am a trained medical doctor. Nowadays, sadly, a woman medical doctor is almost unheard of, but when I finished my training in 1859, it was not all that unusual, though still fairly rare. My father had been so ashamed of me he forced me to marry Albert Wilcox, who promptly dragged me here to Los Angeles, then still a tiny pueblo of five thousand people. Mr. Wilcox bought a vineyard and promptly died, leaving me to make my way as a winemaker who happened to have a talent for the healing arts. I'd been forced to finally reveal myself as a doctor the previous spring. Not everyone, including Marshal Warren, was entirely comfortable with my true vocation.

Marshal Warren was an average-sized man with dark hair and eyes and an overgrown and unruly mustache and beard of the sort that was favored by men of that time. We'd never gotten on well. However, we had developed a grudging respect for each other, and if he did not appear happy that it was me that had come to his aid, at least he wasn't fighting me.

Four men took the marshal on ahead to his house. I told them that I would be there as soon as I checked on Mr. Redona and Mr. Hester. Mr. Hester's wound was superficial and barely needed bandaging. Doc MacKenzie was tending to Mr. Redona. Mr. Redona called out to me. He, apparently, had as little confidence in Doc MacKenzie as I did.

It wasn't entirely fair. Doc MacKenzie had many years of experience, even if he had no formal training. And he would give me the benefit of the doubt, which was more than the other doctors in town would. Fortunately, that day, we were both in agreement that the bullet had passed through Mr. Redona's arm without harming the bone and little more needed to be done beyond stitching the holes shut. I told Mr. Redona to keep the wound clean (which also served to remind Doc MacKenzie that sanitation was of the utmost importance). Then I hurried off to the marshal's house to tend to him.

Mrs. Warren was waiting for me as I ran up. Doctor Skillen came running up and glared at me. He generally approved of me when I tended to the women and children in town. However, he firmly believed that I had no business treating men. But Mrs. Warren told him in no uncertain terms that she wanted me tending to her husband and sent him off.

"How is he?" I asked Mrs. Warren as she led me upstairs.

"Complaining like a little girl," she said, then frowned. "That's good, isn't it?"

"Usually, yes," I said, not wanting to say more.

The case could go either way, based on what I'd seen on the street. He'd been hit in the pelvis. Had the bullet pierced his belly, we would have been facing a long night that would end in a slow, painful death for the marshal.

As it was, I was able to dose him with some morphine and ether, then opened up the wound. The bullet had landed next to his bladder. I got it out, then stitched the wound up, then cleaned and stitched his ear. You'll note, I did not sterilize anything. We didn't yet know. Mr. Lister's and Mr. Pasteur's work had yet to reach our benighted little corner of the world. All I knew was that keeping things clean made it less likely that wounds would fester. I was considered somewhat radical because I used ether and morphine to dull the pain of surgery.

It was a good two hours before I was done. My work apron was a mess, but it couldn't be helped. Fortunately, Juanita, my maid and confidant, worked miracles with blood stains. I was equally happy that I had on my third best riding habit that day, a somewhat faded cotton and wool suit festooned with ruffles around the skirt. I finished washing my hands to find that Mrs. Warren had brought a guest into the room.

He was a tall man, his dark hair neatly combed as it curled slightly around his ears. His eyes were bright blue and rather striking, actually. He wore the usual dark suit which looked fairly new, although there was some dust from the street on it.

"Reverend Jeptha Bennett, Ma'am," he said, nodding at me. His voice was deep and he had a Yankee accent even thicker than my own. "I helped carry the marshal home and have stayed to help bear up Mrs. Warren and the marshal in prayer and spiritual comfort."

"That's kind of you, Reverend," I said, glancing at Mrs. Warren.

She was small and dainty, with a narrow face that often reminded me of a cat. Her hair was coal black, as were her eyes. She was a Mexican, and as such, a Catholic. I'd heard the marshal was, too. Which meant that the Reverend's offer was more kindly meant than practical.

I'd been hearing about Reverend Bennett through the previous months, although I hadn't yet met him. He supposedly espoused the fire and brimstone kind of religion that I do not hold with at all. A traveling preacher, he'd arrived in the pueblo in the middle of the summer and his revival meetings had become so popular, he'd decided to stay indefinitely.

"Father Jimenez is on his way," Mrs. Warren told me, eyeing the reverend with mild annoyance.

"It's a pleasure to finally meet you, Reverend Bennett," I said, returning to cleaning my surgical tools for a couple minutes and hoping he'd recognize this as the dismissal it was. He did not, so I turned to him. "Reverend, I would like to speak to Mrs. Warren privately, if I may?"

"Of course." The reverend bowed his head slightly and left the room.

"How bad is it?" Mrs. Warren asked the second he was gone.

"The good news is that the surgery went well," I said. "We'll have to see if he takes sick from it. We should know in a few hours. I'll wait here with you."

"Thank you, Mrs. Wilcox," she said, going over and stroking her husband's face. "Oh, Mr. Ortiz came by. He thought you might be here and said to tell you that he will tell Mrs. Ortiz not to expect you for dinner."

I couldn't help smiling. I didn't know whether Mr. Ortiz meant Sebastiano or Enrique. They were the brothers who helped me manage my property, with Sebastiano overseeing the winery and Enrique the vineyards. They had started as my workers, but we had become fast friends and I'd recently made them my partners. Their wives managed my household, with Enrique's wife Magdalena as the housekeeper and Sebastiano's wife Olivia as the cook. It didn't matter which of the two brothers had delivered the message to Mrs. Warren, it was clear they knew me well.

"That was a kindness," I said and went back to

cleaning tools. "Are your daughters at home?"

Mrs. Warren's three girls were still fairly young.

"Their grandmother is here but can take them to her house at any time."

I glanced over at the marshal, who stirred. "I'm hopeful, but best keep them close."

Mrs. Warren nodded, her eyes filling with tears. She knew as well as I did what peril the marshal was in, and that it would be best for the girls to be able to say goodbye to their father if need be. Still, he was breathing evenly and his color was good for his condition.

I grew more hopeful as the afternoon wore on. Father Jimenez arrived and sat next to the window, muttering over his beads. Marshal Warren mostly slept. He awoke once just before sunset, chided me briefly, then went back to sleep again. Outside the house, several of the marshal's friends ambled back and forth, waiting.

Mr. Leander Wills, a notary of the local court, came by after dusk to get the marshal's testimony for the court's examination of Deputy Dye, which would be the next day. Mr. Wills was so insistent, I could hear him all the way upstairs. I told Mrs. Warren to wait with her husband and went to the front door.

Mr. Wills was a small man with a rounded belly and pince-nez glasses. He was meticulously clean-shaven and his suits were hand-tailored of the best wool, and his vests usually a shade of blue or yellow. He was wearing one the color of marigolds that evening.

"I am here as an officer of the court," he announced. "I must get the marshal's testimony."

"I'm afraid you're not going to get it," I told him. "The marshal is asleep and neither I nor anyone else, is going to wake him."

Mr. Wills' eyes narrowed. Standing behind him was Mr. King, one of the two men who ran The Daily News. Mr. King did most of the reporting for the newspaper. Mr. Wills harrumphed a couple times. I continued to glare at him. Mr. Wills harrumphed one more time then turned away from the door. As I shut it, I saw him shrug at the reporter.

Half an hour later, Constable Hester came by to visit and was able to speak briefly with the marshal, as did Deputy Redona.

"You should be in bed," I told the deputy. "You could still take sick from that hole in your arm."

Deputy Redona laughed loudly and the smell of whiskey washed over me. It was patently obvious how Doc MacKenzie had chosen to dull Mr. Redona's pain.

"It'll take more than this little hole to knock me down," Deputy Redona said, his body listing slightly to the right.

Deputy Redona did leave shortly after, promising to return, and left Constable Hester in the front parlor to watch. Reverend Bennett stayed with them. Father Jimenez had stayed until dinner time. In fairness, it didn't look like the marshal was going to need last rites. When the family's eight-day clock struck ten that night, I checked the marshal for fever, found he didn't have one, then motioned Mrs. Warren outside the room.

"I can't say for sure that he's out of danger," I told her. "You know as well as I do, wounds can look perfectly all right, then all of a sudden start festering. But I do think it's unlikely at this point. If you want me to stay, I'll be happy to. However, I see little point in it."

"I don't either," she said, looking through the door at her husband. "He just needs rest."

"As do I," I said. "If anything changes, don't wait to send for me. But I'll be back by dawn. Would it be all right if I didn't knock? I don't want to wake anyone unnecessarily."

"Oh, please, just come straight in."

I returned to the room to gather my bag and other things. I almost always carried a large leather bag, not unlike a saddle bag, with me wherever I went. The long strap crossed over my chest and wore my dresses terribly. However, I had my surgical tools and my most useful drugs with me at all times. The gunplay that we'd seen earlier that day was all too common, along with knife fights and other forms of violence. Even if it weren't, malaria, assorted poxes, and scarlet fever lurked everywhere, not to mention typhoid and cholera. Then there were the accidents from runaway horses or cattle or in the mills or on the farms and vineyards surrounding our tiny pueblo. I never knew when I'd be called to the side of an ailing ranch hand or child or young mother struggling to give birth. It was best to keep my most-used remedies and tools with me.

I had folded the work apron into the bag and looked, at least, mostly presentable as I left the Warren house. The crowd outside had lessened to around five or six men. Armando Ortiz, Enrique's eldest son and a strapping youth who had just turned sixteen, was lounging on the porch. He bounced to his feet the second he saw me.

"Tío had me bring the buggy for you," he said softly in Spanish.

"That's a mercy," I replied in the same language. I had already seen the conveyance, hitched to my roan mare, Daisy, and tied up outside the house.

"Tía Olivia says that she will have soup ready for you when we get home." Armando helped me onto the buggy's seat, then pulled himself up and took the reins.

Daisy ambled her way along the street toward my vineyard, winery and home, Rancho de las Flores. The wheel on the buggy squeaked exceptionally loudly and I made a mental note to ask Enrique about it when I saw him.

"I hope she will not be too put out if I'm not hungry," I said. "Señora Lopez made sure that there was plenty of food and insisted that I have some."

Señora Lopez was Mrs. Warren's mother. The Lopez family was one of our more distinguished. They had vast holdings in the area and raised cattle for beef, tallow, and hides. I can't remember if Mrs. Warren was from the third or fourth generation since the family had settled here, but they'd been here almost from the founding of the pueblo in 1781.

Armando shrugged. We both knew that Olivia considered my care and feeding her personal domain and it was equally likely that she would resent the interference from someone else as it was that she'd be grateful that someone had actually taken care of it. Heaven knows, she did not trust me to see to feeding myself, alas, with some justice on her part.

Olivia was waiting on the outside porch of the adobe as Armando and I drove in through the gate of the ranch. The adobe where I and the Ortiz families lived was not far from the gate and across the yard was the huge barn which was our winery. There was a livestock barn just beyond that, which housed Daisy, a pair of mules, a family of goats, and the three ranch dogs. The chickens had a good-sized coop closer to the barracks house, where most of our ranch hands and their families lived.

Armando helped me down off the buggy's seat, then went to lock the ranch gate. I tried to read Olivia's mood. It was not an easy task. However sweet and even merry her heart was, Olivia's face was permanently set in a scowl. Her black hair was sprinkled with gray and her dark eyes were the one clue to whether there would be a tongue lashing in store for me or not.

That night, the soup she had prepared had actually been made in advance of the morning's breakfast, as the weather was turning cold and we'd even had some solid rain the week before.

"I knew Señora Lopez would feed you," Olivia said as she ushered me inside the adobe. "She's a good woman."

Olivia sniffed as if to add that however good a woman Señora Lopez was, her food couldn't possibly match Olivia's.

"It wasn't as good as I'd have gotten here," I said,

dutifully.

Sebastiano, who ran our winery, was waiting for me in the front parlor, which opened directly onto the yard. He was about average size, with broad shoulders and a drooping black mustache. I can't remember if it had started to go gray by that time or if that happened later. His dark eyes usually flashed with good humor, but that night, he was not happy.

"We found two more barrels," he told me.

I bit back the foul words that sprang to my mind. "Two? How many more could there be?"

Sebastiano shrugged. Just over a week before, yet another group of young men had broken into the winery and tainted several barrels of the brandy we'd distilled the year before to make our angelica. It was the local sherry that was made all over the area, although ours was considered among the best. With the harvest done and that year's grapes mostly done fermenting, we needed the brandy to add to the new wine to fortify it so that it kept better.

We were, sadly, quite frequently the target of such vandalism. Sometimes it was from competitors. But mostly it came from men who believed a woman had no place owning a business, never mind that I had no other means of support. Even though I was getting some money for my doctoring services by then, it was hardly enough to keep me in bandages, let alone support my sizable household.

"We have enough good barrels for this year's wine," Sebastiano said. "But just enough."

"I'm assuming you made sure that they are soundly locked up?"

"Naturamente."

I thought for a moment. "Are the chickens locked in their coop?"

"Sí. You want to let the dogs loose in the yard?"

"It can't hurt."

Sebastian smiled. "I was about to suggest it."

"I'm afraid I've got to get to bed," I said, trying to

stifle a yawn. "I told Mrs. Warren I'd get back to the marshal by first light."

"So he's likely to live a while longer?" Sebastiano said, his face rather neutral. He did not like the marshal, with good reason, alas, but he was too kind a man to wish anyone ill.

"It looks that way but we both know how fast that could turn."

I went on to bed. As I had planned, I was up well before the sun. Sebastiano had risen, also, and gotten my roan mare, Daisy, saddled for me. I thanked him and trotted off. The first rays were lightening the sky as I approached the door. The household was still asleep. Deputy Redona snored softly from the sofa in the front parlor. I slid upstairs quietly. Mrs. Warren was asleep in her daughters' room. Senora Lopez had, apparently, gone home.

I knew the second I entered the marshal's bedroom that something was amiss. The covers around him were completely rumpled as if he'd been struggling. A pillow lay at his feet. The marshal's eyes were wide open and he was dead.

CONNECT WITH ANNE LOUISE BANNON

Thank you for sticking it out this long! Please join my newsletter. It's the best way to stay up-to-date on my upcoming projects, blog posts and even games and giveaways.

Sign up here: http://eepurl.com/zH0Ab

Or connect with me on your favorite social media platforms:

Visit my website: http://annelouisebannon.com
Friend me on Facebook: http://facebook.com/RobinGoodfellowEnt
Follow me on Twitter: http://twitter.com/ALBannon
Favorite my Smashwords author page: https://www.smashwords.com/profile/view/MsBriscow
Connect on LinkedIn: http://www.linkedin.com/in/annelouisebannon
Follow me on Pinterest: http://pinterest.com/msbriscow
Follow me on Google+: http://google.com/+Annelouisebannonfiction

OTHER BOOKS BY ANNE LOUISE BANNON

I'm so glad you liked this book! Check out my other novels, available in print or ebook at your favorite retailer:

Freddie and Kathy Series:
Fascinating Rhythm
Bring Into Bondage
The Last Witnesses

Operation Quickline Series:
That Old Cloak and Dagger Routine
Stopleak
Deceptive Appearances

Brenda Finnegan:
Tyger, Tyger

Romantic Fiction:
White House Rhapsody, Book One

Fantasy and Science Fiction:
A Ring for a Second Chance
But World Enough and Time (ebook only)

And I would be honored if you left a review for this and any of my books on GoodReads or any other retail site. It really helps.

ABOUT ANNE LOUISE BANNON

Anne Louise Bannon is an author and journalist who wrote her first novel at age 15. Her journalistic work has appeared in Ladies' Home Journal, the Los Angeles Times, Wines and Vines, and in newspapers across the country. She was a TV critic for over 10 years, founded the YourFamilyViewer blog, and created the OddBallGrape.com wine education blog with her husband, Michael Holland. She also writes the romantic fiction serial WhiteHouseRhapsody.com, Book One of which is out now. She is the co-author of Howdunit: Book of Poisons, with Serita Stevens, as well as author of the Freddie and Kathy mystery series, set in the 1920s, and the Operation Quickline series and Tyger, Tyger. She and her husband live in Southern California with an assortment of critters.